Sweet Land

Sweet Land

New and Selected Stories

WILL WEAVER

BOREALIS
BOOKS

Borealis Books is an imprint of the Minnesota Historical Society Press.

www.borealisbooks.org

The Minnesota Historical Society Press is a member of the Association of American University Presses.

Manufactured in the United States of America

10 9 8 7 6 5 4

♾ The paper used in this publication meets the minimum requirements of the American National Standard for Information Sciences—Permanence for Printed Library Materials, ANSI Z39.48-1984.

International Standard Book Numbers
ISBN-13: 978-0-87351-556-6 (paper)
ISBN-10: 0-87351-556-0 (paper)

Library of Congress
Cataloging-in-Publication Data

Weaver, Will.
  Sweet land : new and selected stories / Will Weaver.
    p. cm.
  ISBN-13: 978-0-87351-556-6
  (pbk. : alk. paper)
  ISBN-10: 0-87351-556-0 (pbk. : alk. paper)
  1. Middle West—Social life and customs—
    Fiction.
  I. Title.

PS3573.E192S94 2006
813'.54—dc22
2006022483

Acknowledgment is given to the following publications in which versions of the following stories first appeared. "Flax," *Milkweed Chronicle* (Winter Issue, 1985), Minneapolis; (revised version) in *Red Earth, White Earth* (Simon & Schuster, 1986); (Borealis Books, 2006). "Sheetrock," *Stiller's Pond Anthology: Fiction from the Upper Midwest* (New Rivers Press, 1991). "Dispersal," *Chicago Tribune Sunday Magazine* et al. (PEN Fiction Project, July 1985). "The Gravestone Made of Wheat," *Prairie Schooner* (1982). "Bad Blood," *Destination Unexpected*, ed. Don Gallo (Candlewick Press, 2003). "Heart of the Fields," *The San Francisco Chronicle* et al. (PEN Fiction Project, 1983). "The Gleaners," *Journal of Gastronomy* 5:2 (Berkeley, California, 1989). "Marked for Death," *Unexpected: Eleven Mystery Stories,* ed. Laura E. Williams (Scholastic, 2005).

Cover image: Ali Selim
Cover design: Adam Waldman

For Ali Selim

Sweet Land

Sweet Land

Flax

"Two-thirds, one-third. And no Sunday farming."

"Deal," Kenny replied to his grandfather, and at the same moment they reached out to shake hands. His grandfather's hand was wide and thick and cool, as if the earth upon which they stood were reaching up through the old man.

His grandfather, Helmer, had farmed these northern Minnesota fields since 1915. But now it was 1982. The last of this grandfather's black Angus were gone to the stockyards in St. Paul. It was Kenny's turn to farm. He had a sudden urge to throw his arms around his grandfather, but their handshake had locked them an arm's length apart. And anyway, Kenny was nineteen now, beyond all that.

The arrangement between Kenny and his grandfather, except for the no-Sunday farming part, was a common one. Kenny would bear all the expenses, provide all the labor. For that he would receive two-thirds of the crop. His grandfather would get one-third, payable at harvest time.

Kenny expected the quiet-Sunday clause. Helmer never farmed on Sunday, believed Sunday was a day of rest for both farmer and land. Unlike his grandfather, Kenny did not read the Bible or attend the Sunday morning gospel meetings, but he could get along without farming on Sundays. He could simply put in more tractor time the other six days. Sunday would be no problem.

"So what are you going to plant?" his grandfather asked, turning to look across the hundred-acre pasture.

"Not sure," Kenny lied.

"Raise a good crop of corn. Oats for sure."

"Have to think on it some more," Kenny said, which was true. For now it was October. There was winter to get through. But between now and spring he would be thinking of flax.

After his graduation from high school last spring, Kenny had taken a brief motorcycle trip to Canada. In Manitoba, at sundown, he had come upon a long field of grain in brilliant, blue bloom, a field so long its blue end was welded to the sky.

3

"Flax," a passing farmer called out with a laugh, checking Kenny's motorcycle plates.

Kenny had taken a sheaf of flax and a handful of the Canadian soil back to Minnesota. No farmers in Sand County grew flax, but no one had ever tried growing it in northern Minnesota, either.

Kenny sent a sample of the Canadian soil and his grandfather's loam to the University of Minnesota for analysis and discovered the two were nearly identical. He saw no reason why flax would not grow well in Sand County, especially in the hundred-acre pasture which had lain in sod, manured by his grandfather's Angus for the last ten years.

Now in October, however, he did not speak of flax. He did not want to argue with his own father about the terrible dangers of trying something new. Anyway, he would need all of his time for work and sleep.

Kenny still lived at home. In the mornings, he arose at 4:30 to help his father with the milking. By 7:00 he was in his pickup, driving to Detroit Lakes where he worked as a maintenance welder in the french-fry plant. After eight hours of welding, he returned home at 6:00 to help his father finish chores. Supper was at 7:30, and then he always took a short walk across the road to visit his grandfather.

Helmer, so long widowed that Kenny remembered his grandmother only vaguely as white hair and the smell of bread dough, sat in his straight-backed chair reading his Bible. Sometimes he and Kenny would talk and sometimes they would read, his grandfather the Bible and Kenny *National Geographic.* Without telephone, television, or radio in the house, the only sound was the whispering slide of their pages and the faint kiss of his grandfather's moving lips. A bowl of ice cream ended their evening, and then Kenny walked home for an hour of TV and bed by ten.

Kenny did not want to live at home forever, or even for another year. But right now it was fine. By helping his father with the Holsteins, he worked out his room and board, plus the use of his father's big tractor and plow. This they had figured out closely. "Money between relatives is like sand between the sheets," his father often said. By keeping close accounts, everybody slept fine. Kenny was able to save his welding money, $280.67 net each week.

On the wall calendar in his upstairs bedroom, Kenny figured out his first season's farming expenses. Each french-fry check bought the equivalent of 20½ bushels of flax seed. He would have his seed paid for by January. February was checked off for diesel fuel and tractor oil. March was marked for plow lays and disks. April allowed for fertilizer and planter expense. May and June were checked for harvest expenses: custom combining and trucking. The month of August, however, was unmarked. There would be no August for Kenny at the french-fry plant. With his flax crop sold he could walk away from his welder for good. With any luck, he could buy a small tractor of his own, perhaps even make a down payment on some land. He would be free, would start his own life.

But first, he knew, there was the winter to get through. It passed quickly, largely because he worked time-and-a-half, including most Saturdays at the plant. Inside the windowless building, under the fluorescent lights, everything was covered with a fine sheen of vegetable oil. All the workers wore blue smocks; men and women were distinguishable only by their caps or kerchiefs over their hair. Beside the river-rush of the transport flumes, the clatter of the cutter, and the heat of the quick-fryers, Kenny welded. Behind his welder's mask, he sometimes imagined himself an astronaut, newly landed on some strange planet inhabited by a ruling class of potatoes—potatoes whose only goal, assisted by large, blue-smocked robots, was infinite multiplication. He was lost in space. He was so far from home.

By April first, the snow, except for slouched, weeping banks on the north side of the farm buildings, had vanished. A week of sunshine and fifty-degree weather followed. By the ninth, Kenny could drive a shovel nearly eight inches into the pasture sod. Tractors and plows began to appear in the farmyards along the road to Detroit Lakes. By April twelfth, a Wednesday, as if by common signal, tractors were in the fields, plowing. Kenny cursed because he was not among them.

But Saturday finally came. At sunup, with only a cup of coffee for breakfast, Kenny turned the tractor onto the sod and lowered the plow. The coulter disks cut six slices into the earth, and the moldboards lifted and turned the shining soil. Stopping only for diesel fuel and a sandwich at midday, he plowed through sundown and then by the tractor's big yellow running lights. By 11:30 that night, insides the tractor's cab with its blue dash lights and the yellow lamps outside shining down the long furrows, Kenny believed the field a long runway. The tractor was a great jet, and with each round on the runway he came closer to taking off over the fence and up into the black sky.

Abruptly he stopped the tractor in midfield. He shook his head to clear it and got out to piss. The cooler air slapped him awake. He surveyed the field. There were only acres left to plow. He could finish that in two hours tomorrow. But then he cursed. Tomorrow was Sunday.

Kenny looked across the field to his grandfather's house. There were yellow lights on in the living room. He knew his grandfather was waiting up, waiting for Kenny to come home. What the hell. He would finish the plowing tonight, keep going. But then he cursed again, involuntarily including his grandfather this time. Though he had only two hours of plowing left, in half an hour it would be Sunday. And a deal was a deal.

Kenny finished the plowing Monday night at ten o'clock. Immediately he hooked onto the field disk. He disked until 3:00 AM Tuesday, then stumbled through chores and work. He disked again Tuesday night. The week became a slow-turning kaleidoscope of tractor's lights, welder's flare, and falling stars. On Friday his father called him at the french-fry plant.

"There's some guy here from Manitoba with 400 bushel of flax seed," his father said. "I told him he had the wrong farm. But he's got your name on the slip. It looks like your writing."

"It's my writing," Kenny said, in the same moment feeling completely awake for the first time in days. He imagined the Canadian, the truck, the brown burlap bags of seed.

"Flax seed? For the old pasture?" his father said.

"Flax. It's all paid for," Kenny replied.

"Flax," his father said slowly, his voice receding in puzzlement, "well, I'll be damned."

Kenny laughed as he hung up the phone. "Not potatoes—flax!" Two of the cutter ladies stared at him. He realized he had spoken aloud. "No more potatoes, no more potatoes," Kenny chanted. In two months this place could fuck itself. His flax would guarantee that.

On Saturday he planted. The shining brown flax seed ran easily through the grain drill hopper, and he was finished and in the house for the ten o'clock news and weather.

April 21: Fifty-five degrees and sunny. Flax seed swelled, some sprouted.

April 30: Warm front slowed over North Dakota and Minnesota. 74° and sunny. Flax sprouts nearing the surface. Could use a rain, though.

May 3: Raining and 54°.

May 5: Flax up! Tiny green needles, millions, billions of them.

May 14: Two inches of rain and the sun out. Black field shading green. Flax finger-high.

May 20: 72°, sunny. One hundred bright green acres. Flax a long hand high.

June 2: 89°, need rain badly.

June 4: 61°, cold front moving in. Keep coming.

June 5: 55° and raining in Sand County and nowhere else. Beginner's luck?

And so Kenny's notes on his calendar and his luck continued. When his flax needed rain, the skies clouded and water fell. When his flax needed sunlight and heat, the frontal systems dispersed, and the sun shone.

By mid-June the field of flax, like a great roadside magnet, began to slow the pickups of passing farmers and draw many to a stop. The farmers got out and walked along the green hedge-end of the grain. They knelt and rolled the flax through their fingers. They chewed the shoots and stared over the field.

Every evening Helmer gave Kenny the Flax report, as they jokingly called it. How many farmers had stopped, the aphid count per square foot. Whether there was rust. For Helmer, it seemed, spent much of his day walking among or along the flax. Sometimes Kenny wondered if his grandfather were not the guardian angel of the field.

But on July eighth, a Thursday, Kenny knew his luck had run out. The temperature and humidity were matched at ninety-two, but a cold front had bulged down from Canada and would meet the warm air in Sand County. Kenny alternated between watching the TV's weather radar and the west sky over the flax. By 7:00 PM the weather woman was predicting high winds.

"—and damaging hail," Kenny's father finished for her. "That's the trouble with flax, you see. Hail catch it right, it'll kill it. But now you take oats or barley, they'll—"

Kenny left the television. Outside he stood among his flax and watched the oncoming weather. Waist-high and blooming blue on the higher swells of the field, the flax's uncertain colors matched the sky. Southwest were the high, shining, cumulus towers—"Holycard clouds," Kenny's mother called them. White heat-lightning shimmered underneath the lumbering warm front. From the northwest came the lower, darker, faster-moving clouds of the cold front. Kenny watched the two fronts, in slow motion, collide. Their clouds tangled and churned and

rolled upward dark and bulbous. Supported by yellow forked legs of
lightning, the fronts now divided and became great spiders, struggling
for control of the prairie sky.

Cold air suddenly washed over Kenny's face. Rain shimmered across
the flax toward him, and behind the rain, whitish and racing, came the
hail. Kenny cursed the sky and ran for the cover of the machine shed.
The rain overtook him, and he was instantly wet through. And once
under the tin eaves of the building, Kenny turned to witness the de-
struction of his field.

But even as he watched, the hail veered sharply south, churned
through a neighboring cornfield, and raced out of sight. It was then
Kenny saw his grandfather. Helmer stood drenched on the front steps
of his house. His arms hung straight down, his palms out, his brown
face and streaming white hair upturned to the sky. His eyes were
closed. His mouth was open. He was either speaking or drinking in the
cold rain.

After the storm, the flax eased into bloom. At first a broad, milky-blue,
the field drew its color from the sky. But then in full bloom, the flax's
color surpassed and gave back a deeper blue to the high crown of the
sky. Past full bloom, the field shaded daily to yellow, then brown, as the
flower petals dropped away and the seed pods formed.

By July twentieth, the seeds, each clutched in their five-leaved cups,
were the size of garden peas. That same week a killer frost burned most
of Manitoba's flax fields brown. And within days, flax futures at the
Winnipeg Grain Exchange began to trade up their daily limits, pulling
the cash price for a bushel of flax to an all-time high of $25.00.

The *Detroit Lakes Sentinel* ran a newspaper article on Kenny and his
flax. The article, entitled, "Gambling and Farming May Pay Off," esti-
mated the flax yield at sixty bushels to the acre.

"That's $150,000, Grandpa," Kenny blurted, as his grandfather
slowly read the article. But his grandfather did not reply or even look
up until he was finished. Then he folded the paper and handed it to
Kenny. Helmer frowned and stared through the west living room window—at the flax, the sky.

"But it's not in the bin yet," he said.

Kenny nodded. He wished the newspaper had not started figuring
his profits because now that figure ran through his mind like a movie.
He could see it all. With $150,000 he could buy land of his own. He

could buy his grandfather a new furnace and a tank of oil. He could buy his mother a microwave oven and a color television. He could buy his father a new pipeline milker. He could buy himself a new pickup. He could—abruptly he stood and erased the pictures from his head. It was nearly ten o'clock, time to hurry home and catch late weather.

By August eighth, with the flax field a golden lake, its seeds hard enough to hold a fingernail dent, Kenny made final harvesting arrangements with a neighbor, Jim Hanson, whose new John Deere would combine the grain. The weather held hot and dry. On August twelfth, a Friday, with clear sky and the next weather front still far off in the Rockies, Kenny cut.

The flax folded golden over the sickle of the swather, golden and steadily like ocean waves. With Helmer watching from a folding chair by the gate, Kenny cut until sundown when the flax began to draw moisture from the cooling air. The sickle pounded in complaint against the toughened stalks, and Kenny pulled away with only a few acres left to windrow.

"Hail can't hurt you now—" Helmer called as Kenny drove through the gate.

Kenny held up his hand in a victory salute. "Nothing can hurt me now!" he cried. Over the noise of the swather's engine he could not hear his grandfather's reply.

Saturday, he finished cutting. Sunday dawned clear, but cool. Tuesday came sunny and eighty degrees which cured the top several inches of the windrows until Kenny could chafe the flax between his palms and watch the shiny brown seeds drop into his lap. Now at $26.50 a bushel, he wondered what each seed was worth.

Tuesday, Wednesday, and Thursday were the days that grainmen, and Kenny, dreamed of: clear and ninety degrees with a hot, dry wind from the southwest. The windrows baked in the yellow oven of the field and shimmered away their moisture. Kenny lined up a parade of grain wagons, trucks, and the auger.

Friday morning at 11:00, two hours later than he had agreed, Jim Hanson came rumbling up the road in his green combine. Kenny ran to meet him. Hanson swung down from the cab. He wore several days of dark beard and a pair of oil-spotted coveralls. He farmed a lot of land, had a lot of machinery, and Kenny often saw his truck at the John Deere dealership in Detroit Lakes. Hanson strode up to the first windrow of flax, hefted an armful, then drew its underside across his nose. He bit into a handful of stems, then looked at the sky.

"Two o'clock," he said. "It won't go until two."

Helmer, who had come up by the combine, nodded in agreement. Hanson climbed back into the cab, shut the door, and slumped backward in immediate sleep. Helmer stepped closer to the combine. He looked closely at the tires, the grease fittings. He stared at the pickup reel, then reached out for one of the spring teeth that rattled to his touch. From his pocket he produced a small pliers and tightened the nut. Hanson did not wake up.

While Hanson slept, Kenny waited and listened to the weather report. It was raining in Omaha, Idaho Falls, Bozeman, and Kalispell.

At 2:30, Hanson sat up, and the combine's engine coughed alive. He slowly brought up the RPMs until the combine shuddered, engaged the pickup reel, lowered the great mouth into the first windrow, and headed downfield. Like a great green beetle, the combine swallowed the flax and spit out a spray of straw behind. Kenny ran alongside. Oblivious to the roar in his ears and the grit in his nose and mouth, he watched on the plexiglass window of the grain hopper the rising brown tide of seed.

Suddenly, as if from the earth beneath, there was a massive thud and then a clanking sound. The combine shuddered to a stop. Hanson leaped down from the cab, threw his cap on the ground, and began to jump on it.

Kenny drove Hanson home. Hanson stared straight ahead with his jaw clenched. Repairs would take three days. Kenny wondered what a new gearbox cost, but did not ask; rather, he was trying to think of other farmers and their combines.

"Fucking flax," Hanson muttered. "Windrows that big, you need that big custom equipment from the Dakotas." Hanson scratched the beard on his throat. "There's a small crew I know that should be around Fargo right now, headed for South Dakota. Flaherty, an Irishman, that's the owner. Maybe he'd detour this way and pick up your flax. He's expensive, though . . ."

"I can pay," Kenny answered quickly.

At six o'clock that evening, with nearly two hundred dusty, new miles behind him, Kenny located Flaherty's crew. Ten miles south of Fargo, the four combines were running a staggered front against the last half of a long wheat field. Kenny's heart billowed with excitement and hope as he closed in on the rumbling, gray Allis-Chalmers gleaners, each of which seemed twice as large as Hanson's John Deere. He drove up to the motor home parked by the fieldside, where a man, hatless, with coppery hair and binoculars to his eyes stood at the fence watching the gleaners. Kenny's heart thumped in his ears; he approached the man and introduced himself.

"Flax, huh?" Flaherty said, again lifting his binoculars to the wheat field. "Don't see much flax around here. But I dunno, a hundred acres isn't much for a day's detour. We're supposed to be down in Sioux Falls tomorrow."

"I'll make it worth your while," Kenny said.

Flaherty lowered his glasses. A slow grin came into the sunburned creases around his mouth. "Oh, you will, will you?"

Kenny nodded. He realized that Flaherty was about the same age as his father.

"This must be quite a field of flax, then."

"Sixty bushel," Kenny said.

Flaherty laughed. He raised his binoculars again. "I've been shakin' grain for twenty years, and I've never seen flax run even fifty."

Kenny suddenly remembered the newspaper article which he had stashed deep in the glovebox of the pickup. He retrieved it and handed it to Flaherty, who fished reading glasses from his pocket and blew away their dust before he read. "Well, hell," he finally said, "I've never yet seen a newspaper could figure bushels. But the pictures look good, yes they do. And you're this gambler fellow they're writin' about?"

"Yessir," Kenny grinned.

"And you want to gamble on Flaherty?"

"Yessir," Kenny said.

By three o'clock Saturday afternoon, Kenny began to think he had gambled wrong. Flaherty's combines had not arrived. He wondered if Flaherty had trouble, gotten lost, or lied to him. Kenny's grandfather sat at his kitchen table so he could see down the road to the west.

"He'll come," Helmer said. "If the man said he would come, he'll come."

But the combines did not come Saturday, nor Sunday morning by the time Helmer had driven slowly off to church. Kenny paced the living room. He listened to the 10:00 AM weather. Rain in Billings and Valley City. He cursed but in the same moment heard trucks. Flaherty's combines, like a caravan of circus elephants, appeared out of a dust cloud from the west. Kenny raced outside to meet them. Flaherty stepped down from the motor home. His eyes were as red as his new beard shadow, and his hands were stained dark with oil.

"On the last forty acres, whatever could go wrong, went," he said, looking over the flax field at the same time. Without waiting for a reply, he walked quickly into the flax. He ran one arm underneath a windrow, the other arm over the top, and hefted the grain.

"Be damned," he said, a grin coming over his face. "I'm in the wrong business. Ought to be growing this stuff instead of shakin' it. Unload those ornery critters," he called to his men, "we've got a real field here."

Kenny started to speak, but Flaherty turned away to direct his men. He looked back at his grandfather's house. The two porch windows were eyes, the door a mouth. He called to Flaherty again, but at the same moment a combine roared alive, and his voice was lost. The crew released the combines from their tether-chains, then lowered the ramps. The combines slowly crept toward the ground, then formed a convoy pointed toward the field. As the last combine touched the ground, Kenny saw his grandfather's truck pull into the yard and then come toward the field. In his dark suit, Helmer walked slowly to Kenny and the combines. For long moments, Kenny met his grandfather's eyes. Then he ran in front of Flaherty's combine and blocked the way.

"We can't do it," Kenny shouted.

Flaherty leaped to the ground. "What the hell you talking about?" he said. "I'm telling you, the grain is ready."

"No, it's not that," Kenny said.

"So what the hell is it then?"

"It's Sunday," Kenny said slowly. "This is my grandfather's land, and he doesn't farm on Sunday." The other drivers climbed down and stood behind Flaherty, who turned his gaze to Helmer.

"Sunday?" Flaherty said. "Old man, are you nuts?" The other drivers laughed. "You've got a field of flax like this one, with rain no more than a day away, and you're worried about Sunday?"

Helmer met the men's gaze in silence.

Flaherty looked away and ran his hands through his hair. "Goddamn but I've never run into this before." He turned to Kenny, pulled him aside. "Look," he said, "Sunday don't matter to us, it sure don't matter to the flax, and it probably don't matter to you. So why not take your granddad back to the house and fix him a cup of coffee or something? We'll take care of the flax and be on our way. And in a few days he'll forget all about it."

But Kenny could only shake his head. "I gave my word," he said.

Flaherty's red-rimmed eyes flared wider. "Look, you hired me. I'm here. If you want me to wait, I'll wait. It's not my flax. But every hour we sit here will cost you the same as if we were rolling."

"I'll pay," Kenny said.

"Bunch of fruitcakes," one of the drivers muttered.

"—get some shut-eye, anyway," another said as they turned away.

Flaherty strode into the motor home, slammed the door, and then there was silence in the field.

That night Kenny lay in his bed upstairs, his eyes open, listening, waiting. The sound that he knew would come fell like a whisper on the shingles, at first so faint that Kenny mistook it for the rush of his own blood in his ear against the pillow. A steady patter. Then a drumming. Rain. Kenny rose from his bed and went to the window. In the yard, under the white glow of the mercury yardlight, the combines shone wetly like great blocks of ice.

The rain continued Monday and Tuesday.

"We can't wait any longer," Flaherty said on Wednesday. He was clean shaven now, his face puffy from sleep. "You're not on our regular route. And we've got to be in South Dakota. Maybe somebody else . . ."

Kenny nodded. He felt older, harder, like some part of him had turned to wood or stone. "How much do I owe you?" was all he said.

"Just for Sunday," Flaherty replied.

Kenny wrote the check. Flaherty looked at it, then across to the flax, and finally to Helmer's house. He suddenly cursed. In one motion he crumpled the check, flung it down, and ground it into the mud with his boot. Then he turned away and waved his convoy down the road.

Thursday the skies cleared, but only for the afternoon. Friday and Saturday the rain came again. The windrows of flax rusted brown, and from their wet weight began to crush their supporting stubble until they lay shrunken and flat on the cold, soaked earth. The rains and mist continued for the next two weeks.

"It's going to clear up," Helmer would say every day. "There's still time."

But Kenny had no words for him, or for anyone. He continued to visit his grandfather in the evenings; they read in silence. He was glad his grandfather spoke no more or less than usual. But often in the early mornings, on his way to the french-fry plant, Kenny saw his grandfather walking along the windrows of flax, poking at them with a fork, stooping to heft their weight. Once at sundown the sky cleared briefly. The orange light slanted harshly across the now-sprouting windrows, and Kenny saw his grandfather standing motionless, far out among the pale green rivers of fire.

September, however, brought Indian summer. The sky cleared, and the sun shone hotly for a week. The flax rows dried on top. If the windrows could be turned to dry their undersides—a hayrake might work—there was still a chance for a partial harvest.

Kenny quit welding again and readied the rake. On a Wednesday, along with four neighbors who had shown up uninvited with their own tractors and rakes, Kenny began to turn the flax.

Still sodden underneath, and heavier than any hay, the flax wound and webbed itself around the reel of the rake. Every few yards it had to be cut away with butcher knives. The rakes' drive belts began to slip, then smoke with the smell of burning rubber. One by one the neighbors' tractors turned away from the windrows. Kenny continued. The drive chains began to chatter and slip and grind away gear teeth. On the steering wheel, his left hand felt wet inside his glove. He saw that he had sliced through the leather with the butcher knife. Suddenly the main chain parted and flopped. Then, at last, he too pulled away from the flax.

He drove toward Helmer and the other farmers by the gate. Helmer waved with his fork.

"Go back—keep going!" he called to Kenny. He waved for the neighbors to turn around, but they looked away.

Kenny got down and walked to Helmer. "It won't turn," he said.

But his grandfather shook his head. "It's got to be turned. When it's turned, then we can get that red-haired man to come back. With his combines he can—"

"No!" Kenny suddenly shouted. He grabbed his grandfather by the shoulders and shook him violently. "It's finished, over, over, over, over, can't you see that?"

But his grandfather would not look him in the face. His eyes were welded to the windrows of flax. Kenny left his grandfather there in the field. He could think only of going to bed, of retreating deep into his quilts. He did not want to speak or even think of anything for a long time.

Kenny awoke, sometime after dark, uncertain of the time. Moonlight shone in his window, and he stumbled toward it to look outside. He thought of Flaherty's combines, wet in the white light. But as he knew it would be, the yard was empty. The only visible movement was some animal far out in his field of flax. Suddenly Kenny cried out as he realized the figure in the field was his grandfather, on his hands and knees.

He raced down the stairs, shouting to wake his parents, and ran barefoot across the yard into the flax.

"Grandpa—" he called, nearing him.

Helmer turned his face to look. A black course of blood ran from his nose across his cheek. Beside him lay his fork.

"Few more hours, maybe," his grandfather breathed, "have it turned . . . get that red-haired man back . . ."

"No—" Kenny cried. He grabbed away the fork, seeing for the first time that his grandfather had turned by hand nearly a quarter mile of one windrow.

"Yes, must turn . . . ," Helmer breathed. He struggled to his feet and caught the wooden handle. "Let me finish. Please. Want to finish this tonight." He pulled against Kenny. Suddenly Kenny was holding his grandfather, feeling his woolen shirt wet with sweat and his old heart shuddering inside his chest.

"You're a good boy, Kenny," Helmer whispered, and kissed him like he used to do when Kenny was small. Kenny tasted his grandfather's blood. But then Helmer slowly pushed him away.

"Stop him—" Kenny's mother cried from behind.

Kenny's father stepped forward, but stopped at Kenny's command.

They watched. Helmer, one forearm clutched across his chest as if to hold his heart, again drove his fork into the grain. Staggering against the moonlight, he slowly worked his way downfield into the dark.

Sheetrock

What first attracted me to *This Old House* was the sound of a saw, or "soar" as Norm Abram says it, which always reminds me of President Kennedy, the way he talked, the long scarves he wore, the way the wind puffed at his hair. I was doing dishes when I heard an electric, hand-held, 7¼-inch blade, circular saw, the kind every carpenter uses. I cocked my head, leaned forward to look through my kitchen window. Up and down the street. Nothing. No one sawing. Just houses, all pre-fabs like this one, that peter out where the hills begin, and a couple of oil rigs sit like black teeter-totters on an empty playground.

My subdivision sits at the west edge of Minot, North Dakota. No construction has ever gone on here. These houses came on trucks. You've seen them on the freeway, half a house on one lowboy trailer, the second half on another trailer behind. The factory staples a big sheet of white plastic over the open middle of each side to keep out road dust and birds, but wind usually tears away the plastic and you can drive alongside and look right into the living rooms, the bedroom. Jim, that's my husband, says hitchhikers are attracted to prefabs. If the plastic doesn't tear by itself they'll cut the sheet, just one razor slit, to get inside and ride. Some prefabs include furniture, like a couch, a kitchen table, a TV-stereo combination, a queen-sized bed. The factory staples the furniture to the floor where they think most people would like it (later, if you want, you can move it) and Jim once saw a bum riding along at sixty miles an hour stretched out sound asleep on the davenport, his hair flapping in the wind. Anyway, when the two sides of a prefab arrive at the job site they're slid onto a concrete slab, then power-nailed together *whacka-whacka-whacka*. Houses like this one, there's nothing to saw.

Still, in my kitchen I kept hearing that faraway whine of a circular saw. I let my hands go quiet in the dishwater. Listened. The sound was like the flip side of a siren. When an ambulance or a fire truck wails by you can bet somebody's dead or hurt, their house is burning, their luck's gone bad. When you hear a carpenter's saw—hear that high, steady calling—you know somebody's life is on the ups.

Which made me look around my own kitchen. The dark, wood-grain paneling. The bowed, plastic strips of floor molding. The muddy white linoleum split here and there, cuts never stitched, from dropped kitchen knives. The cupboard doors with vinyl peeling at the corners like spiked hair. I didn't grow up in a house like this one. Our house was nothing fancy but it was all wood and it didn't come on no trailer.

I grew up in Golden Valley, which is now a part of Minneapolis, on a street with two rows of identical one-story houses all built by Mr. Jenkins. He started with one house, sold that and built another. As soon as the subflooring was down and the plumbing installed he moved his family in. His kids coughed a lot from sheetrock dust, but my father said sheetrock was just chalk and paper, the same they use in school. Every night of the summer Mr. Jenkins's saw was the last thing I heard before I drifted off to sleep. Once my mother complained about the sawing. "That's the sound of progress," my father said, and rattled his newspaper. It was the 1950s then.

I dried my hands and soon enough tracked that faint sawing sound to the den. There the TV was flashing in an empty room. On the screen was a man cutting plywood; another dark-haired fellow held the sheet steady. Big men, with noses and bellies. They wore leather tool belts, jeans and plaid shirts, and scuffed boots that had seen some dust. Two big men working together. Sawhorses, sheets of plywood. A silvery circular saw, its blade eating up the thin red line, the yellow sawdust feathering up behind in a golden drift. I turned up the sound. I sat down. For some reason the scene got to me. Choked me up. There was something about it—the tools, the boots, the wood, the two men working. It was all so real. It was something anyone could believe in. After that, Thursday nights it was Bob, Norm, and me.

T-minus twenty-five minutes.

Bob Vila himself picks each house to be remodeled. He drives around looking for older homes for his next project, and these houses could be anywhere in the United States. Anywhere. Sure, most of the jobs are out East. That's because Norm and Bob are from out East originally. But they have remodeled houses in Connecticut, Tennessee, California, Colorado, Wisconsin, and more. I know because I keep track.

In our den I have a United States wall map and each red pushpin is a *This Old House* project. It took some work, I'll tell you, getting all the sites pinpointed. I had to order the tapes I'd missed, then go through them one by one. But I'm glad I did. Looking at the pins it's clear to me now that Bob Vila could show up in anyone's neighborhood.

Once I was driving west in Minot when I saw a shiny blue crew cab Ford pickup, the driver with sunglasses, coming at me from the other way. For a second I froze at the wheel—then I closed my eyes and spun a louie across traffic. Cars honked at me, which was serious because people in North Dakota never use their horns. I made it across the traffic but there were too many cars and I lost him. Afterward I had to pull over. My heart was pounding. I had to catch my breath.

I bowl, and that night at the lanes I told the girls in my league who I just might have seen.

They laughed. Phyllis said, "You sure it wasn't Elvis?"

Anyway, once Bob picks a house—say it was your house—all the remodeling is free. I have thought and thought about this matter and I believe it to be true. Reason number one, Bob is a wealthy man. He has his television show. He has his videos. He has his books on remodeling. Reason number two, even if Bob wasn't rich, he is not the kind of guy who would take money from homeowners who are struggling to make life better for themselves and their kids, even if they offered him the money.

I don't tell people my ideas on the free remodeling. If you know in your heart that something is the truth, there's no need to broadcast. Besides, it would only hurt Bob and Norm. Imagine how people would try to get close to them, to be their friends. Imagine the women, the things they would do.

T-minus fifteen minutes. I'm knitting with one eye on the clock when Jim pokes his head into the room. The round top of his head shines.

"Yes?" I say immediately and loudly.

"Have I got something for you," Jim says. He is a middle-sized man with a round head and one of those soccer-ball bellies that truckers get from the constant jiggling, the continual pounding over seams in the freeway concrete, which over the years weakens the stomach muscles. Jim holds up his new *Playboy*.

"There's nothing in that magazine for me," I say. I check my watch against VCR time, keep my needles moving.

"Not even an interview with Bob Vila?" My yarn snags.

Jim grins and holds out the magazine.

I make a point of unhooking the snag before I set down my wool, my needles. Then I clutch the magazine. It's heavier than I expect.

I look for the right page, making sure to glance away when the pictures flash up pink. And suddenly there it is, "Twenty Questions with Bob Vila." A picture, too. Bob is standing beside a low red car that I read is a Ferrari. A Ferrari his wife has given him for his birthday.

"I could sure go for one of them Ferraris on my birthday," Jim says from behind me. He puts his hands on my shoulders, begins to rub them. I can feel his belly, round and firm, against the back of my head.

"Well we're not rich, you're not Bob Vila, and it's not your birthday," I say, and hand him the magazine. I check the time on the VCR, then pick up my knitting. I have to focus on my yarn, concentrate, remember the pattern. I crochet newborn caps for the local hospital. Newborn caps are my bowling money.

"My birthday ain't that far off," Jim says softly. He is still standing behind my chair. He takes my head into his hands and begins to run his thumbs slowly over the rims and down the sides of my ears.

I keep knitting, which my girlfriends say I could do through a tornado.

"What if I was Bob Vila and came driving up and knocked on the door?" Jim says. His voice has dropped a note, turned husky. He keeps stroking my ears. He knows what that does to me. And I know that his new magazine has got his batteries charged up.

"Piff to that," I say. It's a nervous saying I have.

"Piff?" Jim says. "That's all?" He laughs once.

"Piff," I say.

Tomorrow morning Jim is leaving for Duluth, Georgia, with a load of durum. When he's gone I stay pretty much in the house; in winter you shouldn't leave a house alone, even for the afternoon. Especially this house. When the temperature drops to twenty below and the wind comes in from Montana and ice knocks down a power line somewhere, it's trouble. Frost grows from the plug-ins, from around the window sills, from the keyhole. It grows like toadstools. I've sat there and watched it move. On those days I wear my parka and one of the newborn caps.

"What if?" Jim whispers. He's leaning down now. His breath is sweet and woody from his Copenhagen, which I'd rather smell than cigarettes.

Summers I stay in, too. I can't take the heat outside so I stick to the den where we have a window air conditioner. I keep knitting. Sometimes if the shades are drawn and the air conditioner is blowing cold I'll forget that it's summer and I'll put on a jacket and one of those wool caps. The caps feel good any time of year really. I can see why black people wear them. And one size fits all.

Jim leans down, whispers in my ear. For a moment my fingers stop; the needles go silent. I look across the living room, see my reflection in the TV. I am low and round and gray. "I used to be prettier," I say.

"You're pretty enough," he says. He keeps stroking my ears.

"I never weighed this much in my life," I whisper.

"It's all the same by me," Jim says.

I can't say anything.

"Really," he says, his voice softer now.

I set down my hooks, my wool, shut my eyes and lean my head back into his belly. Its firmness, heavy as a ripe pumpkin, always surprises me. There are worse things about a man than a belly. When I open my eyes Jim is smiling at me, hopefully, upside down.

"Say I was Bob Vila and it was my birthday besides."

T-minus three minutes.

In our bedroom Jim is breathing hard. I have my arms around him. "Come on, honey," I say. My eyes are on the clock.

The headboard is thumping, thumping, thumping against the wall. It's only half-inch sheetrock. I try to concentrate. "Okay honey!" I call out to him. His eyes are closed; I don't know if he hears me.

I think of the sheetrock. Sheetrock is really billions of tiny dead fossils ground into powder, then rolled out in wet slurry. Pressed flat. Baked. Papered both sides. Then painted white. I saw the whole process once. Bob and Norm visited the quarry and the factory, which were somewhere along a coast in Canada. From the loading dock there were trucks one after another hauling away the finished product, the 4-by-8-foot sheets that we make rooms with, white rooms, rooms so white we have to hang things on the walls. No one can live with bare sheetrock.

Across from the bed there's a calendar with a nature picture. A stream with trees and sunlight. There's no water or trees like that around here; it had to have been taken somewhere else, another state. Below the color picture there is a line of twelve little squares. The months. I can't read their names, let alone pick out the days.

Thump and *thump* and *thump*.

Across the bedroom the digital clock blinks the time. It's T-minus one. I call out to Jim. He hears me this time and picks up speed. I start to feel something, but it's too late for me. So much is late for me that I close my eyes and keep them shut. I concentrate on that thudding sound. Jim goes on and on. After awhile it's like there's someone pounding, pounding, pounding on the front door.

Dispersal

To get to the Matson sale I had to drive through town. On the edge of town I passed the red brick high school where my wife, Ellen, teaches English in the upper grades. Through the school windows I could see students moving about in front of colored posters. I knew that if Ellen weren't teaching I could not be thinking about buying that New Holland hay mower listed on Matson's sale bill. My forty Holsteins are a fine bunch of cows, but if it weren't for Ellen's town job, things on the farm would be tough.

Which made me think of Matson and his family. I didn't really know them—they were strangers to me—but I could tell from their sale bill what had gone wrong. Too much machinery, not enough wheat. Too many bankers, not enough rain. Tough luck all around.

But bad luck draws a crowd like blood pulls flies. Several pickups followed mine as I turned at the red auction flags. Soon up ahead I could see the shiny aluminum tops of Matson's grain bins. Below stood his newer white house and, beside it, lines of pickups stretched from his yard down his driveway and along the shoulders of the highway.

I parked, leaving myself room to turn around, and began to walk quickly toward the crowd. Sales do that to you. Anything can happen at a sale. In Matson's yard cars and trucks had parked on his lawn. Their tires rutted the soggy April grass and water welled up in the zigzag tread marks. Closer to his house, a pickup had backed over a small trimmed spruce tree. The tree remained bent over in a green horseshoe beneath the tire. I slowed my walk. For a moment I thought of turning back, of going home. If everybody left, there could be no sale. But even as I thought, several farmers passed me. I kept walking.

Ahead, the crowd surrounded the auctioneer, who stood atop a hayrack. He wore a wide black cowboy hat, and his tanned, wrinkled throat bobbed like a rooster's craw as he cried the small stuff. Cans of nails. Some rusty barbed wire. Three fence posts. Some half-cans of herbicide. A broken shovel. Beyond the auctioneer, in even lines, was the machinery, mostly John Deere green and Massey Ferguson red. Beyond everything were Matson's long, unplowed fields.

I registered for a bidder's number, then stood in the sunlight with a cup of coffee and looked over the crowd. You shouldn't get in a hurry at a sale. You ought to get the feel of things. The crowd was mostly farmers with a few bankers and real estate men thrown in. The younger bankers wore flannel shirts and seed-corn caps, but I could pick them out right away. Like the real estate guys, their faces were white and smooth and they squinted a lot, as if they were moles who just today had crawled out of the ground into the sunlight. Moles or skunks.

Off to the side I noticed an older farmer picking through a box of odds and ends. He fished out a rat-tail file from the box and drew it across his thumbnail. He glanced briefly around, then laid the file alongside the box and continued digging.

"Gonna spend some of the wife's money?" somebody said to me. I turned. It was Jim Hartley, who milked cows just down the road from my farm. I knew he already had a good mower.

"Not if she can help it," I said.

He grinned. But then his forehead wrinkled and his blue eyes turned serious. "Hell of a deal, a bank sale like this. Imagine if you had to sell out. Had all these people come onto your farm and start picking through your stuff like crows on road kill."

I looked back at the old man with the file. But both he and it were gone.

"Be tough," I said. That old bastard.

Hartley looked around at the crowd. "Haven't seen Matson anywhere. And I can't blame him for that. Good day to get drunk."

"I don't really know the man," I said. "He's a stranger to me."

"He's got some pretty fair equipment," Hartley said. "The combine looks good. And that New Holland mower—it's damn near brand new." He narrowed his eyes. "You could use a good mower."

"Maybe I'll take a look," I said. I raised my coffee cup, took a sip.

Soon enough Hartley went off toward the combine, and I found the mower. From a distance it looked good. The yellow and red colors were still bright, which meant it had always been shedded. Up close I checked the cutting sickle. All the knives were in place and still showed serration, which was like buying good used tires still showing the little rubber teats on the face of their tread. Next I turned the hay pickup reel to watch the sickle move. The knives slid easily between their guards with a sound that reminded me of Ellen's good pinking shears. Then I saw the toolbox and the mower's maintenance manual. The thin book was tattered and spotted with grease and with Matson's fingerprints, tiny whirlwinds painted in oil. Its pages fell open to the lubrication section. There Matson had circled and numbered every one of the grease fittings. I was sold.

I stashed the manual and walked away. I didn't want to linger near the mower and attract other bidders. I bought another cup of coffee and then stood off to the side where I could watch the mower and see who stopped by it. Two men paused by the mower, but they wore wheat seed-caps and smoked, which said they were grain men. Soon they moved to the combine. One stocky farmer slowed by the mower, but he wore high rubber boots and a Purina "Pig-Power" jacket. I was feeling lucky until a man and his son walked toward the mower like it was a magnet and they were nails. Their cuffs were spotted with manure splash. They wore loose bib overalls for easy bending. And they wore caps cocked to one side, a habit dairymen have from leaning their foreheads against the flanks of their cows.

The son turned the pickup reel while the old man held his ear to the main bearing case. After the old man nodded, the two of them crawled underneath the mower and didn't come out for a long time. What the hell did they see under there? Finally they came out and stood off to the side. They stared at the mower and nodded and whispered. I wondered how many cows they milked.

By now the auctioneer was in the back of his pickup and was barking his way along the hay wagons and rakes, headed this way. I went over my figures again. I knew in town that mower would sell for $5,500, give or take a couple of hundred. I had set my limit at $5,000. As long as I stuck to that figure I couldn't go wrong.

"Now here's a mighty clean mower—" the auctioneer called. The hook and pull of his arms drew the crowd forward. "Boys, if this mower were a car, we'd call her 'cherry.' You know what this mower would sell for in town, boys, so somebody give me six thousand to start!"

The crowd was silent.

"Five thousand, then!"

Still there was silence.

"Boys, boys—four thousand to start!"

In the silence somewhere a dog barked. The auctioneer's eyes flickered to the clerk and then to the banker. The banker, ever so slightly, shrugged. He was worried about the big tractors and combines, about the house and the land.

"Boys, this ain't a rummage sale, but somebody give a thousand dollars."

I saw the younger dairyman nod, and the bidding was on. At $1,600, it was between the dairyman and me. The young fellow began to look at his father before each bid. At $1,750 I saw the old man fold his arms and squint. At $1,850 he pursed his lips and shook his head. His son mouthed a silent curse and looked down.

"Eighteen hundred three times—gone!" the auctioneer said and pointed to me. I held up my bidder's number for the clerk to record as the crowd dissolved away to the next implement.

I couldn't believe my luck. Eighteen hundred was a steal, no two ways about that. My ears burned. I felt shaky. I sat down on the mower's long drawbar. I ran my hand along its cold steel. I wondered for a moment if the mower had felt any change, if it knew I was up there. Soon enough that shaky feeling gave way to a stronger idea—that I had to get that mower out of here and home as soon as possible.

I found the clerk's booth and wrote out my check. Then I brought around my truck and got ready to hook on to the mower. Trouble was, Matson had parked the mower in field-cutting position, which meant its mouth was too wide for highway travel. I knew that the drawbar released to swing to a narrower stance. But for the life of me I could not see how. I knew I still wasn't completely over that shaky feeling because if I had been home on my own farm and just sat there a few minutes, I could have figured things out. Not here, though.

I asked another farmer if he knew, but the man was in a hurry to join the crowd around the combine. So there was only one thing to do—find someone who knew for sure. And that was Matson.

I walked up to his house. The drapes were all drawn. I rapped on the door and waited. Inside, I could hear a baby crying. Along the sidewalk was a flower bed. Somebody last fall had done a lot of work planting tulip bulbs, but now their first green spears were drowned in quack grass.

A woman answered the door. She was about Ellen's age, late thirties. She had a bone-white face that said she seldom went outside.

"Is Mr. Matson home?" I asked.

"Yes," she said. She just stood there, looking beyond me to the auction. From deeper in the house I could smell cigarette smoke.

"I bought . . . an implement," I said.

Her pale eyes returned to mine. "Tom—" she called back to the dusk of the hallway.

We waited. There was no answer. No one came forward. She shrugged. "He's back there in the living room," she said, leaning toward the now louder crying of the baby. "Why don't you go on in?"

I walked down the dim hallway into the living room. In the room the TV was a colored bull's-eye. *The Phil Donahue Show* was on, but the picture kept wavering, then skipping ahead several frames. I didn't see Matson anywhere.

"Tom," his wife said loudly from behind me. "Some man's got a question."

Matson slowly sat up. He'd been lying on the couch, on his back. He was fully dressed in coveralls, leather boots, a cap, even his work gloves. He did not take his eyes off the TV.

"And why should we believe you?" Donahue was saying to a man seated on the stage.

"Tom—" his wife said even louder this time.

"I heard," he said.

"The mower," I began. "I bought the mower and . . ."

Matson nodded and walked past me toward the door. I followed. Outside we walked in silence toward the mower. The auctioneer was standing on the platform of the combine. "Boys, I'll buy this combine myself," he was saying. "Then I'll put it on a truck and I'll haul it to North Dakota and I'll make myself ten thousand dollars in one day. Any one of you could do the same thing, you know that, boys."

Matson did not look at the auctioneer. He walked toward the mower like there was a perfectly straight but invisible line drawn in the dirt. I explained my trouble with the drawbar. He nodded and slid underneath. I saw him remove three cotter keys. He handed them to me, then swung the drawbar.

"Now why didn't I see that?" I said.

But Matson still didn't speak. He just stared at the mower.

"It looks like a good mower," I said, then wished I hadn't. I was sure he would ask me how much I had paid.

He was silent. Then, without looking up from the mower, he said, "I'll hook you on."

"You bet," I answered. I got in my pickup. He waved me backward, then held up his hands. I felt him slide the iron pin through the mower's tongue and my bumper hitch, felt the clank in my spine. You know when you're hooked on.

I got out of the pickup again but there was not much to say.

"I appreciate the help," I said.

But Matson didn't reply. He just stared at the iron pin that joined his mower to my truck.

I drove off very slowly, watching the mower and Matson in the rearview mirror. It was like they were on TV. The mower stayed the same size, but Matson got smaller and smaller as the camera pulled away from him.

Suddenly Matson's legs began to move. They moved faster and faster, and Matson grew in size in my mirror. Then he was running alongside my truck, pounding on the side with his fist. Ahead of me was the highway, and I thought of speeding up and leaving him behind. But I stopped. I rolled my window halfway down.

Matson's face was completely white. He paused as if he had forgotten why he had run after me. Then he said, "It was a good mower." His right eye twitched as he spoke.

"I believe that," I said.

"It never let me down," he said.

"That's because you took good care of it," I said. "That's plain to see."

"I did," Matson said. "I worked hard. Nobody can take that away from me," he said. His voice was softer now. I could hardly hear him.

"Nobody I know ever said otherwise," I answered. "When your name came up people said, 'Matson—with a little more luck, some more rain, better wheat prices, he'd have made it.' That's what I heard other people say."

"This is not my fault," he said, swinging his arm at the pickups, at the whole auction. "It wasn't me."

For one long moment I thought of getting out of my pickup and putting my arms around Matson. But you just can't do things like that. We waited there. Finally he turned away.

Out on the highway, I kept the truck at twenty-five. The mower started to sway side to side if I drove any faster. Ahead of me the sun was shining on the dark fields where other farmers were planting. I couldn't stop thinking about Matson. About that run-over spruce tree. His white-faced wife, her tulip bed run to weeds.

I thought about Ellen, about how sometimes in the evenings when there's nothing on TV she reads me poems, poems she likes and uses in her English classes. I thought of one poem in particular, by W. H. Auden. His poem was about a painting in a museum, a painting of Icarus and Daedalus. Even I remembered that story from school. Icarus and Daedalus were prisoners on this island, and they made wings from feathers and wax, strapped on the wings, and flew away. Icarus, however, flew too close to the sun, and the heat melted the wax from his feathers and he fell into the ocean and drowned. In the painting there was a plowman in a nearby field. The plowman saw Icarus fall but he just kept plowing. There was a passing ship, too, but it had somewhere to get to and so it just kept sailing.

Suddenly my truck yawed and shuddered. Behind me the mower was whipping violently side to side—I was driving way over fifty. I hit the brakes hard. Back at twenty-five, the mower trailed straight again. I let out a breath and watched my speedometer from then on.

But I hated driving that slowly. What I most wanted to do was get the mower home, park it in the machine shed, and close the door on it. Then I wanted to eat lunch, sweep up in the barn, feed silage, milk, eat supper, watch the weather report, and go to bed. Because once I had done all those things, this day would be over.

A Gravestone Made of Wheat

"You can't bury your wife here on the farm," the sheriff said. "That's the law."

Olaf Torvik looked up from his chair by the coffin; he did not understand what the sheriff was saying. And why was the sheriff still here, anyway? The funeral was over. They were ready for the burial—a family burial. There should be only Torviks in the living room.

"Do you understand what he's saying, Dad?" Einar said.

Olaf frowned. He looked to his son, to the rest of the family.

"He's saying we can't bury Mom here on the farm," Einar said slowly and deliberately. "He's saying she'll have to be buried in town at Greenacre Cemetery."

Olaf shook his head to clear the gray fuzz of loss, of grief, and Einar's words began to settle into sense. But suddenly a fly buzzed like a chainsaw—near the coffin—inside—there, walking the fine white hair on Inge's right temple. Olaf lurched forward, snatching at the fly in the air but missing. Then he bent over her and licked his thumb and smoothed the hair along her temple. Looking down at Inge, Olaf's mind drew itself together, cleared; he remembered the sheriff.

"Dad?" Einar said.

Olaf nodded. "I'm okay." He turned to the sheriff, John Carlsen, whom he had known for years and who had been at the funeral.

"A law?" Olaf said. "What do you mean, John?"

"It's a public health ordinance, Olaf," the sheriff said. "The state legislature passed it two years ago. It's statewide. I don't have it with me 'cause I had no idea. . . . The law prohibits home burials."

"The boys and me got her grave already dug," Olaf said.

"I know," the sheriff said. "I saw it at the funeral. That's why I had to stay behind like this. I mean I hate like hell to be standing here. You should have told me that's the way you wanted to bury her, me or the county commissioners or the judge. Somebody, anyway. Maybe we could have gotten you a permit or something."

"Nothing to tell," Olaf said, looking across to Einar and Sarah, to their son Harald and his wife, to Harald's children. "This is a family affair."

The sheriff took off his wide-brimmed hat and mopped his forehead with the back of his sleeve. "The times are changing, Olaf. There's more and more people now, so there's more and more laws, laws like this one."

Olaf was silent.

"I mean," the sheriff continued, "I suppose I'd like to be buried in town right in my own backyard under that red maple we got. But what if everybody did that? First thing you know, people would move away, the graves would go untended and forgotten, and in a few years you wouldn't dare dig a basement or set a post for fear of turning up somebody's coffin."

"There's eighteen hundred acres to this farm," Olaf said softly. "That's plenty of room for Inge—and me, too. And nobody in this room is likely to forget where she's buried. None of us Torviks, anyway."

The sheriff shook his head side to side. "We're talking about a law here, Olaf. And I'm responsible for the law in this county. I don't make the laws, you understand, but still I got to enforce them. That's my job."

Olaf turned and slowly walked across the living room; he stood at the window with his back to the sheriff and the others. He looked out across his farm—the white granaries, the yellow wheat stubble rolling west, and far away, the grove of Norway pine where Inge liked to pick wildflowers in the spring.

"She belongs here on the farm," Olaf said softly.

"I know what you mean," the sheriff said, and began again to say how sorry . . .

Olaf listened but the room came loose, began to drift, compressing itself into one side of his mind, as memories, pictures of Inge pushed in from the past. Olaf remembered one summer evening when the boys were still small and the creek was high and they all went there at sundown after chores and sat on the warm rocks and dangled their white legs in the cold water.

"Dad?" Einar said.

The sheriff was standing close now, as if to get Olaf's attention.

"You been farming here in Hubbard County how long, fifty years?"

Olaf blinked. "Fifty-three years."

"And I've been sheriff over half that time. I know you, I know the boys. None of you has ever broken a law that I can think of, not even the boys. The townsfolk respect that . . ."

Olaf's vision cleared and something in him hardened at the mention of town folk. He had never spent much time in town, did not like it there very much. And he believed that, though farmers and townspeople did a lot of business together, it was business of necessity; that in the end they had very little in common. He also had never forgotten how the townsfolk treated Inge when she first came to Hubbard County.

"What I mean is," the sheriff continued, "you don't want to start breaking the law now when you're seventy-five years old."

"Seventy-eight," Olaf said.

"Seventy-eight," the sheriff repeated.

They were all silent. The sheriff mopped his forehead again. The silence went on for a long time.

Einar spoke. "Say we went ahead with the burial. Here, like we planned."

The sheriff answered to Olaf. "Be just like any other law that was broken. I'd have to arrest you, take you to town. You'd appear before Judge Kruft and plead guilty or not guilty. If you pled guilty, there would be a small fine and you could go home, most likely. Then your wife would be disinterred and brought into town to Greenacre."

"What if he was to plead not guilty?" Einar said.

The sheriff spoke again to Olaf. "The judge would hold a hearing and review the evidence and pass sentence. Or, you could have a trial by jury."

"What do you mean by evidence?" Olaf asked, looking up. That word again after all these years.

The sheriff nodded toward the coffin. "Your wife," he said. "She'd be the evidence."

Evidence . . . evidence; Olaf's mind began to loop back through time, to when Inge first came from Germany and that word meant everything to them. But by force of will Olaf halted his slide into memory, forced his attention to the present. He turned away from the window.

"She told me at the end she should be buried here on the farm," Olaf said softly.

They were all silent. The sheriff removed his hat and ran his fingers through his hair. "Olaf," he said. "I've been here long enough today. You do what you think is best. That's all I'll say today."

The sheriff's car receded south down the gravel road. His dust hung over the road like a tunnel and Olaf squinted after the car until the sharp July sunlight forced his gaze back into the living room, to his family.

"What are we going to do, Dad?" Einar said.

Olaf was silent. "I . . . need some more time to think," he said. He managed part of a smile. "Maybe alone here with Inge?"

The others quietly filed through the doorway, but Einar paused, his hand on the doorknob.

"We can't wait too long, Dad," he said quietly.

Olaf nodded. He knew what Einar meant. Inge had died on Wednesday. It was now Friday afternoon, and the scent of the wilting chrysanthemums had been joined by a heavier, sweeter smell.

"I've sent Harald down to Penske's for some ice," Einar said.

Olaf nodded gratefully. He managed part of a smile, and then Einar closed the door to the living room.

Olf sat alone by Inge. He tried to order his thoughts, to think through the burial, to make a decision; instead, his mind turned back to the first time he set eyes upon Inge, the day she arrived in Fargo on the Northern Pacific. His mind lingered there and then traveled further back, to his parents in Norway, who had arranged the marriage of Olaf and Inge.

His parents, who had remained and died in Norway, wrote at the end of a letter in June of 1918 about a young German girl who worked for the family on the next farm. They wrote how she wished to come to America; that her family in Germany had been lost in the war; that she was dependable and could get up in the morning; that she would make someone a good wife. They did not say what she looked like.

Olaf carried his parents' letter with him for days, stopping now and again in the fields, in the barn, to unfold the damp and wrinkled pages and read the last part again—about the young German girl. He wondered what she looked like. But then again, he was not in a position to be too picky about that sort of thing. It was hard to meet young, unmarried women on the prairie because the farms were so far apart, several miles usually, and at day's end Olaf was too tired to go anywhere, least of all courting. He had heard there were lots of young women in Detroit Lakes and Fargo, but he was not sure how to go about finding one in such large cities. Olaf wrote back to his parents and asked more about the German girl. His parents replied that she would be glad to marry Olaf, if he would have her. He wrote back that he would. His parents never did say what she looked like.

Because of the war, it was nearly two years later, April of 1920, before Olaf hitched up the big gray Belgian to his best wheat wagon, which he had swept as clean as his bedroom floor, and set off to Fargo to meet Inge's train.

It was a long day's ride and there was lots to see—long strings of geese rode the warm winds north, and beyond Detroit Lakes the swells of wheat fields rose up from the snow into black crowns of bare earth. But Olaf kept his eyes to the west, waiting for the first glimpse of Fargo. There were more wagons and cars on the road now, and Olaf stopped nodding to every one as there were far too many. Soon his wagon clattered on paved streets past houses built no more than a fork's handle apart. The Belgian grew skittish and Olaf stopped and put on his blinders before asking the way to the Northern Pacific Railroad station.

Inge's train was to arrive at 3:55 PM at the main platform. Olaf checked his watch against the station clock—2:28 PM—and then reached under the wagon seat. He brought out the smooth cedar shingle with his name, Olaf Leif Torvik, printed on it in large black letters. He placed it back under the seat, then on second thought, after glancing around the station, slipped the shingle inside his wool shirt. Then he grained and watered the Belgian and sat down to wait.

At 3:58 her train rumbled into the station and slowly drew to a stop, its iron wheels crackling as they cooled. People streamed off the train. Olaf held up his shingle, exchanging a shy grin with another man—John William Olsen—who also held a name-sign.

But there seemed to be few young women on the train, none alone.

A short Dutch-looking woman, small-eyed and thick, came toward Olaf—but at the last second passed him by. Olaf did not know whether to give thanks or be disappointed. But if the Dutch-looking woman passed him by, so did all the others. Soon Olaf was nearly alone on the platform. No one else descended from the Pullman cars. Sadly, Olaf lowered his shingle. She had not come. He looked at his shingle again, then let it drop to the platform.

He turned back to his wagon. If he was honest with himself, he thought, it all seemed so unlikely anyway; after all, there were lots of men looking for wives, men with more land and money, men certainly better-looking than Olaf.

"Maybe my folks made the mistake of showing her my picture," Olaf said to the Belgian, managing a smile as the horse shook his head and showed his big yellow teeth. Olaf wondered if he would ever take a wife. It seemed unlikely.

Before he unhitched the Belgian, he turned back to the platform for one last look. There, beside the train, staring straight at him, stood a tall, slim girl of about twenty. Her red hair lit the sky. In one hand she clutched a canvas suitcase, and in the other, Olaf's cedar shingle.

Inge Altenburg sat straight in Olaf's wagon seat, her eyes scared and straight ahead; she nodded as Olaf explained, in Norwegian, that there was still time today to see about the marriage. She spoke Norwegian with a heavy German accent, said yes, that is what she had come for.

They tried to get married in Fargo, in the courthouse, but a clerk there said that since Olaf was from Minnesota, they should cross the river and try at the courthouse in Moorhead. Olaf explained this to Inge, who nodded. Olaf opened his watch.

"What time do they close in Minnesota?" he asked the clerk.

"Same as here, five o'clock."

It was 4:36; they could still make it today. Olaf kept the Belgian trotting all the way across the Red River Bridge to the Moorhead Courthouse.

Inside, with eight minutes to spare, Olaf found the office of the Justice of the Peace; he explained to the secretary their wish to be married, today, if possible.

The secretary, a white-haired woman with gold-rimmed glasses, frowned.

"It's a bit late today," she said, "but I'll see what I can do. You do have all your papers in order?" she asked of Inge.

"Papers?" Olaf said.

"Her birth certificate and citizenship papers."

Olaf's heart fell. He had not thought of all this. He turned to Inge, who already was reaching under her sweater for the papers. Olaf's hopes soared as quickly as they had fallen.

"All right," the secretary said, examining the birth certificate, "now the citizenship papers."

Inge frowned and looked questioningly at Olaf. Olaf explained the term. Inge held up her hands in despair.

"She just arrived here," Olaf said, "she doesn't have them yet."

"I'm so sorry," the secretary said, and began tidying up her desk. Olaf and Inge walked out. Inge's eyes began to fill with tears.

"We'll go home to Park Rapids," Olaf told her, "where they know me. There won't be any problem, any waiting, when we get home."

Inge nodded, looking down as she wiped her eyes. Olaf reached out and brushed away a teardrop, the first time he had touched her. She flinched, then burst into real tears.

Olaf drew back his hand, halfway, but then held her at her shoulders with both his hands.

"*Ich verstehe*," he said softly, "I understand."

They stayed that night in a hotel in Detroit Lakes. Olaf paid cash for two single rooms, and they got an early start in the morning. Their first stop was not Olaf's farm, but the Hubbard County Courthouse in Park Rapids. At the same counter Olaf and Inge applied for both her citizenship and their marriage license. When Inge listed her nationality as German, however, the clerk raised an eyebrow in question. He took her papers back to another, larger office; the office had a cloudy waved-glass door and Olaf could see inside, as if underwater, several dark-suited men passing Inge's papers among themselves and murmuring. After a long time—thirty-eight minutes—the clerk returned to the counter.

"I'm afraid we have some problems with this citizenship application," he said to Inge.

When Inge did not reply, the clerk turned to Olaf. "She speak English?"

"I don't believe so, not much anyway."

"Well, as I said, there are some problems here."

"I can't think of any," Olaf said, "we just want to get married."

"But your wife—er, companion—lists that she's a German national."

"That's right," Olaf answered, "but she's in America now and she wants to become an American."

The clerk frowned. "That's the problem—it might not be so easy. We've got orders to be careful about this sort of thing."

"What sort of thing?"

"German nationals."

"Germans? Like Inge? But why?"

"You do realize we've been at war with Germany recently?" the clerk said, pursing his lips. "You read the papers?"

Olaf did not bother to answer.

"I mean the war's over, of course," the clerk said, "but we haven't received any change orders regarding German nationals,"

Olaf laughed. "You think she's a spy or something? This girl?"

The clerk folded his arms across his chest. Olaf saw that he should not have laughed, that there was nothing at all to laugh about.

"We've got our rules," the clerk said.

"What shall we do?" Olaf asked. "What would you recommend?"

The clerk consulted some papers. "For a successful citizenship application she'll need references in the form of letters, letters from people who knew her in Germany and Norway, people who can verify where she was born, where she has worked. We especially need to prove that she was never involved in any capacity in German military or German government work."

"But that might take weeks," Olaf said.

The clerk shrugged. Behind him one of the county commissioners, Sig Hansen, had stopped to listen.

"There's nothing else we can do?" Olaf asked, directing his question beyond the clerk to the commissioner. But Sig Hansen shook his head negatively.

"Sorry, Olaf, that's out of my control. That's one area I can't help you in." The commissioner continued down the hall.

"Sorry," the clerk said, turning to some other papers.

With drawn lips Olaf said, "Thanks for your time."

They waited for Inge's letters to arrive from Europe. They waited one week, two weeks, five weeks. During this time Olaf slept in the hayloft and Inge took Olaf's bed in the house. She was always up and dressed and had breakfast ready by the time Olaf came in from the barn. Olaf always stopped at the pumphouse, took off his shirt, and washed up before breakfast. He usually stepped outside and toweled off his bare chest in the sunlight; once he noticed Inge watching him from the kitchen window.

At breakfast Olaf used his best table manners, making sure to sit straight and hold his spoon correctly. And though they usually ate in silence, the silence was not uncomfortable. He liked to watch her cook. He liked it when she stood at the wood range with her back to him, flipping pancakes or shaking the skillet of potatoes; he liked the way her body moved, the way strands of hair came loose and curled down her neck. Once she caught him staring. They both looked quickly away, but not before Olaf saw the beginnings of a smile on Inge's face. And it was not long after that, in the evening when it was time for Olaf to retire to the hayloft, that they began to grin foolishly at each other and stay up later and later. Though Olaf was not a religious man, he began to pray for the letters' speedy return.

Then it was July. Olaf was in the field hilling up his corn plants when Inge came running, calling out to him as she came, holding up her skirts for speed, waving a package in her free hand. It was from Norway. They knelt in the hot dirt and tore open the wrapping. The letters! Three of them. They had hoped for more, just to make sure, but certainly three would be enough.

Olaf and Inge did not even take time to hitch up the wagon, but rode together bareback on the Belgian to Park Rapids. They ran laughing up the courthouse steps, Olaf catching Inge's hand on the way. Once inside, however, they made themselves serious and formal, and carefully presented the letters to the clerk. The clerk examined them without comment.

"I'll have to have the judge look at these," he said, "he's the last word on something like this." The clerk then retreated with their letters down the hall and out of sight.

The judge took a long time with the letters. Twenty minutes. Thirty-nine minutes. Olaf and Inge waited at the clerk's window, holding hands below the cool granite counter. As they waited, Inge began to squeeze Olaf's hand with increasing strength until her fingers dug into his palm and hurt him; he did not tell her, however. Finally the clerk returned. He handed back the letters.

"I'm sorry," he said, "but the judge feels these letters are not sufficient."

Olaf caught the clerk's wrist. The clerk's eyes jumped wide and round and scared; he tried to pull back his arm but Olaf had him.

"We want to get married, that's all," he said hoarsely.

"Wait—" the clerk stammered, his voice higher now. "Maybe you should see the judge yourselves."

"That's a damned good idea," Olaf said. He let go of the clerk's arm. The clerk rubbed his wrist and pointed down the hall.

Olaf and Inge entered the judge's chambers, and Olaf's hopes plummeted. All the old books, the seals under glass on the walls, the papers, the white hair and expressionless face of the judge himself: they all added up to power, to right-of-way. The judge would have it his way.

Olaf explained their predicament. The judge nodded impatiently and flipped through the letters again.

"Perhaps what we should do for you," the judge said, "is to have you wait on this application for a period of, say, one calendar year. If, during that time, it is determined that Inge Altenburg is loyal and patriotic, then we can consider her for citizenship. And, of course, marriage."

"One year!" Olaf exclaimed.

The judge drew back and raised his eyebrows. Sig Hansen, the commissioner, had paused in the doorway. He shook his head at the judge.

"Christ, Herb," he said, "you ought to run it through, let 'em get married. They're harmless. They're just farmers."

Inge rose up from her chair. There was iron in her face. "Come—" she commanded Olaf, in English, "it is time we go to home."

They rode home slowly, silently. The Belgian sensed their sorrow and kept turning his wide brown eyes back to Olaf. But Olaf had no words for the big animal. Inge held Olaf around his waist. As they came in sight of their buildings she leaned her head on his shoulder and he could feel her crying. They ate their dinner in silence, and then Olaf returned to his cornfield. At supper they were silent again.

Come sundown, Olaf climbed the ladder to the hayloft and unrolled his bedroll in the hay. He wished he could have found some good thing to say at supper, but it was not in him. Not tonight. Olaf felt old, tired beyond his thirty-three years. He lay back on the loose prairie hay and watched the sun set in the knotholes of the west barn wall, red, then violet, then purple, then blue shrinking to gray. He hardly remembered going to sleep. But then he knew he must be dreaming. For standing above him, framed in the faint moonlight of the loft, stood Inge. She lay down beside him in the hay and when her hair fell across his face and neck he knew he could not be dreaming. He also knew that few dreams could ever be better than this. And in his long life with Inge, none were.

Olaf rose from his chair by her casket. That night when she came to him in the loft was forty-five years past. That night was Olaf's last in the hayloft, for they considered themselves married, come morning—married by body, by heart, and by common law.

And Inge never forgot her treatment at the Hubbard County Courthouse in Park Rapids; she rarely shopped in the town, preferring instead Detroit Lakes, which was twelve miles farther but contained no unpleasant memories.

Nor did she become a citizen; she remained instead without file or number, nonexistent to federal, state, or local records. She was real, Olaf thought, only to those who knew her, who loved her. And that, Olaf suddenly understood, was the way she should remain. As in her life, her death.

Before Olaf called the family back into the room, he thought he should try to pray. He got down on his knees on the wood floor by the coffin and folded his hands. He waited, but no words came. He wondered if he had forgotten how to pray. Olaf knew that he believed in a great God of some kind. He had trouble with Jesus, but with God there was no question. He ran into God many times during the year: felt of him in the warm field-dirt of May; saw his face in the shiny harvest grain; heard his voice among the tops of the Norway pines. But he was not used to searching him out, to calling for him.

Nor could he now. Olaf found he could only cry. Long, heaving sobs and salty tears that dripped down his wrists to the floor. He realized, with surprise, that this was the first time he had cried since Inge's death, that his tears in their free flowing were a kind of prayer. He realized, too, that God was with him these moments. Right here in this living room.

When the family reassembled, Olaf told them his decision. He spoke clearly, resolutely.

"We will bury Inge here on the farm as we planned," he said, "but in a little different fashion."

He outlined what they would do, asked if anyone disagreed, if there were any worries. There were none. "All right then, that's settled," Olaf said. He looked around the room at his family—Einar, Sarah, the children, the others.

"And do you know what else we should do?" Olaf said.

No one said anything.

"Eat!" Olaf said. "I'm mighty hungry."

The others laughed, and the women turned to the kitchen. Soon they all sat down to roast beef, boiled potatoes with butter, dill pickles, wheat bread, strong black coffee, and pie. During lunch Harald returned with the ice. Einar excused himself from the table and went to help Harald.

Once he returned and took from a cupboard some large black plastic garbage bags. Olaf could hear them working in the living room, and once Einar said, "Don't let it get down along her side, there."

Olaf did not go into the living room while they worked. He poured himself another cup of coffee, which, strangely, made him very tired. He tried to remember when he had slept last.

Sarah said to him, "Perhaps you should rest a little bit before we . . ."

Olaf nodded. "You're right," he said, "I'll go upstairs and lie down a few minutes. Just a few minutes."

Olaf started awake at the pumping thuds of the John Deere starting. He sat up quickly—too quickly, nearly pitching over—and pushed aside the curtain. It was late—nearly dark. How could he have slept so long? It was time.

He hurriedly laced his boots and pulled on a heavy wool jacket over his black suit-coat. Downstairs, the women and children were sitting in the kitchen, dressed and waiting for him.

"We would have wakened you," Sarah said.

Olaf shook his head to clear it. "I thought for a minute there . . ." Then he buttoned his coat and put on a woolen cap. He paused at the door. "One of the boys will come for you when everything is ready," he said to Sarah.

"We know," she said.

Outside, the sky was bluish purple and Harald was running the little John Deere tractor in the cow lot. The tractor carried a front-end loader and Harald was filling the scoop with fresh manure. Beyond the tractor some of the black Angus stretched stiffly and snorted at the disturbance. Harald drove out of the lot when the scoop was rounded up and dripping. He stopped by the machine shed, went inside, and returned with two bags of commercial nitrogen fertilizer.

"Just to make sure, Grandpa," he said. His smile glinted white in the growing dark.

"Won't hurt," Olaf said. Then he tried to think of other things they would need.

"Rope," Olaf said. "And a shovel." Then he saw both on the tractor.

"Everything's ready," Harald said, pointing to the little John Deere. "She's all yours. We'll follow."

Olaf climbed up to the tractor's seat and then backed away from the big machine-shed doors. Einar and Harald rolled open the mouth of the shed and went inside.

The noise of their two big tractors still startled Olaf, even in daylight, and he backed up farther as the huge, dual-tandem John Deeres rumbled out of their barn. A single tire on them, he realized, was far bigger than the old Belgian he used to have. And maybe that's why he never drove the big tractors. Actually, he'd never learned, hadn't wished to. He left them to the boys, who drove them as easily as Olaf drove the little tractor. Though they always frightened him a little, Olaf's long wheat fields called for them—especially tonight. Behind each of the big tractors, like an iron spine with twelve shining ribs, rode a plow.

Olaf led the caravan of tractors. They drove without lights into the eighty-acre field directly west from the yellow-lit living-room window of the house. At what he sensed was the middle of the field, Olaf halted. He lowered the manure and fertilizer onto the ground. Then, with the front-end digger, he began to unearth Inge's grave.

Einar and Harald finished the sides of the grave with shovels. Standing out of sight in the hole, their showers of dirt pumped rhythmically up and over the side. Finished, they climbed up and brushed themselves off, and then walked back to the house for the others.

Olaf waited alone by the black hole. He stared down into its darkness and realized that he probably would not live long after Inge, and yet felt no worry or fear. For he realized there was, after all, a certain order to the events and times of his life: all the things he had worked for and loved were now nearly present.

Behind, he heard the faint rattle of the pickup. He turned to watch it come across the field toward the grave. Its bumper glinted in the moonlight, and behind, slowly walking, came the dark shapes of his family. In the bed of the pickup was Inge's coffin.

The truck stopped alongside the grave. Einar turned off the engine and then he and Harald lifted the coffin out and onto the ground. The family gathered around. Sarah softly sang "Rock of Ages," and then they said together the Twenty-third Psalm. Olaf could not speak past "The Lord is my . . ."

Then it was over. Einar climbed onto the tractor and raised the loader over the coffin. Harald tied ropes to the loader's arms and looped them underneath and around the coffin. Einar raised the loader until the ropes tightened and lifted the long dark box off the ground. Harald steadied the coffin, kept it from swinging, as Einar drove forward until the coffin was over the dark hole. Olaf stepped forward toward it as if to—to what?

Einar turned questioningly toward Olaf. "Now, Dad?" he said.

Olaf nodded.

Swaying slightly in the moonlight, the coffin slowly sank into the grave. There was a scraping sound as it touched bottom. Harald untied the ropes and then Einar began to push forward the mound of earth; the sound of dirt thumping on the coffin seemed to fill the field. When the grave was half filled, Einar backed the tractor to the pile of manure and pushed it forward into the hole. Harald carried the two bags of nitrogen fertilizer to the grave, slit their tops, and poured them in after the manure. Then Einar filled in the earth and scattered what was left over until the grave was level with the surrounding field.

Olaf tried to turn away, but could not walk. For with each step he felt the earth rising up to meet his boots as if he were moving into some strange room, an enormous room, one that went on endlessly. He thought of his horses, his old team. He heard himself murmur some word that only they would understand.

"Come, Dad," Sarah said, taking Olaf by the arm. "It's over."

Olaf let himself be led into the pickup. Sarah drove him and the children to the field's edge by the house where Einar had parked the little John Deere.

"You coming inside now?" Sarah asked as she started the children toward the house.

"No, I'll wait here until the boys are finished," Olaf said, "you go on ahead."

Even as he spoke the big tractors rumbled alive. Their running lights flared on and swung around as Einar and Harald drove to the field's end near Olaf. They paused there a moment, side by side, as their plows settled onto the ground. Then their engine RPMs came up and the tractors, as one, leaned into their work and headed straight down-field toward Inge's grave.

The furrows rolled up shining in the night light. Olaf knew this earth. It was heavy soil, had never failed him. He knew also that next year, and nearly forever after, there would be one spot in the middle of the field where the wheat grew greener, taller, and more golden than all the rest. It would be the gravestone made of wheat.

Olaf sat on the little tractor in the darkness until the boys had plowed the field black from side to side. Then they put away the tractors and fed the Angus. After that they ate breakfast, and went to bed at dawn.

Bad Blood

I knocked on the door.

Waited.

Inside the farmhouse I heard a radio go quiet, then shuffling sounds. I had a good feeling about this place; it was set well off the road, and the old lady appeared to live alone.

She opened the door partway. "Yes?" Her voice was thin and croaky from lack of use.

"Good morning, ma'am," I chirped. "My name's Jared Righetti and I'm looking for summer work. Painting, lawn mowing, odd jobs?" One good thing about being an undersized sixteen-year-old is that I can pass for thirteen. I try to see beyond her, into the house.

"No, nothing for you," she said, and stepped back from the screen door. The shades were half drawn—what is it with old people and daylight?—so I couldn't see much. However, it smelled like an old person's house—stale, fruity, soggy tea bags, flowers, cats, all of it mixed together like the odor of old carpet.

"Okay, ma'am," I said. I flashed her my winning smile (learned from my old man). "Sorry to bother you." I headed down her porch steps and pedaled off with my lawn mower in tow—except that I went only a short way before turning back.

"What is it now?" she said. She was still at the screen door. "I told you I have no work for you."

"I understand, ma'am," I said. "But I'm in the Boy Scouts, and we get pins for doing volunteer work. I'm wondering if you'd mind if I mowed your lawn for free? It won't take me long. It's part of the Boy Scout oath—to do volunteer work."

She was silent, then cleared her throat with a raspy sound. "Okay. But just that front part."

"Thank you, ma'am!" I said, and saluted.

Boy Scouts. Ha.

As I started up my mower, I felt her gaze on me. When I began to move back and forth across the shaggy lawn, her white head peeped from behind the window. Her fuzzy white hair looked like the dandelion seed globes that my mower scattered in the wind.

I had spotted this place when my family first landed in this lame, white-bread Ohio town. I almost said Iowa; we've moved around so much, sometimes I forget where we are. Anyway, I was riding my bike, casing the town—which I had to admit looked perfect for us. My father was a genius in choosing places such as Oakville, population 7,500. Here people left their car windows open, left their garage doors up in the daytime, and left their kids' bikes lying on lawns. It was one of those little towns that the real world hadn't caught up to yet—a petty thief's dream.

Trouble was, my father had drummed into me that we were not petty thieves. Thieves, all right, but not small-timers. "The dollar bill is lying on the table, and all you have to do is reach over and pick it up. But it's not the dollar you want, or the ten-spot, or even the whole wallet. Set your sights higher, son." But stealing was in my blood. I didn't see a woman shopping; I saw her purse loosely slung over her shoulder. I didn't see a man walking down the street; I saw his wallet peeking from his hip pocket. I didn't see a photographer shooting a sundown scene; I saw his camera bag unattended. It was genetic.

Anyway, back to the old lady. That first week here I had biked all the way to city limits and a little beyond—which was scary. All that open space, all those cornfields with tall, tight, shadowy rows. My parents had warned me about midwestern cornfields, about kids getting lost in them and never found. Big fields and open horizons gave me the creeps—give me honking taxis and narrow streets any day (also probably genetic). So just as I was about to pedal like mad back to town, I saw a narrow driveway, and beyond—back off the road at least a block—an old white farmhouse. Saggy barn. Tall hay shed, along with various cribs and coops. And a lawn in major need of mowing. Elmer A. Anderson, the mailbox read.

Even as I looked, this little white-haired lady shuffled onto her porch to water some red flowers in a window box. I sank low in the ditch so she wouldn't see me and I watched her for quite a while. I got the feeling there was no Elmer around. At age sixteen I already had a nose for lonely old widows; sometimes I amazed and disgusted myself at the same time.

Today when I finished mowing, I rattled my mower back to my bike. On Mrs. Anderson's porch steps sat a tall glass of iced tea. "I wouldn't feel right without giving you something for your trouble," she said from behind the screen.

"Whew! It's hot—thank you so much, Mrs. Anderson," I exclaimed.

"How'd you know my name?" she asked suspiciously.

"The mailbox?" I answered.

She was silent.

I took my time with the iced tea, but finally finished the last, long, cold swallow. I approached the screen door with the empty glass.

"Just set it on the porch," she said.

"Thank you. Bye, Mrs. Anderson," I called cheerfully over my shoulder. Through her watery little eyes I imagined seeing myself: a smallish brown-haired kid on his bike, heading down the driveway towing his lawn mower on a rope. The image should be a Norman Rockwell painting. *Summer Job* would be the title. That or *Honest, Hard-working Young Man.*

However, as far as I could see, there hadn't been any honest, hard-working men in my family for generations. My great-grandfather, whose last name was unpronounceable (it had several Zs and Ys), was some kind of King of the Gypsies back in immigrant days in New York City. His pickpocketing skills bordered on magic and what's called the dark arts. People not only didn't miss their wallets or coin purses; they forgot they ever had them. (My father knows the moves but won't teach them to me—his own son. "They'll just get you in trouble, and besides, son, you've got to set you sights high in this world." If I hear that one more time, I swear I'll become an actual nice, honest young man just to punish him.) My grandfather, Alphonse Szymoro, founded the so-called Travelers, the world's largest fly-by-night roofing and home repair company. It's based in Skokie, Illinois. Don't believe me? *Sixty Minutes* did an investigative report on the Travelers but all CBS got were some blurry long-distance photos of white Ford F-150 pickup trucks carrying ladders and cans of roofing tar. Most of the segment was interviews with geezers all weepy about paying thousands of dollars for roof repairs and still needing rain buckets in their living rooms. When Mike Wallace began to talk about money—how the Travelers wives all drove Cadillacs—my mother gave my old man the evil eye. "Always said we should have stayed with the family," she said. (Her family was eastern European as well—thick as thieves, you might say.)

"Nonsense," my father said. He was a tidy, dark-haired man with brown eyes and an open, likeable face and a sense of humor that tended to one-liners. His favorite: "America's biggest problem is that it's overrun with private property." (It is sort of funny, considering.) Anyway, now he continued, "You don't see *Sixty Minutes* peeking in our windows, do you? The bigger you get, the bigger target you make. The three of us—we're on nobody's radar, and every penny we make, we keep."

"Right," I muttered sarcastically. I happened to know that my old man had been drummed out of the larger clan for cheating them. In other words, not only was my father a crook, he was a dishonest crook. But he was a great father. Hey—you can't have everything.

My mother had nothing more to say about her imaginary Cadillac, because in many ways my old man was right. Here we were in a nice rented home, a three-bedroom rambler, with a green lawn and bright flower beds. We had settled quietly into this neighborhood and now were just another family on East Maple Drive. Okay, slightly darker skinned, and brown-eyed rather than blue, and a foot shorter than most of the corn-fed Swedish and German stock around here. But we passed for Italian (Righetti was my favorite name so far), and Italians get a pass in the Midwest because they are associated with Italian food. Nobody eats more than midwesterners; it's why they're so fat.

Anyway, there was always the question of jobs—how my family supported itself—but as usual my father had that covered. My mother was an interior decorator (the perfect job for casing houses) and my father was a wholesaler involved in supplying olive oil to Italian pizza joints across the Midwest. I didn't know exactly what scam he had going right now, but he was very cheerful of late, and I got the feeling he was closing in on something big.

But then again, so was I.

The next part I'll skip through, because it's as boring as a public television documentary on life in the Midwest. See me mowing Mrs. Anderson's lawn, front and back, the next time. See me returning once a week to Mrs. Anderson's farm. See me trimming the hedge. See me painting the porch railing. See me trying to get a look into the outbuildings, but see her always watching me from her chair on the porch. See me raking her leaves in the fall. See me shoveling snow in the winter. See me working in her garden the next spring. See me waiting for my chance—at what, I didn't know. See me inside her gloomy house, having my snack, politely munching a sugar cookie and sipping my iced tea. See me checking drawers in the kitchen, desks in the living room the first time she leaves me alone. See me notice, one day, through the parlor doors (never opened quite this far) a photo on display on the wall—like a shrine in a church—except this was a shrine to a soldier.

"That man on the wall, is that your husband?"

Mrs. Anderson stiffened. "No," she said abruptly, and hurried to shut the parlor door.

Next week when I arrived to work, I knocked and knocked. It wasn't locked, so I stepped inside. Mrs. Anderson was in the parlor, just sitting, staring at the soldier on the wall. It's like she hadn't moved for an entire week.

"Hello? It's me, Jared," I called.

She turned slowly; it was as if she didn't recognize me.

"I'm going to start on the garage today," I said cheerfully. "Scraping and painting."

"It's his birthday," she murmured.

I stepped forward to the parlor entrance. For the first time I got a good look around. It was like a museum filled with antiques—valuable antiques.

"His birthday?" I said.

"Garry," she said to the wall. Creepy-like, as if she was talking to Garry.

I looked closer at the shrine. There were several photos of Garry, one with helicopters and a jungle in the background.

"Garry, my son," she murmured, as if calling out to him.

There was a framed and yellowed newspaper clipping. "Local Marine Garrett Anderson Killed in Vietnam." I got it: her dead son.

"He would be fifty today," she whispered. "Fifty years old. Isn't that amazing."

"Yes, it is," I agreed as I made a note of the antiques: some great old lamps, a lion's head rocking chair, an actual wind-up Victrola phonograph, plus an eight-track tape deck and a shelf of clunky, oversized eight-track tapes: Bob Dylan; Crosby, Stills, Nash and Young; the Byrds; others with faded daisy and psychedelic designs. Eight-tracks were worth a lot of money nowadays; people collected them.

Mrs. Anderson blinked; she seemed surprised to see me standing there. "I'm starting on the garage today," I said again. Loudly, cheerfully. As always.

She didn't seem to hear me and turned back to look at the soldier on the wall. Which gave me the opportunity—at last—to case the outbuildings without her spying on me.

The garage was gloomy and full of spiders. It looked like a museum of rusty tools and shovels, not a hundred bucks' worth of goods. So I slipped over into the barn.

The door creaked and pigeons clattered out of the hayloft. My heart pounded; the damned birds scared me. It took a while for my eyes to adjust to the light, which revealed a long row of rusty cow stalls and a few old shovels and forks lying here and there. Zilch. Zero.

Coming out of the barn, I looked around. The only other building was a hay shed: a metal roof supported by tall poles, and open sides. I still don't know why I walked over to it and certainly can't explain why I walked around back, behind it. The thief in me, I guess.

A few bales had sagged and spilled out to the ground. They were black and rotted. I kicked at them. Just when I was about to give up on finding anything of value, I spotted a different kind of green in the haystack. Some kind of canvas or tarp. I tugged loose a couple of bales and looked closer. The canvas, mouse-chewn so badly it looked shot by a machine gun, was draped over some kind of wooden frame. Beams, heavy ones. Some kind of secret garage.

I got down and dug out some bottom bales until I could slip underneath the canvas. Inside the canvas enclosure it was dark except for the bullet holes. Standing up, I hit my head on something hard; suddenly I had plenty of light—as in stars—little arcing pinwheels of white.

To steady myself I reached out and felt curving metal sticky with some kind of grease. "Ack," I muttered, and wiped my hand on the scratchy hay.

I needed more light so I crawled backward out of there and began to remove more bales. Soon I had a double doorway–sized area clear, and found a corner of the canvas. It was nailed to the bottom of the wooden frame. I glanced around; seeing or hearing no one, I yanked it upward.

With a ripping sound, the canvas came loose; light spilled into the secret garage. Inside was a car.

A small car covered in grease.

A small, squat car with lines and curves that anyone would instantly recognize: an old Corvette.

I sucked in a breath. It's not the dollar bill or the ten-spot or even the whole wallet! Peeking around the hay shed toward the house, and seeing nothing of old lady Anderson, I stepped inside the secret garage and tried the car door. Grease, everything coated with grease, as if painted or broomed on, but the door opened. The low cockpit sat empty, its stick shift with its little round knob sticking upright between the seats. I wiped dust from the dashboard, the gauges. The odometer read 562 miles. The *bumpa-bumpa* of my heart echoed louder inside the dim cab. A classic Corvette with less than a thousand miles on it. The car had to be worth twenty or thirty grand.

In the glove box were some papers. A faded green title sheet with all the information. Make: Chev. Year: 1964. Model: Coupé (Stingray). Owner: Garrett Elmer Anderson. One other paper, a yellow sheet of tablet paper, fell out of the title papers.

Dear Mom and Dad,

Take care of my 'Ray. When we win this war, which shouldn't take long, I'll come home and I'll drive you down Main Street in the Fourth of July parade.

I promise.

Love, Garry

The rest of that afternoon I loudly and cheerfully scraped window trim on the garage. I whistled while I worked, and kept one eye on the house. Finally the old lady came out on the porch. She seemed older in just two hours and walked bent over as if she carried a hundred pounds on her bony shoulders.

I thought she'd never bring out an iced tea, but finally she remembered. I joined her on the porch. We sat there in silence.

"Hot one today," I said. "Whew."

She was silent.

"But I'm happy for the work," I said.

She stared off across the fields. Her eyes were cloudy today.

"I'm saving money for college, you know."

She had nothing to say.

I took a deep breath. "That and a car."

No response.

"If I had a car, I could drive out here anytime you needed me," I added.

She blinked, seemed to consider that. "Garry had an old car," she murmured, still looking across the fields. "Funny little thing, it was. He worked summers at the gas station to buy that car. Was so proud of it."

Then I took a chance, a big chance. "There's a little old car in the hay shed," I said. "Would that be it?"

"Car in the hay shed?" she repeated. "You mean a tractor?"

"No, a little old car," I replied as if I was uninterested—as if this were the most boring topic in the world.

"I don't know what Garry did with his little car," she murmured. "So hard to remember everything."

"Just a little old car in the hay shed," I drawled, and pretended to check some paint chips under my fingernails.

She looked through the parlor at the soldier on the wall, then around her house. "I hardly drive my Pontiac anymore," she said. "I certainly don't need two cars."

I felt a little shaky; things were happening fast; things were coming together. It was a major adrenaline rush—and I suddenly understood why the men in my family could never hold straight jobs.

"Why don't you take it, Jared?" she said.

"The little car in the hay shed?" I asked. My voice was suddenly as thin and shaky as hers.

"Why would I need two cars? I hardly drive the Pontiac anymore."

I swallowed, then took a gamble. "No, Mrs. Anderson, I couldn't do that. You've been awfully nice to me, too, and while the car probably isn't worth much, I just couldn't accept a gift like that."

"Why, you're always helping out around here," she continued, like she hadn't heard me. She actually came over and patted me on the head—it was the first time we had touched. "This place would have fallen down without you. Such a nice young fellow. I think you should take it. Why would I need two cars? I hardly drive the Pontiac anymore."

"I'll . . . think about it," I said. I was so excited that I almost tipped my glass. "Right now I'd better get back to work."

"I hardly drive the Pontiac anymore," she murmured as I left.

Outside, I let out a deep breath. I hurried back into the secret garage and examined the title page again: it was clear that if I could get her signature in a couple of places, the Corvette was mine. I couldn't believe my luck. I did a crazy little victory dance—wait till my old man saw this car.

Then I heard a sound and peeked back around the hay shed; I saw her shuffling across her porch, so I stuffed the title papers inside my shirt and resumed work on the garage. I watched her lift a watering can to her petunias. Her arms shook so badly that she spilled most of the water. I turned away—I couldn't watch.

That night, at home, my father asked, "So how's the old lady?" He had come to be a little puzzled at my loyalty to Mrs. Anderson. I think he worried that I was turning into a nice, young, honest fellow.

"Better and better," I said, trying to sound sly. In truth, I had this weird mix of emotions swirling in my head.

"Great," my father answered. He flashed a white-toothed smile (sometimes I swear he could pass for Omar Sharif and be in the movies). "Anything you'll need help with?"

"If I do, I'll let you know." I was suddenly crabby.

He nodded. "Remember, son—" he began.

"I know, I know. Nothing illegal, nothing I can't walk away from, don't get greedy, blah blah." I'd heard all that one too many times.

"That's right," he said gently. "Good luck."

I shrugged. It was difficult to stay angry at him. "Anyway, it's in the bag," I said.

He patted me on the head. "I'm proud of you, son."

Later, in bed, I lay in the dark with my eyes closed. I saw myself cruising in Garry Anderson's Corvette. At first it was just me, then me and a girl—a blond college coed. Then I must have drifted off, because I was in college, studying to be a doctor or an astronaut—something all-American—and it was clear that the blond girl and I would be married and have two perfect children, and I would take my family for Sunday afternoon drives in the Corvette, and when we passed, people would look up and remark, "Such a nice family."

The next night I had another Corvette dream. It started out with the blond girl again, but then it was me at the wheel, and Mr. and Mrs. Anderson were in the back seat. People were gathering for a parade. Firecrackers and fireworks kept going off, in loud booms and sharp machine gun–like rattles, then the parade began. It was the Fourth of July, and I was driving proudly down the street, wearing a Boy Scout's uniform and saluting all the people waving and clapping—except in the crowd I kept seeing flashes of this ragged-looking soldier. He was burned or injured somehow, and he just kept staring at me. From this dream I woke up with a start; my heart was pounding.

The third night I had a dream that made no sense. I was in this health club, in the weight room with all these bodybuilders. Me, an undersized, pencil-necked sixteen-year-old who couldn't lift one of the massive iron plates they were pumping. I watched them in awe (me watching them would have made yet another Norman Rockwell painting). Then I went up to the biggest guy and in a cheerful, totally optimistic voice said, "Excuse me, sir. I want to change how I look. If I start lifting weights today, how long do you think it would take for me to look like you?"

The buffalo-necked guy glared down at me, then lifted me by the scruff of my neck with one hand and examined my scrawny body. "How long would it take for you to look like me? I'd say at least three to four generations." Everyone in the club laughed wildly.

The next day I felt hyper, felt shaky—like today was the day it had to be done. Now or never. Fish or cut bait.

I biked out to Mrs. Anderson's right away in the morning. She looked like she had been wearing the same dress all week. She didn't even get out of her chair when I came in.

"Garry!" she said.

"No, Jared," I said loudly.

She blinked; then her eyes filled with water. "I'm sorry, Jared. Don't know what I was thinking."

"It's okay," I said quickly. I drew up a chair and produced the title sheet to the Corvette. "I've changed my mind; I'd like to have the little car in the hay shed," I said.

She stared at me.

"The one you offered to me," I added.

"That would be fine," she murmured. "I don't even drive my Pontiac anymore."

"You'll have to sign on the title page," I said clearly and loudly. "Do you understand?" *Nothing illegal, nothing you can't walk away from . . .*

"Yes, I understand," she said.

I had a pen ready. If I hadn't, if one thing had gone wrong—say the pen ran dry—I swear I would have bolted.

But I didn't.

"There," she said. Her handwriting was crampy but legible.

"And date it," I said. I wanted everything in her handwriting, everything legal.

"What is the date?" she asked.

I told her the day and the year.

She looked up quickly. "How is that possible?" she murmured. "That means Garry is fifty."

"Right there," I said, pointing to the line. "Fill in the date right there." My voice was high and faster now. I was sweating. Images of my dream Fourth of July parade filled my head. Garry on the wall stared down at me. I thought I might throw up.

But then it was done. "Thank you so much," I said. I touched her bony hand—it was cool, almost cold. I drew back, then hurried to the door.

"Jared?" she called after me. "Garry?"

Mrs. Anderson croaked only two weeks later. I was the one who found her, which I prefer not to talk about, other than that she was on the kitchen floor. Her false teeth had come out, and the place didn't smell so good. I guess I knew she was going to tip over sooner rather than later, so to be honest it wasn't a surprise.

Looking back, I could have taken advantage of the situation and cased the entire house—maybe she had money under the mattress—but that would have been a mistake. "Never get greedy," my father always said. "It only calls attention to yourself."

So I called 911, did all the right things. Me, the yard boy who had worked for Mrs. Anderson for nearly two years—loyal to the end. Even some of the distant neighbors, who I didn't know had been watching, knew of my work for her. "More than work, a relationship with Mrs. Anderson," as the attorney for the estate described it. He and the neighbors supported me when some long-lost Andersons appeared at the funeral (which I attended along with my mother and father) and then stayed in town for the reading of the will.

"It always happens," the attorney muttered to me. "Somebody dies all alone, and then the relatives come out of the woodwork." There were objections to the signatures and dates on the Corvette's title, but in the end it was no contest—and anyway, the distant relatives ended up with the farm, which they immediately put up for sale.

My father was beside himself with pride. "You've got a great future, son," he kept saying as we loaded the Corvette onto the trailer. "This was masterful. Couldn't have done better myself. And being there at the funeral—what a great touch."

"Thanks," I muttered.

He was so happy he didn't hear me.

As we drove out of the driveway, I looked back at the old white house, at the sagging, shabby buildings, at the dead flowers on the porch. Then we headed onto the highway and picked up speed. As we passed the endless rows of corn, for an instant I thought I saw bony, tattered arms reaching out at me, but they were only corn leaves fluttering in the wind.

My father began to whistle as he drove. I turned to look at him. My father the crook. My grandfather and great-grandfather, all crooks. *At least three to four generations,* the bodybuilder had said. I looked behind at the little car on the trailer.

"So, I've found this dealer in Wisconsin who specializes in muscle cars. He'll give top dollar," my father began.

I cut him off. "We'll see," I answered.

He looked at me, surprised.

"Hey, it's my car," I said. "Has my name on the title, if you recall. Which means I can do with it what I want."

His face turned dark with anger, then a moment later opened in a great laugh. "Okay, I get it. Chip off the old block, yes? Just like your old man?"

"Maybe," I said. I looked down the highway ahead of me. "Then again, maybe not."

Heart of the Fields

The hunters were all Hansens. They were all dressed in red and stood in the snow near their pickups. Benny's father said again, "You're sure there was nothing."

"Nothing," Benny said.

Benny's father cursed; his breath smoked in the December air and a clear droplet spun from his nose.

Benny turned away. He leaned on his rifle and tried to get his breath without taking the frozen air too deeply into his lungs. Beside Benny, three of his cousins were lying back on the snow, their coats open at the throat and steaming. Benny and they had just finished driving the big timber where the snow was hip-deep in places. Benny's father, his uncles, and his grandfather had been on stands waiting for the deer to break out. There had been no deer.

Benny looked down the field to his grandfather. The grandfather's gray Ford sat parked in the northeast corner of the hay field, alongside a low patch of brush. The brush broke the outline of the Ford, shielded it from the timber and from the eyes of any deer that might try to come east across the open snow. A yard-wide oval of carbon blackened the snow beneath the Ford's tailpipe. To keep warm, his grandfather ran the motor all day. By its constancy, the Ford's dull, thumping idle was a part of the landscape of pines and snow and fields, a sound that, like a steady breeze, went unnoticed until it died. But during deer season, the Ford's pumping rhythm never ceased.

Benny wondered if his grandfather got lonely, there in the car all day. He knew his grandfather took with him only a cold egg sandwich, a thermos of Sanka, and the old twelve-gauge shotgun with a single slug—"In case one tries to come east," as the old man said every year.

The grandfather no longer carried his own deer rifle, the silvery Winchester Model 94. Benny had it. Benny's father and uncles decided those things. They awarded the rifle to Benny because they believed the grandfather's eyes were too dim to make good use of the rifle, and because, at age thirteen, Benny was the oldest grandchild.

Benny drew his glove along the worn walnut stock of the Winchester. He thought of walking on to the Ford to talk with his grandfather, but in the failing light the snowy road lengthened even as he watched. Today, however, was the last day of deer season. They would not have to hunt tomorrow, and Benny would visit him then. He would make lunch, scrambled eggs and toast and cranberry jelly and Sanka, for his grandfather. And then they would sit together by the oil burner and listen to the radio.

"Well—that's it for this year," Benny's father said, and cursed again.

Benny turned. Across the blueing snow, two fluorescent orange hunting caps swam out from the timber's shadow. Drawing light from air, the hats bobbed toward Benny and the others in separate rhythms. They were the last of the drivers. There was now no chance for deer.

"Weren't nothing in there," one of the cousins muttered from the snow.

"The hell," Benny's father said quickly. "There's deer tracks goin' into that timber but none comin' out. What does that tell you? It tells me you drivers got too spread out and the deer got back through you."

None of the drivers said anything because Benny's father was right. Some of the cousins, disoriented by the gray, sunless sky, had wandered in and out of the drive line. Other cousins, tired of the deep snow, walked the higher ridge trails instead of working through the bottom brush in the draws and holes. The deer, a great buck along with some does, had not stirred.

Hell, maybe the deer weren't in the timber in the first place, Benny thought. Though he had seen the buck's tracks earlier in the day, had seen the buck himself in the alfalfa and cornfields all that fall, by now Benny barely believed in the gray-brown ghosts.

A hundred yards away, the orange caps rode bodies now, Benny's Uncle Karl and another cousin. "So where'd they go?" Karl called across the snow as if to get in the first word.

Benny's father spit.

"They didn't cross south," Karl continued, waving his rifle. "They didn't go west because of the lake. And they didn't come north because you were there. Unless you didn't see 'em."

"They didn't come north," Benny's father said, a tic of anger working his forehead.

The cousins were all standing now.

"Hell, I don't know," Karl muttered. "Maybe they're hiding under these goddamn pickups."

His boot thudded against the fender and snow fell over the tire.

"Maybe they came east, through here . . ." one of the cousins said.

"Then Grandpa would have seen them," Benny answered immediately.

The hunters all looked, first at Benny, and then down the field at the grandfather's Ford. They had forgotten the grandfather.

But Karl turned his back on the grandfather's car. "Hell, the way his eyes are these days, he couldn't see a deer if it jumped over his car."

Benny turned quickly to his father, who only looked down and kicked snow from his boots as he nodded in agreement.

"Honk the horn for him," Karl said, jerking his head toward the Ford, "let's go home."

"I will! I will!" Two of the youngest cousins scrambled to be the first into the pickups. The horns blared across the fields and their echoes wavered back from the timberline. The others began to case their rifles but Benny remained standing, angered at his father and uncle. He waited for the Ford's brake lights to blink on red, for the race of the engine and the black blossom of exhaust.

But the Ford's idle pulsed evenly on. There was no blink of light, no black smoke, nothing. From the side of his eye Benny saw his father, gun half cased, look up and freeze. The others straightened and stared downfield at the Ford. White-faced and wide-eyed, the cousins at the pickup horns now looked about as if they had done some terrible wrong.

"Honk again," Benny's father said with an old slowness.

The horns blared and the timber honked back the faded replies.

"Again," Karl said quickly.

At the third honking there was motion near the Ford, brown motion from the brush alongside the car. Three deer uncoiled from the bushes, their white tails flagged up and bouncing. Behind Benny someone scrambled for a rifle. "No—" Benny's father shouted.

The big buck and two does leaped a car's length in front of the Ford and then ran straight away north. The buck's antlers flashed through a last slant of sunlight and then all three deer disappeared into the shadow of the timber.

"Holy Christ—" someone began, but stopped. In the silence, the Ford's thumping idle beat in the air like the heart of the fields.

"Grandpa!" Benny cried. He ran toward the Ford, tearing off his coat for speed, outdistancing the others. As he neared the car he saw his grandfather slumped in the front seat. Benny tore open the door.

"What? Whoa!" his grandfather exclaimed with a start. "You scared me there, Benny!"

"Grandpa! Are you—didn't you hear us honk?"

The grandfather blinked. The white wisps of his eyebrows moved as he thought. "I don't rightly know," he finally said. "I guess I heard, but then I thought I was dreaming. Or something like that. I wasn't sleeping, nosir. But I was dreaming, somehow . . ." His voice trailed off. The others were there now, crowding around the car. Benny held on to his grandfather. He buried his face in the roughness and the woody smell of the old wool coat and held his grandfather tight.

"Here now, Benny," the old man said, "where's your coat? It ain't July."

One of the cousins had retrieved Benny's coat, and he stood up to put it on. His grandfather squinted around at the hunters. "Any luck today, boys?" he said.

No one said anything. Then Benny's father said, "No, no luck today, Dad."

The grandfather shook his head. "Guess we'll have to eat track soup this year. And that's thin eating, I always said."

Benny's father nodded.

"Everybody's out?" the grandfather asked, peering across to the timber he could not see.

"Everybody's out," Karl answered.

"I'll drive on home then, and get myself a hot cup of Sanka."

The Ford's engine raced briefly, then the car lurched forward; on the snow was a dark rectangle of wet leaves and grass. The Ford receded up the snowy field road toward the yellow yard light and buildings. The hunters stared after him. "I'll be damned," one of the men murmured.

Karl turned away to inspect the deer beds, three gray ovals in the snow, and beside them the scuffed hearts of the leaping hooves. But darkness had fallen and the hunters soon pressed on to their pickups.

Benny's father led the caravan. He drove in the grandfather's tracks that led up to the old house and then beyond, to the country road that forked away to their own farms and homes.

But tonight the chain of headlights behind Benny and his father did not pass through the grandfather's yard. One by one the trucks turned in and parked. Doors thudded. Laughter hung in the frosty air as the Hansens, all of them, converged on the yellow lights of the grandfather's house.

The Gleaners

That first season the gleaners came out only at sundown. They parked their vehicles, battered Chevrolets and rusted Datsun pickups, well away from each other on the road along the potato fields. Caps pulled low across their foreheads, gunnysacks flat shawls across their backs, the gleaners crossed the ditch and entered the field. Under a pink and blue sky, the air belled with September chill, the gleaners hurried along the black, heaved furrows, the damp and tangled vines at their feet. They had come to look for potatoes that the great mechanical harvesters had missed or discarded.

There—a fat, muddy russet, big as a man's hand.

There—in the empty trough of the irrigator's wheel, another fat one.

There—in a clump of vines, two keepers.

Ahead, beside a heavy stone brightly scarred, among a small maze of boot prints and a blacker stain of oil, a whole peck of spilled potatoes!

Stoop, stoop, and stoop again, in this way the gleaners moved steadily downfield. They measured their progress against the dark silhouette of the irrigator, its long drooping lengths of pipes and tall stilt legs. Intermittently, like prairie dogs remembering to look about, the gleaners stood fully erect: they glanced at the other pickers, to the road, and to their own cars—after which they dipped ground-ward again and kept moving. In the bluing twilight their bags humped darker and darker on their backs.

Later, the gleaners staggered through the last, plum-purple light to their cars. Sacks thudded and trunk lids slammed. Engines raced and gravel chattered sharply against wheel wells as their vehicles accelerated away, without headlights, toward the highway.

The second season the gleaners came out earlier in the day. Some appeared already in the afternoon, and the boldest waited in the cars beside potato fields as harvesters worked the last rows. Word was that Universal Potato Company had nothing against gleaning. It had bigger things to worry about—like hot spots in the new storage bins, like nailing down the Burger King contract, like the union sniffing around. Universal Potatoes wasn't about to bother people who picked up a few stray spuds. Just don't drive in the fields or otherwise pack down the dirt—that was the unofficial word. Otherwise, have at them, plenty of spuds for the taking, enough for the whole town of Sand Lake (population 2,650)—that was the word in the cafes and stores on Main Street. With spuds free for the picking, why would a person even fool with potatoes at home in the garden?

That second autumn better vehicles drove slowly along the potato fields, newer and shinier Ford sedans, late model Pontiacs, an occasional older Cadillac. Often they stopped, amber parking lights on, radios playing faintly through open windows as their occupants watched the gleaners. The spectators were mostly older retired couples, people like Shirley Kelm and her husband, John.

"Look at them," Shirley remarked, staring past her husband at the gleaners. "Don't it remind you of the Depression?" She was seventy-four, had short white curly hair, and wore a gauzy blue head scarf tied loosely over her permanent, knotted tightly at the chin. She was neatly dressed in knit pants, blouse, and sweater. From the side of her eyes she watched for her husband's reaction.

John's heavy white eyebrows drooped slightly as he squinted. He remained silent, his heavy knuckles wrapped around the steering wheel.

"You wouldn't think, in modern times like these, a person would ever see this, would you?" Shirley said, clucking her tongue briefly. She watched as a heavyset woman stooped for a potato, then another and another like a fat old hen picking her way across a chicken yard. She speared six spuds in quick succession. Shirley felt her heart pick up a beat.

"Depression days are coming again," John said. He clenched the steering wheel harder; his fingers reddened. "Things can't go on the way they are!"

"Some people would agree with you," Shirley said quickly. She didn't want to anger him, have him drive off. It had been difficult enough getting him to take her on the dirt roads past the potato fields. Shirley did not drive, had never had a license. Their car was a white 1976 Oldsmobile with 24,532 miles on the odometer and no rust spots or paint chips, a town car.

"I mean, why can't people raise their own food, like we do?" she added, turning the angle of her vision an inch, watching him closely. He continued to stare somewhere into the field.

Shirley turned her eyes back to the gleaners. The fat woman dragged her gunnysack forward. Shirley's heart beat slightly faster still. She put her hand inside her jacket pocket, felt the cool plastic there.

"Easier to steal them, everybody steals nowadays—" John said, pointing. His voice rose sharply.

Shirley swung her gaze away, out her side window and across the road to a drifting hawk which she pretended had caught her interest. With John she had to go carefully. At age seventy-nine he was an increasingly silent, unpredictable man. Conversation with him was like speaking with their son who lived in Alaska. His phone was hooked up to a satellite, and the words had to bounce off something (was it the earth or was it the satellite? she could never remember), then float back. There was a delay. You had to wait. You couldn't talk fast and you couldn't interrupt.

"Though," Shirley said evenly, looking back to the potato field, "you couldn't really call it stealing, could you?" She paused. "I mean, Universal would just plow them under, wouldn't they?"

John stared across the field. Shirley watched the fat woman shake a clump of potato vines. Dirt showered in the sunlight.

"Their potatoes are poison," John said. "The chemicals!"

Shirley waited. She watched the big woman stoop five more times, then drag her bag forward, leaning into the task, using both hands now.

"Oh I'm not sure about that," Shirley said, drawing in a little whistle of air through her teeth to show that she wasn't in any way serious about the topic at hand. "Some people say they taste just as good as homegrown." Inside her pocket she gathered up the heavy plastic bag.

A car came from behind. Shirley quickly turned to look. A battered pickup rattled past, its dust rolling briefly upward, then tilting slowly toward the ditch. John, staring into the sunset, did not even turn his head.

She eyed her husband for a long moment, then said, "Maybe we should give them potatoes a try." She laughed briefly—loud enough so that he was certain to hear. "Why don't I just step out there and find a couple of spuds for our supper?"

In the silence a small airplane droned overhead. Its single red light blinked slowly across the sky, crawling toward the Dakotas. Suddenly John's hand dropped from the wheel onto the gear shift and the car lurched forward.

They passed a second potato field where a shiny blue car parked in the shallow ditch drew Shirley's eyes. A car from town. A familiar car, though she couldn't put the person's name to it. The owner, a well-dressed woman about her own age, with white hair and a gauzy pink scarf, was a few yards into the field. She carried a white plastic grocery bag which only could be gotten from Marketplace Food and Deli, the new grocery store in town. Shirley leaned forward through her window to squint at the woman who, at the same moment, looked toward the road. It was Thelma Haynes, a widow who worked in the floral shop at Marketplace Food and Deli. Their eyes locked. Thelma turned quickly away toward the field; Shirley ducked her head out of sight below the car's window.

John turned to stare at her. Shirley pretended to see something on the floor, then sat up straight again. The car moved on.

As they drove she kept her eyes peeled, as usual, for cars over the center, for farm implements or stray animals on the road, but her mind was filled with another vision: Thelma Haynes's plastic grocery bag. It bloomed white on top but hung dark and heavy below (she thought of a bull's scrotum) with potatoes. Shirley's gaze swung around to the interior of the Oldsmobile. She stared at the steering wheel. The dashboard. The levers. She watched the pedals, how John positioned his feet. She knew which pedal stopped the car, which gave it gas. Two pedals, two feet. She looked at the shift lever. The little window above the steering wheel said "P R D 2 1," and momentarily she thought of the *Wheel of Fortune* game show, the bonus round. How Pat gave people the letters "R S T L E." How, often well before the contestants, she figured out the words.

Later, as they drove on blacktop, a sharp smell drew up her gaze. They were passing Universal Potato Company, the long, new, airport hangar–sized building that stood at the edge of town. Its walls were concrete, windowless panels, and high atop the gray front was the company's logo, a giant potato that radiated yellow sunbeams. Above the logo, steam billowed from vents and shiny turbines that spun out a hot, starchy odor of french fries.

Universal Potatoes had come last year to northwestern Minnesota from Idaho where the land was tired and the water expensive. Around Sand Lake the soil, graded perfectly flat by some long ago glacier, was loam on top with clean gravel below and a water table that rose up to within twenty feet of daylight. The combination was ideal for irrigation and big machinery. It was a wonder, Shirley thought, that farmers around here had not thought of growing potatoes themselves.

But people, especially farmers, were creatures of habit. Before potatoes this land had supported only dairy cows, and barely enough of them for farmers to scratch out a living. Shirley had grown up on such a farm—the white house, the red sheds, the black, winter hills of manure that rose up behind the barn. In spring the manure went back onto the fields and the whole country stank so strongly that, while waiting for the school bus, her eyes ran tears; and if she tied her head scarf across her face, bandit-style, to cover her nose, then when she arrived at school her hair smelled of cow shit. There were kids, rough-looking boys and tomboy girls, who always smelled of the barn because they did chores before school, and she steered clear of them. Her friends were town kids.

After high school Shirley took a teller's position at First Farmer's Bank and married John Anderson, who ran the hardware store. Her bank was the most modern building in town with its fluorescent lights and a continual cool, humming breath of air conditioning. In town the only time she had to smell manure was when farmers came in for their loans.

Looking back, something Shirley did often after she retired, she saw a trend among the farmers who came to the bank. It had to do with the smell of manure. In the 1950s only a few farmers came in for loans, and they stank strongly of cow dung and occasionally of DDT. In the 1960s more farmers came for loans. They smelled sweeter and dustier with the scent of commercial fertilizers such as nitrogen, phosphate, and sulfur, along with the orange-rind flavor of 2,4-D, the brush-and-slough grass killer. In the 1970s, when First Farmer's grew in assets from one million to six million, the farmers had come in droves. More chairs were added to the waiting room, and their fabric soon gave off the sharper, nose-itching smell of ag-chemicals. Herbicides. Pesticides.

Atrazine, Roundup, Lorsban. By the end of the 1970s the odor of manure was gone altogether. Farmers dressed better, sometimes even
wearing ties for their meetings with the loan officers. By 1980, when
First Farmer's built its new building and simplified its name to First
Bank, the farmers had at long last joined modern times. And Shirley,
as retired chief teller, was proud to have played a part.

Of course with changing times some things were lost. The twenty-
cow dairy farm disappeared by 1975, and even forty-cow farms were rare
nowadays. But an omelette could not be made without first breaking
the eggs; it was survival of the fittest—that's the way Shirley saw it. The
farmers who could adapt changed to irrigation. Square fields rounded
under central pivot irrigators that sprinkled corn day and night
through July and August. Dairy barns, empty of cows, stanchions removed, now leaked #2 yellow corn from their window sills and ventilators. Farmers read market news, went to seminars in Minneapolis or
Fargo, stayed in touch with world events.

Those who didn't, lost out. Went under. In the bank Shirley had
seen it close up. It was sad initially—especially the dispersal auctions—
but a farmer losing his land wasn't as bad as people made it out to be:
by then the potato growers had arrived. Universal Potato Company
gave top prices for irrigable land, and usually gave the farmers jobs besides. Farmers stayed on in their own homes, continued to work their
own land. Now they drove tractors and harvesters that belonged to
Universal Potatoes, and they no longer had to worry about maintenance, about breakdowns, about the high price of parts. In the evening
there were no barn chores, no more getting up at midnight to birth a
calf. For the first time in their lives the men had time to watch TV, to go
fishing, to drive their families on a Saturday afternoon to the mall in
Fargo.

In Sand Lake the stores improved. A Hardee's came to town, and
Marketplace Food and Deli followed. An antique store opened on Main
Street where old milk cans and separators were the best sellers. Sometimes Shirley browsed through the store, clucking her tongue at the
things people bought. A pedal grindstone. Blue mason jars. Wooden
kraut cutters. Washboards. She wondered what had become of things
like her family's old ice chest, the crank phone; some items were worth
an astounding amount of money. But antiques were a laugh. Shirley
had grown up with antiques. Why would she want to buy them back?

She had no desire to return to the old days. To Depression days. To the flat frozen fields, the black winter mountains of manure.

The next morning, early, Shirley woke up with a vision of white. Frost. She sat up in bed, remembering she had not covered the squash or the muskmelons. Quickly she dressed, put on a jacket and rubber boots, and went out. A white rime of frost coated the steps, and beyond it— she saw immediately—the tall squash plants lay flattened and brown in the garden. On their shrunken vines the cantaloupes sat up high and shiny like skulls.

Among the wet, flattened garden the only green was the row of peas and carrots that John had planted. Somehow, in planting, he had gotten the seeds into the same trench. In June the row came up frothy green like a wave of sea water rising from the garden, threatening to spill over everything. By late July the row crested, collapsed under its own weight, and delivered no peas and no carrots. It remained now in September so dense and jungle-like that even frost could not penetrate it.

No matter. The garden was finished now, and good riddance, Shirley thought. She looked briefly back to the house, then across to the neighborhood. The houses around were narrow, white, and tall with dark, steep pitched roofs and caragana and lilac bushes rising up untrimmed toward the windows where shades remained pulled; their neighbors—all older couples like themselves—were still sleeping. They weren't worrying about gardens and frost. All of them had long ago figured out that it was cheaper to buy food. John and Shirley had the only garden in sight.

Now she walked along the mess of pea vines and carrots to the four rows of potatoes where there was a plant here, a plant there. Long gaps of weedy dirt between. Had he planted them too deeply? Cut the seed potatoes wrong, left them with no eye? Put the eye staring down, sent its white shoot on a death march to China?

Shirley went to get the wheelbarrow for the squash and melons. In the garage she paused by the Oldsmobile. In the dim window light its paint glowed whitely. She ran a finger along its roof, then down the cool window glass to the chrome door handle. Quietly opening the door she eased into the driver's seat. She raised her hands to the steering wheel, felt her palms dampen. The little grooves—how well they fit the fingers! She turned the wheel left and right. She sat there staring through the windshield and the garage window, beyond which she could see only sky and the vague, darker peaks of the neighbors' roofs. She sat there until she heard shouting in the garden.

Shirley blinked—then scrambled from the car. In the garden she saw John in his pajamas, with no jacket, no shoes.

"The kids, they're stealing again!" he shouted. He waved his arms.

"Here! Hush!" Shirley called. "Stop that crazy talk!"

"The kids," John said. "Look at the garden. It's all gone."

"There's no stealing because there's nothing to steal," Shirley said. She grabbed his arms, and her words came out faster than she wanted but she couldn't slow them or pull them back.

"That stealing stuff is all in your mind because your mind is not so good anymore—you can see that by the way things are planted."

John let his eyes slowly fall to the thick green row of peas and carrots.

"You're too old to plant a garden just like I'm too old to work in one," Shirley said. "Things change and you've got to get that into your head. Don't you see?" she said, softer now, "we're old! Old."

In a long, slow turning of his head John brought his gaze around to hers. The morning light shone in his eyes, and for an instant she saw him when he was a young man, with coppery hair and shiny blue eyes. Now he looked down, down to his own hands. He stared at his fingers, his palms, turned them over, then back, then over again.

She went to him. "Come on in now," she said.

He let himself be led to the house.

Later in the morning, since it was Saturday, they went grocery shopping as usual. John drove. Shirley watched him warily but he drove well enough and they arrived at Marketplace Food and Deli without trouble.

"You want to come in this time?" Shirley said.

John looked across the parking lot to the new store. Marketplace had slanting, coppery-colored angles to its metal roof and several colored flags flying on top; it was what Shirley imagined a Spanish train station must look like. There was also a drive-up window for grocery pick-up that kept people out of the rain and snow and sun. Under one roof there was a bakery, coffee shop, florist's shop, video section, film processing station, a delicatessen plus grocery aisles that went on and on under bright fluorescent lights.

"Too big," John said. "A person could get lost in there."

"Well sit there then," she said with some relief. "I'll be right back."

Halfway across the parking lot she looked back to see him, alone in the car, nodding yes.

Inside the store, from the smell of the bakery Shirley realized she had not finished her own breakfast. Now she had to shop on an empty stomach, something she tried never to do. She found a cart, and before moving an inch made herself read aloud the list. "Crisco. Yeast. Baking soda. Flour. Milk. Turkey (leg). Navy beans. Hand soap."

In vegetables she passed by eggplants, jalapeño peppers, kiwifruit, artichokes, gingerroot, guavas—who in this town ate such things? Briefly she hefted an avocado, then put it back. At home she had jars and jars of perfectly good green beens and tomatoes and pickled carrots. She found Idaho red potatoes, a ten-pound plastic bag for $3.99! She hefted the bag, held it up toward the light. The potatoes were all as firm and round as apples and scrubbed a fresh, chapped red. She thought of the scattering of her own potatoes—droopy, sprouted, and brown—which remained in the root cellar. She let the bag of Idaho potatoes balance on the edge of cart. She turned it sideways for another look. Finally she thudded the sack back onto its shelf.

In fruits she passed baby coconuts, Asian pears, and papayas on her way to the California seedless grapes. Though down a nickel since last Saturday, they were still sixty-nine cents per pound. She moved on. Blue plums caught her eye; she stopped to smell of them, to squeeze their little purple bellies. Her stomach growled. She swallowed, checked her list, then tore off a plastic bag and chose two of the fattest plums.

The turkey leg took longer. "Most people want the breasts," the manager said cheerfully. He was a round-faced man who wore a white plastic hat with a short bill, and as he dug through the freezer bin, the round white packages clacked against each other. "I'll have to look in back," he said.

As she waited she added up the total so far, then thought about eating one of the plums. But it would not be washed, and besides, someone might think she was not going to pay for it.

The manager appeared in the doorway. "Fresh or frozen?"

"Frozen," Shirley said quickly.

Heading toward hand soap she passed through the feminine-products section, shelf after shelf of shields, liners, rinses, all packaged with drawings of women in white dresses in sunny fields of daisies or at the seashore where their long hair blew lightly in a breeze. She thought of her own cotton that she had washed every month, of it hanging on the far end of the clothesline, waving in the wind during the summer, swinging stiffly in winter. Today there was none of that for her. As she passed by the little plastic boxes and packets she had to look twice to figure out what some of the things were for.

In the soap section she sneezed twice—had to steady herself against her cart until the dizziness passed. After some searching she found the single bars of Ivory. She paused to look at the woman and her baby on the blue-and-white soap wrapper. She had read once that one of the models was a notorious actress in pornographic films. What a laughable notion! The things one heard! A young mother with two stumbling toddlers turned to stare. Shirley quickly covered her mouth, pretended to cough.

Coming down the final aisle Shirley was so hungry that she held tightly to the cart and let it pull her along. Rounding the corner she smelled flowers, and at the same moment saw Thelma Haynes. Thelma was dressed in a white apron with a fresh carnation on her blouse, her hair done up far too blue; she stood polishing the glass counter of the floral shop.

"Shirley Kelm," Thelma called out in an artificially cheery voice, "what can I do for you today?"

"Me? I'm here for groceries," Shirley said.

"Special on fresh carnations," Thelma said brightly.

"I grow my own flowers," Shirley said immediately. The fool idea that she didn't drove away, for the time being, her hunger.

"Well they are cheaper that way," Thelma said, lowering her voice. A young manager fellow passed. He wore a short-sleeved white shirt and a thin black tie, and Thelma turned quickly to adjust some dried flowers in a fancy teakettle pot.

"Everything is too high priced here," Shirley said, loud enough for the manager to hear.

Thelma fussed with the stems—weeds, really, just spray-painted weeds—until he passed around the corner.

"I agree," she whispered.

"Take potatoes," Shirley said to Thelma, narrowing her eyes slightly. "Nearly forty cents a pound."

Thelma's small, blue eyes flickered briefly around her before they came back to Shirley. "I guess it depends on where you get them," she winked.

"Yes, I suppose it does," Shirley said.

Thelma leaned forward. "You know how many potatoes I've got?" she whispered. Her eyes widened with a sudden surge of light.

Shirley held tighter to the cart's handle.

"Twelve bushel. Maybe fifteen. They take up the whole closet and part of the bedroom of my apartment," Thelma whispered. She giggled briefly.

Shirley felt the grocery cart push her backward an inch, as if it moved by itself.

Thelma leaned closer. "I tell myself I won't go out there again," she whispered, "but the next thing I know, there I am again."

"You could give some away!" Shirley said.

Thelma was silent.

"Other people, who can't get around by themselves, people who don't drive—they might like some of those potatoes," Shirley said.

Thelma turned sideways to wipe at something on the glass. "I've got myself to think of."

"But fifteen bushel!" Shirley breathed.

Thelma looked up at Shirley, then to the store behind—the aisles, the displays, the people with their carts, the children. She turned her gaze back to Shirley and lowered her voice. "No one knows what's going to happen," she whispered. "I could live on potatoes if I had to."

At the till Shirley waited behind a heavyset woman with a cart topped off with two twelve packs of Mountain Dew. She breathed lightly through her mouth as she watched the cashier swing the items across the red light that burned beneath the counter. The beeping went on and on. To speed up things when her turn came Shirley counted out exact change, $13.68. She clutched the money. Her hand shook slightly. Ahead, as the beeping of her groceries went on, the fat woman stood leafing through a *Teen Beat* magazine; she had no idea of what things cost, Shirley realized. What kind of person did not know the price of things? She felt a fine cool sweat come on her forehead.

When Shirley at last passed through the electric doors, the grocery boy behind her, the wide parking lot outside for an instant tilted—then righted itself—then tilted again.

"Lady, are you all right?" the boy said. His voice sounded far away.

"Of course I'm all right," Shirley said. "Just a little hungry."

For some reason he grabbed her, roughly, and the next thing she saw was his face staring down at her. She was lying on the asphalt.

"Call 911!" the boy was shouting.

"No!" Shirley said sharply. The potential cost of an ambulance gave her a surge of energy and she managed to sit up. "Those are my groceries—" she barked at the boy. Her sack lay tipped over on the asphalt. She struggled to her feet and shook her finger at him. "I paid good money for those!"

That afternoon, as John read the local paper, she tried to nap. She kept thinking about prices. The high price of things. How prices never stopped rising. How they went up day after day. When she closed her eyes she saw price tags. She saw herself drifting down endless aisles where the prices on their own, untouched by human hands, went higher and higher; as she reached for things—the California grapes— little wheels of numbers ratcheted upward at a dizzying pace: she set herself, then lunged for the grapes but they jerked upward out of reach.

She sat up and blinked. Her hand waved high in the air, as if she were asking to be recognized. As if she had a question. But what was it?

Across the living room John sat tilted back in his chair, the paper limp across his lap, his mouth slack. Her hand jerked back to her body and she caught her breath: for one long instant she thought he was dead.

At twilight that same day, in the chilly, silent yard, Shirley stood beside their bedroom window and listened. John snored on; he was out for the night.

Wearing one of his old caps and carrying a flat flour sack over her shoulder, Shirley went to the garage. There she stowed the bag in the trunk of the Oldsmobile, then got behind the wheel. Taking a deep breath, she started the engine.

Its noise made her flinch and duck her head for a moment. Then she looked up, swallowed, and began to back from the garage. On the street she paused to catch her breath, then put the little arrow on "D" and got ready. She wrapped her fingers tightly around the wheel, her fingernails biting back into her palms, and felt her heart beating around and around the wide, hard hoop of the wheel. Or maybe it was the humming pulse of the engine she felt. Swallowing once more, she took her foot off the brake.

She crossed Main Street without event. On the side streets, each time a car approached she held her breath and at the last moment as they passed, jammed shut her eyes. Remarkably, when she opened them, the street was clear again.

Heading toward the city limits, two cars flashed their lights at her. Then a third. Was she too far over? What was she doing wrong? Cars passed her from both directions, sometimes tooting, sometimes flashing their lights. The headlights! She began to pull buttons along the dashboard—the wipers came on—until yellow beams shot down the road in front of her. After that she set her jaw and brought the Cutlass up to forty.

In a few minutes she began to look for the dirt road which turned west toward the potato fields. In gray dusk everything was smaller, narrower, farther off, a flat dusky plate with an occasional looming grove of trees, and she almost missed the road. Turning sharply the car tilted over the corner, bounced once on something—a stone—that clunked underneath, then found the gravel road again. She drove another mile, then another and another. About to turn back, she saw, in silhouette, stretched across the field, the long black spine of an irrigator.

A car was just pulling away from the field. Shirley sped up suddenly, then braked to a halt near where the car had been parked. In the bottom of her sack she lifted the cool heavy cylinder of the flashlight, checked its beam, then headed quickly down across the ditch. She had not walked twenty steps before the narrow beam of her light speared a potato.

Then another.

And another.

Rapidly she plucked them into the sack.

But they were so small. In the next moment she realized that these were potatoes other people had passed by. She dumped them from her sack, headed deeper into the field. Ten minutes later she found a furrow that no footprints followed, and began to find better potatoes.

Heavy-bodied russets. One would make a meal. She began to think of them in that way. Meal.

Meal.

Meal.

Meal.

She hurried forward, following her light, stooping and stooping again, the sack bouncing on her back. It what seemed no time the neck of the sack began to chafe sharply across her shoulder. And her arm was cramping.

She stopped. She looked back toward the road where the Oldsmobile, small and faraway, drew light from the falling dark and glowed like a lighthouse beacon. She pressed on. Three more, she told herself. Three more good ones, that was. One by one she found them—five, actually—then made herself turn back.

By the time she reached the Oldsmobile her breath came in short gasps. Her arms were numb. She slumped against the car and tried to breathe evenly. It took her several minutes to regain her strength. As she stared off across the dark she gradually came to see how few lights there were on the land. A white pinprick of a yard lamp here and there. Four, possibly five farms if she looked in all directions.

She thought of neighbors from her childhood. The van den Eykels. The Lanes. The Grunheims. The Niskanens. The Petersons. She wondered what had become of them. Other memories, images from childhood rose up from the darkness. The bright Surge milking kettle that her father swung from cow to cow. The oiled leather surcingle strap from which the milker hung like a second belly beneath the cow. The Watkins salesman with the glass eye and his sweet jars of orange and purple nectar that her mother sometimes bought. The slivers of ice her father chipped from the blocks that he fished, with black tongs, from beneath wet sawdust. The April melting, the wide, field-ponds where she and the other farm kids had sailed shingle boats with cornshuck sails. Where had it all gone?

Turning, she looked back toward Sand Lake. The new sodium vapor street lamps threw up an orange umbrella of light over the whole town. Foolishness. No town needed to be lit up so brightly, and certainly not all night. Nowadays the town was too light, the land too dark.

She raised her flashlight and turned its beam to the fields. Where its light stopped, the present ended and the past began. Her yellow beam trembled. Quickly she swung the light back into the trunk where its yellow glow was brighter. There she emptied her sack and began to count the potatoes; the light bobbed across the night's gleaning, but too soon she was finished. Afterward she took up her empty sack and followed the short yellow trail of her light back into the field.

Marked for Death

When I walked into gun safety class, some of the boys laughed, their thirteen-year-old voices croaking like tree toads.

"Hey," a pimply faced one said, "aren't you in the wrong room?"

I pretended to check my registration sheet. "No, I'm in the right room—but the dermatologist is just down the hall."

A few other boys snickered, and not at me. Pizza Face, aka "Tanner" (we had to wear stick-on name tags), looked at me dumbly. "Forget it," I said. I glanced around, then took a desk near the front; since I was the only girl, I might as well be a cliché.

The instructor, Mr. Johnson, soon came into the room. "Good Saturday morning, class!" he said. He was a high school industrial arts teacher, but today he was all geared out: he wore a camo cap and a Dorks Unlimited shooting vest and carried two long guns plus a bunch of handouts under his arm.

"Don't be afraid; they're only guns," Tanner said.

I glanced at them. "Looks like a .22 rifle and a twenty-gauge shotgun," I replied. "Though I prefer a sixteen-gauge myself. The dram load is a little light for ducks and geese, but it's perfect for partridge hunting—wouldn't you agree?"

"Huh?" he said to me. He was staring at the guns, this undersized, scruffy kid with all the wrong clothes.

"Well, well, well!" Mr. Johnson said, his eyes lighting up as he saw me. "If it's not Miss Samantha Carlson."

"Sam," I said. Please. Spare me.

"Samantha's father happens to be a professional hunting guide and one of the top shooters in the Midwest," the instructor said loudly. "If she's anything like her father, you boys don't stand a chance."

There were a few uncertain chuckles.

"Maybe you could just turn a big spotlight on me?" I muttered.

This got a big laugh from the boys; Mr. Johnson drew back, cleared his throat, and moved to a different spot in the room.

I checked my watch. I had to pass this class in order to get my gun safety permit, which meant I could go deer hunting—real hunting, as in carrying my own gun. For midwestern kids, this is a big deal. The even bigger deal was this: I'd be hunting with my father. Just me and him. He wasn't around much; right now he was guiding in Kodiak, Alaska—fish in the spring and summer, big game in the fall—but we had been planning this for years. "When you turn thirteen, it's just me and you, honey," he always said. My brothers, Jake, Ben, and Andrew, had their turn; now it was mine.

First, however, I had to get through this day. Stuck inside a school classroom on a hot August Saturday (the last one before school started) was bad enough, but most of my friends from La Crosse were off to the Mall of America in Minneapolis on one last shopping trip for school clothes. Growing up with three brothers, I constantly worried about becoming Jo March from *Little Women*. On the other hand, I wasn't a full-time girly girl like most of my friends. To be honest, my life in that area was kind of a mess.

"Today's class will cover the basic principles of firearms operation and hunting safety," Mr. Johnson droned as he distributed handouts. I sighed again. My family lives in Wisconsin, in the countryside north of La Crosse, and we target shoot right in our backyard. My father got me started with a BB gun when I was about five. I wish he could have seen me smoke 24 of 25 sporting clays the other day with the Browning twenty gauge he bought me last Christmas, but these days he's gone almost all the time. My parents seem kind of married, kind of not. I don't ask. I only know that my mother has made a big deal of me knowing how to do all the stuff my brothers can do, such as ride a horse, clean fish, and use cables to jump-start a car with a dead battery. She's a real outdoors woman herself; after deer hunting season, she always gets a manicure because deer blood chaps her hands, her cuticles especially (a beauty tip you won't get from reading *Teen Beat* or *Glamour*).

"There will be a test at the end of the day," Mr. Johnson said, "so pay attention—unless you think you know it all."

He glanced sideways at me; I pretended to study the handouts, which anyway were easier on the eyes than a room full of thirteen-year-old males. After the teacher moved on, I sneaked another look around. The boys looked like they had all been dropped as babies. Some had noses and ears way too large for their faces; some had no chin, or too much jaw; some were tall, some (like Tanner) were small in their desks; some had patches of whisker fuzz and croaky voices while others sounded like canaries. Not a pretty sight. Tanner had drawn something rude on his desk and was trying to get the kid next to him to look at it.

"We'll start with the fundamental, number one issue of handling a gun: muzzle safety," the instructor said. He held up the small rifle. "If the bore, or 'business end' of a gun is never pointed at a person, no one can ever be shot accidentally." Then he took ten minutes saying the same thing ten different ways. *We get it, we get it!* I checked my watch again to make sure its battery wasn't dead.

After muzzle safety, it was on to more bonehead facts and information, including a filmstrip (I thought they went out with the last century) on moving safely through the field while carrying a gun. "Always be sure of your target, and never, *ever,* run with a gun."

Yawn.

"The next part of our class contains graphic images," the instructor said as he set up his slide projector.

"All right!" Tanner said to anyone who would listen.

"These photographs were taken at the scene of actual hunting accidents."

"Even better!" Tanner whispered.

Everybody ignored him. If Tanner were a character in an action movie, he would be marked for death—you know, the swimmer who paddles away from the others in a shark flick, or the camper who wanders into the woods at night in a slasher film.

"Fair warning: some of these slides are explicit, or, as you youngsters might say, 'gross,' " Mr. Johnson said.

No one said anything.

"Their purpose is to shock you," he continued, taking his time, making us wait. Clearly this was his best stuff. "I want you to see the effect of a rifle bullet or a shotgun blast on human flesh."

I got ready by squinting my eyes. The first slide was of a hunter face-down in brown leaves with a big black splotch on the back of his blaze orange jacket; compared to the computer games that Jake, Ben, and Andrew played, it was pretty tame.

"That's what he looked like in the field," the instructor said. The next slide flashed onto the screen—I looked away but not in time—and there was a sucking in of breath around the room. "This is what he looked like in the coroner's office."

A stainless steel table. A totally naked guy lying on his stomach with a huge, *Little Shop of Horrors* flower growing on his back: white, fatty petals at the edges, bulging red stuff in the middle, things that looked like black tongues. I felt my breakfast Cheerios move in my stomach.

The slides continued. I watched the next one from the very corner of my eye: an arm blown away just below the elbow, flaps of skin hanging like a fringed skirt on a doll. "This hunter bled to death," the instructor announced.

Two dead hunters were enough. We got the picture—at least I got the picture—and while the boys watched the rest of the freak show, I watched them: it was a great moment to observe the species. With each new image, Tanner's jaw dropped a degree lower until I could hear him breathing through his mouth.

"Okay, that should be enough," the instructor finally said. He shut down the projector and turned on the lights. There were exhalations and murmuring and thumping about in the desks. After another short filmstrip on target shooting and safety, at last it was lunchtime.

Even better, we got to go outside.

On the elementary school playground we took our bag lunches toward some grass. Tanner carried only a twenty-four-ounce Mountain Dew. "Hey everybody, did you see that dead guy's butt?" he said. Everybody ignored him. We sat down. Tanner kept looking for a group to join, but nobody would let him in. Being a sucker for birds and chipmunks fallen from nests, I was just about to give in and make room for him, when he raced across to the swing set. He took a swing and began to pump himself higher and higher. Gradually we turned to watch him. Soon, at high arc, the chains began to slack and he free-fell with harder and harder jerks. "Hey everybody, higher?" he called.

"Yeah—way higher!" several boys called, and snickered.

"What a jerk," one of them said, and turned away.

Tanner stood up in the swing and pumped. I held my breath.

"Anybody, want to see me jump?"

"Yeah—for sure!" several guys called; the boys turned as one to get a good look at Tanner breaking his neck. I'd had enough; I ran over to the swing set and grabbed at the chains as they flashed by. "Tanner, cut it out! You're gonna get hurt!"

His head jerked sideways and he stared down at me. Then he looked at all the boys, and I realized I'd just made things worse for him. Luckily for all of us, Mr. Johnson stepped through the door. "The bus is here," he called; in an instant, the boys raced off, leaving me with Tanner.

"Hey everybody, wait up!" Tanner shouted.

I waited as he braked himself in a cloud of dust, and then jumped. He did a running flip, and landed on his back with a thud. For a second his mouth went fish-lips as he sucked at the air, and soon he sat up, gasping.

"See, what did I tell you?" I said. "Those guys just wanted to see you get hurt."

He looked at me, and for a second his eyes were not crazy and jumpy. It was like there was a normal kid buried somewhere inside his head. But really deep inside.

"Race you to the bus!" he said.

The yellow school bus took us to the local target range for actual shooting—in other words, the fun part of the day.

"I've never shot a gun before," Tanner said; of course he had to sit by me.

The boys all looked at one another, then rolled their eyes.

"Does it kick?" he asked me.

"Some," I said, "but just keep the butt of the stock tight against your shoulder. That and your cheek tight on the wood." I thought for sure he'd make some lame joke about "butt" and "cheek."

"I'll try to remember that," Tanner said. I looked twice at him. Tanner was possibly the only thirteen-year-old boy in the world who didn't mind taking directions from a thirteen-year-old girl. The boys rolled their eyes again; however, as the shooting range approached, they all began to stare out the bus windows. I got the feeling that many of them had never shot a gun.

First, everyone shot the little .22 caliber, single-shot rifle. Three shots in the three main positions: prone, sitting, and standing (off-hand). The first boy couldn't figure out the sitting position; that is, which elbow to place on which knee. When my turn came I took time to get my breathing right—it's best to squeeze the trigger in that dead moment just after exhaling—and put all three shots, in all three positions, in the bull's-eye black. "What did I tell you, boys," Mr. Johnson said.

Soon we moved to the shotgun and clay pigeons. Mr. Johnson let me "demonstrate" by going first. I figured he'd try something sneaky, and from the corner of my amber shooting glasses saw him adjust the bench-mounted thrower to "rabbit," meaning a ground-skipping clay.

"Ready?" he asked.

I nodded. "Pull!" The clay came out low and fast, but I led it right—and puffed it—just before it flew out of range. By the end of the day I had twenty new friends, Tanner in particular, plus my Hunting and Gun Safety certificate and badge.

For the boys the big question was where to sew on their badge: cap or hunting jacket? They even included Tanner in that debate. I slipped mine in my pocket and got out of there.

"How'd it go?" my mother asked. Her name is Amy, and she was waiting for me in the parking lot beside our Jeep. Tanned and lean with a sandy brown ponytail, she wore her usual Saturday outfit: jeans, dusty cowboy boots, and the leathery, soapy smell of Penny, our horse.

"She can shoot like heck!" Tanner called across to my mother. "She's cool!"

I shrugged. "Tanner, my new best friend."

My mother smiled. "Thatta girl." She put her arm around me right there in the open.

"Please, Mom," I said.

"Sorry," she said, and let go.

I watched the other boys head off with their fathers, all except for Tanner, who got on a battered bicycle with a wobbly back tire. My mother started the car and we drove away. I kept looking back.

"What?" she asked.

I was silent.

"You miss your Dad," she said.

I shrugged. "Do you?"

She paused a moment too long. "He'll be home for a while real soon."

She drove on and we were both silent. We never talked much about him; there was lots of unsaid stuff about him being gone. I think she thought I blamed her, and maybe in some ways I did.

When I got home I left my father a voice mail message about passing the gun safety class; he hardly ever answered his cell phone, but then again if you're a hunting guide, the last thing you need is your phone to start beeping. Sometimes I called his number just to hear his voice message.

The first day of school was a disaster. Everybody except me had grown a foot taller and several bra sizes bigger; I was wearing bright new Adidas when all the girls in the Tara-Melanie group were wearing strappy sandals (how come I didn't hear about that?). And the bad news didn't stop there. I was standing with Tara and Melanie, in the eighth-grade hallway, when a loud voice called, "Sam—hey Sam!"

I looked over my shoulder. I froze.

Tanner came rushing up. His pimples were somewhat better, and he had on a clean shirt, but he was wearing old, busted-out tennis shoes and ratty jeans and his hair needed a major washing. The girls around me drew back.

"It's me, Tanner! Remember? From gun safety class?"

"Oh yeah," I said. I checked my watch.

"Hey Sam, I was thinking—maybe we can go hunting some day!"

I felt my ears begin to burn, and could only imagine their new color. "We'll see. Actually, I gotta go to class," I said.

"Okay, see you around, Sam," Tanner said cheerfully, and turned away.

"Who was *that?*" the girls asked in unison.

"Just this . . . kid," I said, and felt my face turn really red.

As school continued that first week, Tanner ricocheted from group to group. Nobody wanted anything to do with him, so I ended up talking to him a couple of times. From his lineup of mostly special classes, I could tell he was a "consonant kid" (I once heard a teacher use that phrase)—hyperactivity disorder (HD), behaviorally and socially challenged (BSC), etc. The only conversation he could really stay with was about hunting. Going hunting. Someday even owning a hunting gun. I tried to be nice to him but he was like a stray dog: feed him and he only comes back more often; chase him away and you feel like dirt. One day I asked him about his parents.

"My foster parents or my dead ones?" he said.

I swallowed. "Whichever."

"My foster parents are okay. But my real parents died a long time ago."

"I'm sorry."

"My father, that is," he added. "My mother's in California in this drug treatment place."

I tried to think of something to say.

"Actually, it's a prison," he added. "She's in prison." He looked straight at me. "Usually I lie about her."

"Well, I'm glad you didn't," was all I could think to say, but with Tanner that was enough. He smiled like he was the happiest kid in the world.

After that, Tanner attached himself to me like a wood tick. Like a leech. Like a lamprey. I swear he was sucking my blood, and he certainly didn't help my hall life. Tanner and the fact that my father was never around. Once Tara asked, "Is your mother, like, a single mom?"

I laughed as if that were the funniest thing I'd ever heard; none of the Mary-Kate and Ashley group (as I sometimes thought of them) laughed with me.

As October rolled around, and with it the opening of small game season, Tanner pestered me daily about going hunting. "Mr. Johnson said he's going to find someone to take me grouse hunting," he said. "When we go, want to come with?"

"We'll see," I said.

"You could show me how to wing shoot and stuff like that."

"We'll see," I muttered. It was the only answer that worked with Tanner, the only response that made him go away. Not yes, not no. "We'll see."

Then the leaves turned yellow and red and brown, geese honked high overhead as they flew south for the winter—and my father blew home with them. Suddenly one day there he was in his dusty black Ford Explorer, waiting for me after school right there in front of the busses and everybody.

"Daddy," I shrieked. I raced into his arms. I didn't care if anybody saw me. In fact, I hoped they did.

"Sam, honey!" he said, and lifted me off the ground and swung me around. He smelled like cigar and leaves and wood; his trimmed beard had flecks of snow in it, a speckled whiteness that I never noticed before. There were also new, fine wrinkles around his eyes, which were tired, and a little sad, as if he'd been working too hard or lost something important. "I'm home to do some scouting for deer season," he said, flashing his old smile and holding me tight with one strong arm. "Hope you haven't forgotten our date."

I began to cry.

"Honey, honey, what's the matter?"

"Nothing," I said, rubbing away my tears.

"Well, I certainly hope not," he said.

"Hey, is that your Dad?" a loud voice said.

Tanner. Tanner lurched up beside us.

"Hello there young man," my father began.

"Go away!" I said suddenly to Tanner.

Tanner flinched as if I had kicked him. My father looked at me with disappointment—which only made the moment worse. I rushed into the Ford and slammed the door. My father came around and settled into the driver's seat.

"What was that all about?" he asked.

"Just . . . this . . . boy," I blubbered.

My father smiled and started the engine. "Oh, that," he said.

"No—you don't understand," I said, even more annoyed. I looked out the window; Tanner was still standing there, staring after us with his mouth-open-deer-in-the-headlights look.

For the rest of that week, the one before deer season, my father picked me up every day after school. And every day, Tanner found some excuse to be there. "What's the deal with Tanner?" my father said.

I shrugged. "I met him in gun safety class this summer. He just sort of attached himself to me."

"He's new in school?"

I nodded.

"Does he have any friends?"

"I'm it," I said sarcastically.

My father looked in his rear view mirror at Tanner, then across to me. "I'm proud of you, honey."

On Wednesday afternoon, when I came to meet my dad, I saw the gun safety instructor, Mr. Johnson, talking with my father. When I approached, their voices dropped to a murmur, then became hearty and false.

"Hello Sam," Mr. Johnson said way too cheerfully.

"Sam, Sam, guess what?!" Tanner shouted as he raced up behind me.

"What," I said flatly.

"Mr. Johnson says I might get to go deer hunting with you and your father! Isn't that right, Mr. Carlson?"

On the way home I sat as far as I could from my father and stared out my window. I wouldn't let him see my face.

"It's not like that, Sam," my father said again. "And anyway, what could I do? Bob Johnson tells me this kid's story—how he's bounced around foster homes all his life, how he came to the gun safety class all on his own. The one thing the kid wants to do is go deer hunting. What could I say?"

"Like, 'No'?"

My father sucked in a breath. "I considered that. But sometimes we have to . . . share what we have. Share the luck. Share the gifts. Think about it: this kid has no one. For starters, you've got two parents."

"Sort of," I said.

My father fell silent.

I glanced over at him. His eyes had a hurt look, and they stared straight down the road.

"I'm sorry," I said. I felt my own eyes burning again.

"It's okay, baby," he murmured, and touched my hair.

"It's just that you always said—" I began, but my voice broke.

"I know, I know: 'just you and me.' But it will still be almost like that. I've got it figured out. I'm going to make a blind for Tanner that's way away from us. You and I will take the tree stand, and I'll check on him once in a while. It will all work out, okay?"

I bit my lip. I didn't say anything.

On Thursday night after school, my father took Tanner and me to the shooting range. "I just want to make sure he knows what he's do-ing," my father said to me. I made my statement by staying in the truck. And anyway, my gun, a twenty-gauge shotgun set up for deer hunting was long-since targeted in. Tanner was using one of my brother Andrew's old ones, a single-shot "starter" twenty gauge. The range was busy with last-minute shooters; guns boomed and crashed. Tanner's first screw-up was to wave the muzzle sideways across the line of bench shooters—including my father. I sucked in a breath. A couple of hunters drew back and glared, and my father snatched the muzzle downward. I flashed on the dead hunter on the autopsy table. But the gun was not loaded, and I saw my father mouthing stern words to Tan-ner—who hung his head. Then my father got Tanner situated at the bench and the gun pointed in the right direction. At first Tanner flinched and jerked each time he fired. Dust kicked up yards below the target, but gradually he began to lean more tightly into the stock, and keep his cheek on the wood when he squeezed the trigger. My father glanced at me; I looked away. When the round of firing stopped, and hunters walked forward to check their targets, Tanner raced wildly downrange and came rushing back against traffic waving the target.

"Look, Sam, I hit it three times!" Tanner shouted.

"Great," I said without expression. He had shot at it ten times.

"Not that bad your first time with a new gun," my father said, as they returned to the truck.

Still holding the gun, its muzzle waving, Tanner hopped up and down with excitement. My father quickly took the shotgun from Tanner. "What did I tell you? Never jump or run with a gun!"

"Sorry," Tanner said with that instant kicked-dog look in his eyes. My father glanced at me.

"But you did all right today," my father added. "Saturday morning, if you promise to be safe and remember what you learned, we'll go hunting."

"I promise, I promise! Oh man, I can't wait!" Tanner said.

My father smiled, but something in my stomach clenched, and it had something to do with my father. But he was a pro. He had worked with hunters of all kinds. He had to know what he was doing.

We dropped Tanner off at his foster parents' place, a double-wide trailer with several battered plastic tricycles lying about.

"What time will you pick me up Saturday morning?" Tanner asked.

"Let's say 5:00 AM."

"I could be ready earlier," Tanner said.

My father patted Tanner on the back and shooed him out of the pickup. "5:00 AM. I'll be here."

Tanner raced up the double-wide. At the door he braked and brought up his hand as if to knock. Then he changed his mind and rushed inside, slamming the door so hard the wall quivered.

My father stared after him. Then he looked at me. I looked out my window.

"Hey, you want to get a Dairy Queen or something?" my father asked. "Just you and me?"

On opening morning we drove into town to get Tanner. It was chilly and pitch-black outside, and the streetlights were bright as we entered La Crosse. In the trailer park with its curving streets, Tanner was the only moving thing. He stood outside, stamping his feet up and down against the cold, and puffing frosty breaths.

"Wow am I glad to see you!" he said, leaping into the truck. He shuddered with cold, and there was frost on his eyelashes.

"How long you been waiting?" my father said, turning up the heater fan.

"Not that long," Tanner shrugged.

North of town, at the dark edge of the woods we owned and would hunt, my father let the truck coast to a stop. "It's very important to enter the woods quietly," my father said to Tanner. "I'll take you to your stand."

Tanner nodded continuously. He could not stop grinning. "I can't believe this," he said to me.

"Shhhhhh," my father said. "Deer have great hearing. They're already listening to us."

Tanner looked at the dark woods.

"Remember, you'll stay there until I come for you," my father said to him. "It takes patience to wait for a deer."

"Why can't I, like, track them and sneak up on them?"

"That comes later, with more experience," my father said. "Most hunters start out on the stand, or a blind."

Tanner nodded with some disappointment.

"Sam and I will take the tree stand. Whistle if you need help of any kind, all right?"

Tanner nodded, and then the two of them headed off into the darkness. My father's little flashlight bobbed along the trail like a firefly. It became a little speck, then went dark. I sucked in another breath.

After ten minutes or more, my father's bobbing light reappeared, and I began to relax. My father and I went to our stand. It was a platform about six feet off the ground, sort of like a tree house with two chairs. It had a tiny little heater if we needed it, and a railing on which to rest our guns. We settled in, and after we were quiet, the forest gradually came alive: invisible ducks whistled overhead; an owl went "*who-who*"; there was a sharp skittering sound in the leaves below.

I tensed and gripped my rifle.

"Squirrel," my father whispered.

Gradually the light came. First to appear were the silhouettes of spruce trees, then a broad duskiness spread downward from their points. The grayness softened and slipped closer to the ground, like a giant scrim curtain being raised; soon we could see the deer trail that ran parallel to our stand. My father checked his watch. "It's legal shooting time," he whispered. And almost on cue I heard soft steps coming down the trail.

"Get ready," my father said softly.

I clicked off the safety.

The shape of a deer appeared; at walking speed, it was moving right toward us.

"Let's see what it is first," my father whispered.

The deer was not large, but there was a pale flash of horn.

"Spike buck," my father murmured. "Let's let him pass."

As we watched, the buck stopped to paw for some acorns, then dipped his head for a mouthful; he chewed audibly—a muffled crunching—as he looked around. His erect ears pivoted like pointed radar dishes. Then his tail flickered white, and he moved on, disappearing as if absorbed by the bushes and trees.

"A good sign," my father said. We settled back to wait for a bigger and better deer. My pulse was rushing in my ears.

By 10:00 AM we had seen nothing but chickadees, a pileated woodpecker that chipped popsicle stick chips of wood from a dead pine tree, and at least a dozen gray squirrels. By noon, with full light, the woods went gradually quiet. Dead. It was like everything—all the birds and critters—were taking their nap. We relaxed, too, and my father told me stories about his job as a guide, how some people were great but others were total slobs and jerks.

"Same with school," I said. I was about to tell him about my friends—at least I thought they were my friends—when "*Boom!*" went Tanner's gun.

My father and I looked at each other; then we heard Tanner's whistle.

"I'd better go check," my father said quickly.

"Be careful!" I said suddenly.

"Don't worry, honey, I'll be right back."

I waited alone in the stand. I could hardly get my breath; I kept having this terrible feeling, but soon enough my father's orange cap and coat blossomed on the gray trail. He climbed back into our stand shaking his head and smiling.

"He says he saw a deer of some kind, and had a good shot. But we looked all over and couldn't find blood. I'm sure he missed him cleanly."

We settled back into our chairs. The sun was out now, though still low (it was November), and by 2:00 PM the woods slowly lost its brightness. Began, like the tide going out, to grow dusky again. My father dozed for a little while; it was nice waiting there, holding my gun while he napped: it was like I was on guard for him.

When he woke up, we continued talking, about my friends this time, about boys I liked. I was surprised to be telling him stuff.

He nodded. "When I was a junior in high school I was dating this really hot senior girl," he said. "She sort of picked me, you could say. Anyway, we went to her senior prom, and then parking in my Chevy afterward. She wanted to go all the way that night, but I wasn't ready, so we didn't." He glanced sideways at me.

"So, Dad, is that my lecture on abstinence?"

He said nothing but I saw the smile in his eyes. We turned to stare out at the forest in comfortable silence.

Suddenly there was a scattering, crunching sound on the trail; it was grayer now, and the air colder—the woods were coming alive again.

"Get ready!" my father whispered.

Two does bounded along with their brown and white tails erect.

"There must be a buck close behind," my father whispered.

Hot on their tracks came a buck with tall antlers—at least eight points. He was moving too fast for a good shot, and in a couple of seconds went out of sight in Tanner's direction. I let out a disappointed breath and lowered my muzzle.

"That's okay, honey. You didn't have a clean shot. Who knows—we might see him again."

Or not. "*Boom!*" went Tanner's gun.

My father looked at me. Then we heard Tanner's voice calling for us. "I hit him, I hit him," he shouted faintly.

"Wait here," my father said. "I'll go check."

"Be really careful, Daddy!" I said again.

He looked at me oddly. "Sure honey," he said. And left.

I watched him disappear down the trail.

Several minutes passed; nothing in the forest moved. I could hardly breathe.

"There he is," Tanner suddenly shouted. "I see him!" His voice was to the east now, and moving; he was running through the woods.

Then "*Boom!*" again.

And a hoarse scream; a wailing.

"Daddy!" I shouted. Dropping my gun, I leaped to the ground and raced through the loud leaves underfoot, past the slapping, stinging branches. "Daddy!" I kept crying.

"Over here, Sam!" my father called. His voice sounded terrible—as if he couldn't breathe.

I rushed into a clearing. Beside a fallen, mossy log, my father was slumped over—slumped over Tanner, who lay on his back in the brown leaves.

"Look, Sam! I got him!" Tanner said to me, struggling to sit up. He pointed. Twenty yards away a large buck lay brown on the brown leaves; an antler curved up darkly.

Tanner held his other hand over his stomach. His face was bone pale and his eyes white and sort of pop-eyed. My father said, "Sam—we have a shooting accident here. I want you to run back to the stand—my cell phone is in my backpack. Call 911."

"I'm sorry!" Tanner said to us. He started to cry. "I reloaded, then was running, I must have tripped . . ."

"Go, Sam!" my father said.

I ran as fast as I ever have—made the call—then rushed back up the trail toward Tanner, now following the blood on the leaves. The deer's blood or his blood, I couldn't tell. So much blood, spatters of it on the brown hands and fingers of the oak leaves.

My father met me before I could see Tanner again. He blocked my view. "Sam, I want you to go back to the truck," he said slowly. "Wait for the ambulance, then show them the way here. I'll wait with . . ." Then his voice broke, and he drew me fiercely into his arms and held me tight.

At Tanner's funeral, we put the deer's antlers on his coffin. Melanie and Tara and some of their friends from school attended; at first I was pleased, and we all hugged, but later I saw Tara whisper something, then giggle under her breath at the others, who cried continuously, as if Tanner were their best friend. For a second I hated them, but then let go of it.

The preacher was bald and had a voice like the teacher on the Simpsons (twice he called Tanner "Tyler"). The eulogy was mainly clichés about "the less fortunate among us" and life as a "flickering candle." Tanner's foster parents were there, but their baby began to wail, then throw up, and they had to leave. Quickly the service was over. Tanner's body was to be shipped somewhere, Minneapolis I think, so there was no trip to the cemetery, no burial. After the church service there was punch, coffee, and cake in the chilly church basement. The lunch was hosted by a flock of blue-haired old ladies who chattered cheerfully among themselves in the kitchen. There were more church ladies than people who actually came for Tanner.

I stayed close to my father, as did my mother. I hadn't seen them together, dressed up, forever. They held hands, too. Mr. Johnson, the gun safety teacher, came up to us. "Well, Tanner got his deer," he said.

I realized one thing about funerals: adults say incredibly stupid things.

"He wasn't ready," my father said, staring across the room. "I should have known that."

"It's all he wanted to do—go hunting just one time," Mr. Johnson said.

"Excuse me," my father said; I could see the pain in his eyes.

"Let's go, Daddy," I said.

He nodded and let me take him by the arm and out the door. My mother followed. It was bright now, the sun breaking through patchy clouds, and the three of us drove home in silence.

At home we all ate dinner in more silence. My brothers used their best manners.

"I've been thinking," my father said. "I have an offer to manage a sporting goods store here in La Crosse."

My mother looked up quickly.

He swallowed. "I'm thinking of taking it."

We all stared at him.

"The owner wants to sell eventually, and I've got some ideas on new sports lines, new gear."

My oldest brother, Jake, perked up. "Hey, you could hire us!"

"And go broke immediately," my father replied. "But seriously, what do you think?" he said, turning to my mother.

"Could you stand being inside a store all day?" she asked.

"I'd do some Midwest guiding on the side—if I could find good help for the store."

Andrew, Ben, and Jake took their cue and began to poke and laugh at each other.

"I think I'll take the offer," my father said suddenly. He looked at me. "Life's too short."

I looked down; my eyes felt hot and then they spilled over.

"Hey, what's a matter with her?" Andrew called.

"Nothing's the matter with her," my father said, and under the table took my hand. I held on tight, and kept crying; my brothers, after glances among themselves, went back to eating. Maybe crying is a girly kind of thing, but I was home and it felt right and nobody minded. Soon enough I needed to dry my eyes, which meant I had to let go of my father's hand. There's an art to hand-holding, even if it's with your dad; someone has to let go first, but tonight neither of us were in any hurry.

You Are What You Drive

One bright winter morning in February of 1969, in the Deerlake, Minnesota, Chevrolet/GMC/Ford/Chrysler/Buick Dealership where the tall windows were reduced to portholes by brilliant white frost, Mrs. Fulton G. Anderson drew one finger across the roof of the new Buick LeSabre. Its paint was black and smooth. Sunlight bloomed golden in the chromed mirror. From below, she could smell the leather of its seats, the fresh rubber of its tires.

Mrs. Anderson swallowed. Her husband, the Reverend Anderson, had died suddenly the previous year, in December; his life insurance money was sitting in the bank. The Andersons' present car, a Ford, was on its second hundred thousand miles. In winter, ankle-biting drafts leaked through the floorboards; in summer, dust. Mrs. Anderson's only child, Beth, a thin, studious girl with a long neck, was already a senior at Luther College in Decorah, Iowa, and had good prospects for teaching high school English (though no prospects whatsoever for a husband unless she began to take more pride in her appearance; but unwashed hair, floppy hats, purple sweatshirts, and long black skirts would pass, Mrs. Anderson believed, because children went through phases). Right now Mrs. Anderson wished Beth were here. They had always included Beth in family decisions.

"Go ahead," the auto salesman said. He was a young fellow, Beth's age, with big teeth and tiny dried razor nicks on his Adam's apple. "Put yourself behind the wheel," he said with a grin.

Mrs. Anderson drew back her finger, kicked a tire.

That afternoon Mrs. Anderson wrote Beth.

Her daughter's letter came by return post. Beth wrote that the Buick seemed like a lot of money for just a car. She said that a luxury car like the LeSabre was, considering the division of wealth in the world, one of the most repugnant of American metaphors. She wrote that, rather than buying the Buick, Mrs. Anderson ought to donate the insurance money to the Maryknoll nuns laboring in Central America, then use public transportation to get around Deerlake.

After Mrs. Anderson read Beth's letter she looked out the kitchen window to the bird feeder. Several chickadees pecked at cracked corn. She watched the little birds without really seeing them, just their brief gray flutters, their minor comings and goings in the periphery of her mind, and waited to be visited by her true opinion of Beth's letter. Suddenly a single fluffed-up chickadee, a big fellow, lit squarely in the yellow corn and stared straight at her through the glass. Mrs. Anderson blinked. She squinted and leaned closer to the window. How truly gray his grays, how sharply drawn his blacks and whites!

She found a pen and wrote Beth a brief note reminding her there was no public transportation in Deerlake, never had been.

The pastor at First Lutheran encouraged Mrs. Anderson to buy the Buick. First, he said, the way the Indians drove—especially during the autumn ricing season—one needed a safe car, and it was the big front-engine American cars like the LeSabre that always came out best in head-on collisions. Second, he said, she was already sixty-three. The Buick would be the last car she'd ever have to buy.

That night Mrs. Anderson sat bolt upright from a deep sleep: in her own room she had heard someone say, loudly,

"Yes!"

In nine years Mrs. Anderson drove the LeSabre 18,142 miles. During this time Beth went on to graduate school in English, first for an MA at Iowa City and then for the PhD at Purdue. Beth returned home to Deerlake regularly at Christmas and Easter, always alone, and talked endlessly about a French novelist called Alain-Fournier who had died tragically—heroically, actually—at age twenty-eight. Fournier was perhaps the first man killed in World War I. Beth had written her dissertation on Fournier, and now was enlarging the dissertation into a book because she had decided she wanted to be an essayist or a novelist; publishing the Fournier book, even with a small house, might be her big break. Summers, Beth traveled by train or Greyhound bus back and forth across the country to college writers' conferences. There she stayed in low redbrick dormitories for two weeks at a time and got tips from famous writers during wine and cheese hours.

Each Christmas and Easter Mrs. Anderson listened to Beth talk on of Fournier and of other things one could write about. A hot topic the year before had been depression, Beth said, but she hadn't realized it until depression had peaked and the magazines had gone on to breast cancer. After a few years of this, whenever Beth began to talk of Fournier or of writing, Mrs. Anderson's mind automatically shifted into reverse, to Beth back in high school, Beth winning at debates and at spelling bees. However, by Easter of 1978, when Mrs. Anderson was seventy-two, she thought mainly about who it was who was to take her grocery shopping. In the previous year, the year of depression, Mrs. Anderson had begun to drive the LeSabre an inch too close to things.

To the drive-in window at the bank.

To the pumps at the gas station.

To both sides of her own garage.

People from church, especially those with small children who rode bicycles around town, now drove Mrs. Anderson about Deerlake. Any time, anywhere, they told her, just call.

Of course Mrs. Anderson didn't need to call when Beth was home. Beth drove her mother about in the Buick. Beth drove and complained about a funny ticking noise somewhere in the car. Try as she might, Mrs. Anderson could not hear the noise.

"That fellow Sylvester Harjula," Mrs. Anderson said. She was surprised to have remembered his full name. "The dark-haired fellow you went to high school with. He has a mustache now. Maybe I should have him look into it—they say he can fix anything." Mrs. Anderson looked over at Beth. At her daughter's long neck, her thin blond hair that needed a good washing and then a body perm. "He's not a bad-looking man either," she added.

"Really, Mother!" Beth said. Her neck colored pink.

When Mrs. Anderson turned seventy-five she happened onto a *Reader's Digest* article, "The Cruel Cost of Aging." The next day, without writing Beth, Mrs. Anderson dusted off the windshield of the LeSabre and drove it carefully back to the dealership. There she learned firsthand a lesson about depreciation—how when a person puts the key into the ignition of a new car, one thousand dollars flies out the window. (She imagined green dollar bills streaming out the window and fluttering down the road behind.) She also learned that people preferred smaller Japanese and German cars these days.

Mrs. Anderson took the check for the LeSabre and walked three blocks to the bank's drive-in window. There she placed the check in the little tin tube and pushed the button. With a hiss her check disappeared down the pipe—which suddenly reminded her of another

Reader's Digest article: the similarities between rural banks of today and rural banks of the 1930s.

She spoke into the microphone, then waited. Her heart pounded. After a long while the pipe hissed and the little tube popped into daylight. Mrs. Anderson retrieved, in cash, one half of the LeSabre money. At home she placed the money in a one-pound coffee can which she then stored in the freezer beneath several square packages of frozen corn dated 1969.

At the dealership the LeSabre was scheduled for the body shop. It needed front and rear bumpers. New chrome door guards. Rocker panels. Quarter panels. Paint. That same morning Big Ed Hawkinson was driving his Kenworth logging truck past the car lot when from the corner of his eye he spied something different. Something black. He set the air brakes and skidded his rig to a stop. Big Ed was a logger, a Christmas tree farmer, and an auto body man during the coldest months of the winter. Every fall during ricing season he made a few bucks selling junkers to the Indians. At the moment, however, Big Ed was looking for a better-than-average unit, something a notch or two up. His oldest boy, Elvis, was getting his driver's license this very week. Big Ed never knew exactly what he was looking for in a car until he saw it, and what Big Ed was seeing, there next in line at the body-shop door, was the old Anderson widow's LeSabre.

Elvis Hawkinson drove the LeSabre home and straight into Big Ed's body shop. Elvis had plans for the LeSabre. He saw it painted metal flake blue, saw it with rear leaf-spring risers and Cragar mags, saw inside red shag carpet on the dash and a Jensen stereo system that would tear your scalp off. But there was one problem. The LaSabre was a four-door. Four-door cars were for women hauling around curtain climbers and bags of diapers and Kotex.

Elvis worked thirty hours straight. He knocked off the rear door handles and fiberglassed the holes. He welded the rear doors shut, then sanded smooth the welding bead. With a toilet plunger he popped out the rear quarter panels. He stripped all the chrome, glassed the screw holes, sanded everything again, then taped the windshield and all the glass. Toward morning of the second day, he shot the whole car with rust-colored primer.

After breakfast Elvis led Big Ed and Jimmy out to the shop.

"So what do you think?" Elvis said happily. He held a screwdriver and was about to open the gallon of blue metal flake.

"Well . . ." Big Ed said. He ran his hand through his hair.

"You ask me, it looks like a sixty-nine four-door LeSabre with the back doors welded shut and then primed," Jimmy said.

Elvis looked at the LeSabre. At Big Ed. At the can of blue metal flake.

That fall Elvis drove the LeSabre, still primed, with no Cragar mags and no Jensen stereo, back and forth to International Falls Community College where he took classes in diesel mechanics and hydraulics. The drive was 125 miles one way. At the end of two years the LeSabre had 62,879 miles on it and Elvis Hawkinson had enlisted in the air force.

Jimmy Hawkinson, Elvis's younger brother, put chrome wheels on the rear of the LeSabre and added twelve-inch risers to the rear leaf springs. The risers caused two problems. First, the rear bumper now stood forty-two inches off the ground, and Jimmy, who was five feet five, or only sixty-five inches tall, could not jump high enough to reach into the trunk. Second, the rear risers also threw the headlight beams directly onto the highway, like two floor lamps. But these were not large problems. Jimmy built a small wooden step stool which he carried on the back seat, in case he needed to get into the trunk; and when driving at night he simply left the headlight beams on bright.

Jimmy further customized the LeSabre. He tore out the front bench-type seat and welded in its place two bucket seats he had gotten from a wrecked Datsun 280Z. To the dashboard he added an eight-track stereo. He was saving for a gallon of red metal flake, but his car payment made things tough.

Every week Jimmy sent thirty dollars to Ensign Elvis Hawkinson, Third Diesel Support Squadron, c/o Fourth Tactical Squadron, Fifth Fleet, Pensacola, Florida. He sent the thirty dollars for two weeks. He missed the third week because he had bought the chrome wheels. He made the next week's payment, but could muster only twenty dollars the following week. Missed the next week. Missed the week after that. At the end of three months he stopped sending anything, though he did write to Elvis asking what exactly were the dates when Elvis would be home on leave.

Elvis showed up for Christmas two days earlier than planned, but Jimmy and the LeSabre had left the day before. A business trip. Jimmy left a note for Elvis and for Big Ed, saying that he was heading out to work in the gas fields in Wyoming. A week later he wrote again, a card postmarked Buffalo. He didn't say what outfit he was working for. He did write that there was so much natural gas in Wyoming it came up in water pipes; that you could turn on a faucet, light a match, and have fire and water coming from the same tap.

In March, Jimmy wrote Big Ed that Wyoming was deader than road kill and he was heading down to Texas, to the oil fields. He said that's where the work was.

In May, Jimmy Hawkinson hitchhiked into Deerlake from the south. He found Big Ed working on the Kenworth boom, hunkered over the bright spark of the welder. When Big Ed finally tipped back his mask and saw Jimmy, he stood up. Father and son grinned at each other. They shook hands. Jimmy didn't remember ever shaking hands with Big Ed. In a rush of words, Jimmy told Big Ed that he was ready now to work with him in the body shop or in the woods or trimming Christmas trees, wherever he was needed. Jimmy felt dumbshit happy and more than a little like crying. He told Big Ed that he'd always wanted to work at home with his own father, but for some reason he had to get way far away before he saw it. And one more thing: Could he borrow the Kenworth to drive down to Minneapolis to pick up the LeSabre?

Sylvester Harjula, a bachelor with deeply bitten fingernails, was the sole proprietor of a one-banner used-car lot at the Deerlake city limits. He bought the old Anderson LeSabre off the Hawkinson truck for ten tens cash. He would have paid more—a lot more, for here was the car Beth Anderson herself had driven. Here was the car that finally would give Sylvester a real excuse to talk to Beth Anderson when she came home for Christmas. But a hundred bucks was a hundred bucks.

The LeSabre was cold iron stew. The engine had thrown a rod through the block and clear into the battery. The trunk lid was gone. The left rear door was punched in with the outline of a parking meter. The transmission bled red through its seals like a lung-shot deer, and the odometer was a dead clock stopped at 17,847 miles. Yet none of this necessarily bothered Sylvester. With cars, where other people saw rust,

Sylvester saw Bondo. Where other people saw blue oil smoke in the exhaust and turned away, Sylvester saw piston rings and maybe sleeves. SYLVESTER HARJULA'S NO PROBLEM USED CARS, DEERLAKE, MINNESOTA, his business cards said. Within two weeks Sylvester found an engine from a junked LeMans which used a quart only every five hundred. He found a door, though no trunk lid. He gave the Buick a quick coat of black enamel, inside the trunk as well, so everything matched, and had the car on the lot stickered at $295 just in time for ricing season.

Sylvester sat in the square wooden office he had built himself. He wore a yellow shirt and a yellow tie. It was October. Sunlight slanted through the single window. Sylvester leaned back in his chair and smoked a Camel. His fingers smudged the white cigarette paper. He looked out the window at the shiny black LeSabre. He glanced at the calendar. Beth Anderson was thirty-nine this year. He wondered if she'd found a man yet. He nibbled at a thumbnail, then stopped himself. He looked at his hands, his fingernails. He glanced over at the calendar again. Briefly he lifted the cellophane sheet and looked at the tanned blonde on the beach. He looked at the untanned parts of her. Then he let her bathing suit fall back into place, and turned the pages to November and December. His fingers left little black lilypads on the corners of the pages. He examined his hands again. Another three weeks, four at most, he'd have to start work on his hands if they were to be clean in time for Christmas. He swung around to his desk, found a notepad and stub of a pencil. "Gojo" he wrote. After that he doodled a minute. He drew a tall, thin girl with a long neck.

When Sylvester looked up some time later, there were Indians in the lot. A whole covey of them, like blackbirds, had lit around the Buick. Two kids perched on top of the LeSabre, another kid jumped up and down inside the lidless trunk, longer legs poked from beneath the car and several heads were visible inside the Buick.

Sylvester stood up. In the small mirror above his desk he checked his hair, adjusted his yellow tie. Then, humming a little tune he had made up himself, Sylvester stepped outside into sunlight. The Indians' hair gleamed like crows' wings.

At the river John All Day steered the Buick backward to the big Norway pine. When the bumper hit wood, he killed the motor and set the brake. He always parked that way to cover up the license plate and,

more important, the gas cap. Sometimes on the reservation he forgot
to park that way. Then his first stop had to be a gas station, which was
his own fault for not parking right. Now as the bumper rocked once
more against the Norway, John All Day felt the long back of the old
tree come into his own body. Felt its roots in his own legs. Old Man
Pine with the long legs.

The rest of the All Days, including Bobby All Day, John's brother,
and several of their children, climbed out the rear windows of the black
car. The kids ran to the shore and began to throw stones into the water. John and Bobby untied the canoe ropes and the long duckbill pole.
They left the car radio on while they loaded the canoe.

In a still moment between songs, they heard, far out on the lake, the
whump-whump of rice sticks on canoes.

Bobby straightened up to listen. "Dammit, we better hurry," Bobby
said, and clattered the duckbill into the canoe.

John All Day laughed at his brother and continued to load the canoe at the same pace. Lastly he went to his wife, who was watching
from the soft front seat of the black car. He put his hand on her belly.
Inside, the baby kicked like a little calf. "Whoa!" John said.

His wife grinned. Her face was round and smooth and shiny, like
the aspen trees on the bank, only darker and smoother, like walnut.

"Stay in the car and sleep," John said. "Honk the horn if you need
me. I'll come, hey?"

"You better, mister," she said. They smiled at each other.

John and Bobby pushed off from shore. The canoe scraped on sand,
then went silent on water. An Elvis song played from the black car's radio. On the shore the children waved and threw rocks after the canoe.
At first their stones splashed close beside the canoe—one rock clinked
on tin. "Devils!" Bobby said without looking behind him. But soon the
splashes fell farther and farther behind. John All Day watched his children and the black car grow smaller. He wondered if things disappeared when they went out of sight. If they really went away.

Ahead was the rice bed, a long feather of green in blue water. As they
neared the rice, John took from his pocket two pieces of pink bubble
gum. He tossed one to Bobby, and they chewed the sweet gum soft. Soon
the bow of the canoe entered the tall grass with a soft scraping sound.
The rice stalks leaned away from both sides of the canoe. John swung his
long stick and brought the rice heads over the mouth of the canoe.

"Little Mahnomen men," John said to the rice, and with his other hand brought down the flail.

Bobby poled.

John beat grain. Once a rice beard flew into the corner of his eye. Bobby stopped poling while John took the bubble gum from his mouth, held open the eyelid and pressed the gum to his eyeball. He took away the bubble gum and blinked his eye rapidly; the lake wobbled back into focus. John popped the gum back into his mouth and nodded to Bobby, who leaned into the pole. The little rice beard crunched in the bubble gum. "Mahnomen man," John said. From across the water, out of sight, came the faint laughing cries of his children and music from the black car's radio.

That afternoon at three o'clock Bobby poled the canoe slowly back toward the landing. The canoe rode low in the water.

When they came closer, John saw on the shore his two boys jumping up and down like young crows trying to fly from a tree. They flapped and called to him. "Hurry," they shouted. "The baby!"

Bobby leaned into the duckbill pole.

"In the car—" the boys shouted.

John leaped from the canoe and ran through the shallow water. From the car his wife groaned. Her feet stuck out the driver's side window. They were wide apart and her brown toes were curled like snail shells.

"It's coming," his wife said. She had bitten her bottom lip and there was blood on her chin.

"Dammit, you should have honked!" John said.

"The horn don't work," she said. She groaned again.

"It works, I tried it—" John said.

"Not for me, it don't work," she said.

"Forget the horn, man!" Bobby said from behind them.

John leaped in beside her and turned the key to start the engine. The battery clicked once and was silent.

"Goddammit!" John shouted. He tried again. Not even a click this time. Then he heard a noise, a faint faraway noise that was at the same time close up. He looked down at the dashboard. The radio volume knob was turned all the way up. He leaned his ear toward the speaker. A song. "Jesus, you listened to the radio all day!" John said.

"Why not?" she said, then groaned again.

"Why not? Why not? The damn battery, that's—"

His wife's groan rose to a shout. "It's coming, I can't stop it."

"Bobby—run to the highway—flag somebody down," John called.
Bobby's shoes kicked up dust as he ran. John knelt between her legs
to help. The children gathered around.

Twenty minutes later a dusty pickup jolted down the road toward
the shore. Bobby rode standing up in the rear, hanging on like a
bronco rider. He leaped from the truck before it came to a stop and
raced forward. John came slowly from the front seat of the black car.
He was grinning and holding, wrapped in his shirt, his new baby,
Manny, whose full name was to be Mahnomen, which in Ojibwe
meant wild rice. John's wife lay in the front seat, resting. The two
biggest boys stood with pine-bough fans by the open windows of the
black car and made sure no flies or mosquitoes bothered their mother.
The smaller kids had returned to the shore and were throwing pebbles
into the water.

The pickup's driver, an older farmer with a limp, walked forward.
He looked into the front seat, then at the baby. "Well, I'll be dipped,"
he said. He spit long and cleanly to the side, then bent down for a
closer look at the baby. John held the baby forward. The farmer
brought up a thick finger and touched Manny's nose. "You little bug-
ger," the farmer said, "you little acorn, you."

John smiled and nodded.

Then the farmer looked at the Buick. "We better get your car started
anyway," he said. He went to his truck and dug behind the seat for a
pair of dusty jumper cables.

Bobby took up one pair of the cable grips.

"Nope—I'll do it," the farmer said. "Don't want my alternator
burned out."

Bobby shrugged and let go his end.

Leaning against the big Norway pine, his bare back on the bark,
John All Day held his son and watched. He felt the old man pine come
into him again. Grandfather Pine. John's back was Grandfather's back,
John's arms were Grandfather's thick, curving limbs, and John's baby
was a pine cone, a sticky, sweet-smelling pine cone full of seeds of his
own, seeds enough for a whole forest, seeds and life for anyone or anything who touched Grandfather Pine.

"Ready?" the farmer called to Bobby.

Bobby got in the driver's seat of the black car. Its rear bumper remained pressed against the big pine; from its nose, battery cables stretched forward, drooping power lines, to the farmer's truck. Bobby held up his hand.

"Here we go," the farmer called; he touched metal to metal.

John All Day felt something pass through his own body, something like the flow of river water against a canoe paddle, the way moving water pushed up through the paddle handle and into your hands and arms and shoulders and finally into your back where it turned around your spine and then you pushed it back to where it lived, where it never needed recharging or batteries or wires, that weight in the river—or in the bite of axe on wood or in a full wind against your face that pushed against you but pulled you forward at the same time—John All Day felt it pass up the chain of wood and iron and men's hands, and the black car's engine coughed alive.

After the farmer had gone, John returned the baby to his wife. Then he drove the black car down to the shore, to the canoe. He left the engine running while Bobby shoveled the rice into the open trunk. There was only one shovel, so John watched. The rice flew, each shovelful thudding onto the last, onto the rising green mound. Bobby began to sweat. "Slow down, man," John said, "you always in such a damned hurry. Running around like a damned crazy man."

Bobby straightened up fast to glare at his brother, then saw that John was smiling.

The All Days drove the black car, which sagged in the rear, out to the highway. First John took the baby and his wife home to her mother; he waited outside the house until her mother came and said everything was okay. Then he and Bobby drove fast to Deerlake to have the rice weighed while it was still wet.

The rice weighed 210 pounds.

The price was ninety cents a pound.

John and Bobby took the check and cashed it at Doc's Inn, on Main Street. The tavern was loud and warm and smelled like lake water and beer. People danced. Rice beards hung on the shirts and pants of everybody but the bartender. John bought a drink for everyone, and people clapped. Other people danced, sometimes Indians and whites together. Tiny pale green rice worms shook loose from cuffs and pockets, and left slippery spots on the dance floor. John grinned and sipped the whiskey. He watched his brother and he watched the other dancers and he watched the beer light, a circle of seasons—spring green, summer gold, fall orange, and winter white—painted on a plastic plate turning with a grinding noise around a yellow light bulb. John watched and he chewed the bubble gum that was crunchy with rice beards and now tasted like the whiskey and now like the lake. John sipped his whiskey and he watched the dancers go around and around.

On December 10, Sylvester Harjula repoed the LeSabre. All Day had paid $150 down with $145 due when the rice was sold. Sylvester knew for a fact All Day had cashed his rice check at Doc's Inn—like any businessman Sylvester kept track of his customers—and Sylvester hadn't seen a dime of the $145.

Which didn't necessarily bother him. He called Ken Edevold, a high school pal who was also the deputy sheriff. He caught a lift with Ken out to the reservation. The All Day house was a white government prefab with a sagging roof and smudges all around the siding as high as children could reach. In the snowy yard sat four rusted 1966 Bonnevilles. Doors and trunk lids from three of the Bonnevilles had migrated to the blue Bonneville, which sat closest to the front door. The LeSabre sat off to the side with a drift of snow down its hood. It looked like a frozen skunk.

Sylvester knocked on the metal door. There was no storm door. Inside, a dog barked. A TV played loudly. A baby cried. Someone peeked briefly out the window, then the TV went silent. No one came to the door. Sylvester knocked again. He heard whispering. Finally he turned away and walked to the LeSabre. He had a key. He kept a key to every car he sold to the Indians and to whites as well; business was business, particularly with used cars. The LeSabre's battery was deader than an icehouse pike but Sylvester had jumper cables and a spray can of ether. Five minutes later Sylvester was driving the LeSabre off the reservation and back toward Deerlake.

In his shop Sylvester examined the LeSabre. The seats were covered with dog hair and stank accordingly. The front seat was ruined; somebody had spilled what looked like a gallon of ruby port. The trunk was covered with snow and rice hulls and frozen green worms. But none of this was a problem. Come spring he'd steam-clean the whole unit, find another front seat and a trunk lid, touch up the black enamel, and the Buick would sticker out at $325, minimum. If it didn't sell until fall, that was fine. The All Days might even buy the Buick again, which was fine by Sylvester. He felt nothing one way or the other about the All

Days. They had the Buick car for ricing season, and now Sylvester had it back. And none too soon.

Beth Anderson rode into Deerlake on the Greyhound bus the snowy evening of December 22. Sylvester Harjula sat parked across the street in his personal car, a fully restored '51 Merc. He ran the wipers to keep the windshield clear of snow. He saw Beth get down from the bus; his heartbeat picked up RPMs. She wore a long black coat and dark stocking cap pulled low across her forehead. Her neck was bare and for a moment caught light from the street lamps. Sylvester's heartbeat picked up speed. A man came down the steps close behind Beth; Sylvester's heartbeat raced. There was some accelerator in his chest and he felt short of breath. But the headlamps of a waiting car blinked on and the man waved and turned toward the light. Sylvester, slightly dizzy, let out his breath. Beth waited for her small black suitcase, then walked, leaning into the snow, the two blocks to her mother's house.

The next morning Sylvester drove slowly by the Anderson house. He looked for tracks in the snow on the front steps, but saw none. Which was no problem. He knew her routine. He parked down the street.

At two o'clock Beth came out of the house. She swept snow from the steps, not the whole width but just enough to make a path for her own feet. She continued sweeping in this manner down the sidewalk. At the street she turned and for a long time stared at the house she had grown up in. Then she let the broom fall in the snow, and walked downtown.

Sylvester followed her in the Merc a block behind. She looked closely at each house she passed. Once she stopped to stare up at a big elm tree, its naked branches, the white knots of snow where the black limbs joined the trunk. On Main Street Beth walked slower. She paused by every store window. Eventually she turned into Kinder's, the old soda fountain from high school days.

Beth Anderson took a stool at the long counter. Kinder's was empty but for two high school kids in orange-and-black letter jackets who stood jolting two pinball machines with the butts of their hands. Magazine racks to the side. Booths, probably empty, to the rear. The booths were where high school couples necked. She didn't remember ever sitting in the booth section of Kinder's.

Old Man Kinder, bald now, his mouth caved in, turned from the television set and came her way. He paused in front of her. He waited in silence. He did not recognize her.

"Cherry Coke," she said, which was the only reason she'd come here in the first place. Cherry Cokes at Kinder's did not come from a can.

Old Man Kinder turned back to the TV as he filled her glass. One rattle of ice. One long squirt of cherry that raced a red spiderweb among the cubes. Then the brown flood of cola.

She sipped the Coke. Its sweet blossom filled her nose and made it tingle. She drank half, then slowed, and looked out to Main Street. The square front windowpane was shrunken by frost to a single clear oval. A porthole in a submarine. Outside, a brown jacket passed; she saw its quilted pattern as the coat drifted by only inches from the glass, like some large, unidentifiable sea mammal.

Beth thought of Sylvester Harjula. Creepy Sylvester. He was still around, she supposed. Sylvester had been a regular at Kinder's ever since high school. Back then he had some sort of radar for her. She looked past the counter into the mirror. She took off her stocking cap and shook out her hair, except that it didn't shake. She had forgotten, again, to wash it. She replaced the stocking cap and looked away from the mirror. Mirrors were not her friends, never had been. Mirrors in truth were no one's friends, for they reflected appearance to the neglect of reality. Mirrors saw no inner life, and it was the inner life of people, other people, that had always interested Beth. She was a people-kind-of-person, always had been.

She thought of herself. Her own life. From Deerlake to a dissertation on Alain-Fournier, the doctorate, a comp/lit teaching position at Northwestern in Chicago. Not too shabby, as her students might say. Northwestern was not the University of Chicago, but with a book or two in print, anything was possible. And of course, had she been born, say, to a family of Georgetown diplomats who spoke three languages at dinner, she doubtless would be at Harvard. And often on the MacNeil/Lehrer news. One of Robert MacNeil's favorite sources, one who spoke in short but perfect paragraphs and so made his blue eyes shine; she would certainly remember to wash her hair for the "MacNeil/Lehrer NewsHour."

She glanced down at the pinball players. She looked at the ceiling. An oval water stain, brown-rimmed and weepy at the corners, stared back at her. She turned to look out the frosted glass to Main Street and thought again of her own life. She had come, several years ago, to believe that Deerlake was a mistake. That, somewhat like Shirley MacLaine, she should have been born in France, preferably in 1890 in the village of Epineuil-le-Fleuriel, France. Then she would have met Alain-Fournier. They would have been childhood friends, then schoolmates; then, in adolescence, the wonderful confusion of friendship and deeper passions; and much later, because of her—Beth Anderson (though her name would have been different, perhaps Beatrice)—the drums of World War I would have sounded to Alain faint and far away. He would have remained in Epineuil. Alain, dear Alain, would have loved honor less and her more, and so would not have gone off to the front—at least not so quickly—and because of Beth and her letters, a correspondence of aesthetics atremble with desire, a correspondence surpassing even the letters between Alain-Fournier and Jacques Riviere—all because of Beth, Alain would have returned to his writing desk. To the white paper. The dark ink.

Alain was commanding officer that day. There was ragged fire from a hostile wood. Alain had led the charge, pistol upraised; he had taken a ball in the hand or the arm, had fallen, but then risen and pressed on into the smoke, the dust, the noise. Into memory, history, dream. "Oh Alain," she whispered, "dear dark burning Alain—"

Suddenly a voice beside her said, "Beth Anderson—long time no see!"

She turned. Her mouth fell open. The dark hair across the forehead, the eyebrows, the deep-set burning eyes, the mustache. It was Sylvester Harjula.

"Welcome home," Sylvester said. He extended a chapped hand.

Beth caught her breath. Her cheeks warmed. She took the hand— there was no choice. It felt like a coconut. Like Sylvester soaked his hands in pickling brine.

"Mind if I?" Sylvester said, sitting down, leaving one stool between them.

"No—I mean, go ahead," she said. She looked back at her Coke.

They sat in silence for a while. Sylvester ordered a chocolate Coke. Creepy Sylvester.

"So when did you get in?" he asked.

"Last night."

"All by your lonesome?"

"I enjoy traveling alone," she said.

Sylvester was silent for a moment. "It's a good time to think about things, I suppose," he said.

She looked up at Sylvester. She never imagined he thought about anything except cars.

"I was thinking about you recently," Sylvester said.

Beth looked down and swirled her cubes.

"I've got the LeSabre now," Sylvester said.

In the mirror Beth saw him smile at her as if he expected to be congratulated for something. "The LeSabre?" Beth said.

"Your mother's old car," Sylvester said.

"Oh—I'd quite forgotten," Beth said.

Sylvester's smile faded. He turned back to his chocolate Coke. "Of course it's pretty well beat," Sylvester said. "Mainly an Indian car now."

Beth turned. She had forgotten about the Indians.

"Why are they so hard on cars?" she said.

Sylvester shrugged. "They don't see cars like we do. They don't care what they drive, long as it goes," Sylvester said.

Beth was silent.

"They're kind of beat down, themselves, I guess," Sylvester said. "As a race, I mean. Maybe it's like that old saying, 'You are what you drive.'"

Beth swirled her ice cubes once around her glass. "I don't have a car, so what does that make me?"

"Well," Sylvester began, "I . . ." But there was no more. His neck reddened.

For an instant Beth felt sorry for him and ashamed of herself. She shouldn't have been so quick, so sharp. All her life she'd been that way. It was not an admirable trait.

"Maybe not having a car could be good," Sylvester said. "You wouldn't have payments, upkeep, insurance."

She turned to look at Sylvester.

"You'd be more free," he said, staring straight at her.

Then her eyes fell to his lobster hands. She turned back to her watery ice cubes.

After a long silence, Sylvester said, "So how's your mother?"

"Not good," Beth said. She told him about the diabetes. The heart trouble. The forgetfulness.

That night, after fixing hot milk for her mother, who was, strangely, not at all sleepy by eleven o'clock, Beth finally went to bed. She was slipping toward sleep when something Sylvester had said came into her mind. Indians and cars. "You are what you drive," Sylvester had said.

Beth opened her eyes. For the Indians, a car was not a car at all, but a metaphor. A cultural metaphor. More than that: it was a Weltanschauung. And the fact that Indians cared not a whit for cars was not necessarily a sign of cultural decay; in fact, it was the opposite. Indians who drove junked cars and left them along the road when the motors burned out were the real, that is, the nonassimilated, the true Indians.

Beth switched on the lamp, got up and began to pace the bedroom. Of course Sylvester was right—you are what you drive. But she was right, too. She was righter. She was a writer, that is. For wrapped up in her mother's disgusting old LeSabre—Sylvester had told her all the details—was the whole Indian Problem.

Rapidly she dug in her suitcase for a yellow notepad and a pen. At the top of the page she wrote in bold letters "The Indian Problem, by Beth Anderson." As she waited to be visited by the next sentence, downstairs her mother gave out a groan and died.

After the funeral there was the matter of the house and her mother's belongings. For want of acquaintances her own age—Beth realized how few friends she had had in high school (not any, really)—she called Sylvester Harjula.

Sylvester appeared at her door twenty minutes later. He carried a long tool box. He said he imagined there were things of her mother's that Beth would want shipped, and he had brought along lumber, saw, hammer, nails, and strapping tape.

"Well, there is the china cabinet," Beth said.

Sylvester sawed and hammered. He made a marvelous crate; Beth found old blankets to drape the cabinet. Mid-morning, Beth made a pot of coffee. At noon they drove downtown for lunch in Sylvester's Mercury. The Mercury was scented sharply with a Pine-Tree air freshener; its seats were deeply soft and upholstered in burgundy velours, a combination Beth imagined that one might find in the waiting room of a bordello. She also realized, as they turned downtown, this was the first time she had ever ridden alone with a man her own age, in his car, down Main Street in Deerlake.

At the cafe she ordered a broasted half-chicken in a basket.

Sylvester ordered the same, though with potato skins rather than fries. They waited for the food in silence.

"I have a house now," Beth said to herself. She looked out the window for a long time.

Their chicken came. As they ate, Sylvester intermittently spoke, but Beth often missed what he said and didn't remember to reply. She stared out the window. Whenever she stopped eating, Sylvester paused as well. Finally she turned to Sylvester. "Would you watch the house for me? This winter?" she asked.

"Well," Sylvester began.

"For remuneration, of course," Beth said. "Then when spring comes I'll organize some sort of estate auction. However, for the short term I need someone to watch the house."

"It'd be an honor and a privilege," Sylvester said.

Beth stared at Sylvester. Then she laughed.

Sylvester's eyes widened; he looked down, into his chicken basket.

"I'm sorry," Beth said. "It's just that you sounded so . . . formal." She laughed again, and tried to cover her mouth with her hand.

"I really am very sorry," she said. She giggled.

"It's okay," Sylvester said. "I know how tough it must be."

She laughed again, louder this time, because she had entirely forgotten about her mother. She was thinking, rather, of herself. Herself, at thirty-nine years of age, sitting in Deerlake, Minnesota, picking at cold broasted chicken and fries with Sylvester Harjula of Harjula's No Problem Used Cars. She continued to laugh. She couldn't stop. She upset her water glass and laughed louder at that. Sylvester helped her up from the table and out the door into the cold air. On the way home she tipped over on the seat and kept laughing harder and harder until Sylvester realized she was crying.

The next day Beth prepared to leave. Sylvester had a key. Everything was in order with the electricity and water departments, the heating oil truck driver. She took a last look around the house. In the basement a faint humming noise caught her attention. She touched the furnace. The water heater. The white side of the chest-type freezer, which vibrated beneath her fingers. She had forgotten about the freezer. Ice squeaked as she lifted the lid. The freezer overflowed with large cauliflowers of frost, and beneath the frost, years' worth of food. Frozen vegetables. Meat. Berries. Packages of arm roasts, round steak, hamburger; containers of crystalline raspberries, purple chokecherries; layers and layers of hard bags of yellow corn. Among the corn was a single red coffee can which rang emptily to her touch. She lifted the can and shook it; something rustled inside with a sound like dried leaves. She pried off the plastic lid and found inside the can fifty green twenty-dollar bills. One thousand dollars in cash.

In January, back at Northwestern, Beth happened to glance through the travel section of the Sunday Tribune. She began reading about sun vacations to Mexico and the Caribbean. She noticed how some of the advertisements slipped the word singles into their sentences; how really quite inexpensive they were.

The next day Beth booked a single's package to Club Papagallos, which meant Club Parrot, on Grand Cayman Island, which was seventy nautical miles south of Cuba. There Beth was walking along the beach with her head down to avoid stepping in the crude oil that had washed ashore and rolled itself into little black sandy balls that resembled Russian tea cakes when she bumped full-length against a tall, thin man with a Lincoln beard.

"One thousand dollars for a vacation and the damned beach is no better than a goose yard," the man said. "Look at my feet!"

Beth did.

The man was a full professor at the University of Chicago, was recently divorced, and had written two books and eighteen critical papers about Gustave Flaubert. At dinner that night he told Beth things about Flaubert that few people knew, for example, that Flaubert's saliva was perpetually blackened by mercury treatments for venereal disease. He also told Beth his former wife read nothing but James Michener, which was the straw that finally broke the back of their marriage. "Not that I didn't bring home good literature for her to read," he said twice that night.

Beth and Henry Ridgecraft were married in February in the office of a judge in a civic building overlooking Lake Michigan. As they left the office, Henry made a joke about the number of Chicago judges caught in recent police stings.

Beth moved into Henry's town house. And to that address, every

other week, came a letter from Sylvester Harjula. Sylvester wrote on his
small, brown "No Problem" stationery. His writing, always in blue ink,
was cramped both in penmanship and in style, yet contained no sentence fragments or comma splices. Henry, for a good laugh, always
read the letters aloud. He pointed out faint oil smudges on the pages.
After a month of this Beth kept Sylvester's letters to herself.

In his letters, Sylvester wrote about the house. He said now that
winter was here he worried about the furnace going out. About the
pipes freezing. Since he had a key, he wrote, he sometimes slept
overnight in the house. He said it was a warm house and a quiet house
for sleeping, a good house all around.

Beth wrote Sylvester in return. She thanked him for being a scrupu-
lous caretaker. She assured him that he was welcome to stay in the
house, regularly if he wished. She did not, for some reason, tell him
about her marriage to Henry Ridgecraft.

In his next letter Sylvester asked if she would address her letters to
him in care of her mother's house. He said regular mail was important
to the safety of an empty house. Also he would get her letters a day earlier, in case there was anything urgent that she wanted from him or
wished to tell him. He said he hoped she wouldn't feel funny sending
letters to him at her old address.

"Not strange at all," Beth wrote, though in truth it was. At first she
felt as if Sylvester had become part of her family. After two or three cy-
cles of letters, however, of Sylvester's reports and her thank-you notes
in reply, Beth felt at ease writing to Sylvester at her old home address.
She began to add occasional anecdotes, as she had to her mother,
telling Sylvester of her students; of teaching them to write; of making
them ponder, for at least fifty minutes a day, things they read.

Sylvester wrote back that he had liked Zane Grey and Jack London
from school days. Now he sometimes picked up a Louis L'Amour pa-
perback at the grocery store. He asked if she could recommend to him
some books along that line.

Beth wrote back to suggest Hemingway and Faulkner, then on second thought crossed out Faulkner. She explained that Faulkner might
have won the Nobel Prize but his sentences would never win any As in
her freshmen composition classes.

Sylvester wrote back and included in his letter one particularly long
sentence from *The Sound and The Fury*, which he had found in the Deer-

lake Library. He said he could see what she meant about Faulkner. He also said that he had read *The Old Man and the Sea*. He had put the "closed" sign on his office building and read the whole book in one day. He said it was a good book, which to him meant the type of book he could see reading again sometime.

Beth wrote back immediately a rather excited letter, saying that he had hit upon the best definition of art—writing or painting or music that held up under repeated scrutiny, that got better with age. After that, Beth wrote less about the house and increasingly whatever came into mind—mostly about growing up in Deerlake. She told Sylvester things. How she had hated the choir director, Mr. Kinney, and his ugly pipe. How she thought the cheerleaders were an embarrassment to themselves. How she really had not liked school and could not wait to turn eighteen and graduate.

Sylvester wrote that he remembered her well from school. He said it had always seemed to him that she enjoyed school. And if someone like her hadn't enjoyed school, then who ever did?

"Maybe no one," she wrote back. "Maybe no one ever is really happy with her life," she wrote. She was tired and it was late when she wrote that; when she should have been Hemingway, she was Faulkner. She wrote about her studies, about Alain-Fournier, a long rambling letter that held up her life in Deerlake to Meaulnes's life in Fournier's novel. She wrote that she, too, always felt like an outsider " . . . even to myself," she wrote. "Sometimes I feel as if there's an explanation to my life that continues to escape me; that I've missed something noble, something sublime; that in some way I have cheated myself . . . life is so strange, so harsh," she wrote.

Sylvester wrote back that he could find nothing by the Fournier fellow in the Deerlake Library, but said he was going to a used car auction at the Minneapolis Auditorium, and he would try a bigger library down there. As far as life went, he agreed it was an odd business, but he couldn't really agree with her about no one being truly happy, because here he was, Sylvester Harjula, writing letters to her, Beth Anderson. He wrote that since high school, perhaps from the first time he saw her, he had admired her more than she ever knew. He said that April first, when she was to arrive back in Deerlake, was only two weeks away, and seeing her again would make him happier than she could know.

Beth finished reading his letter and looked up from her desk. Henry

knelt by his stereo grooming one of his jazz albums with an electro-
static roller; the turntable circled emptily, waiting. "Oh dear," Beth
said.

Beth and Henry Ridgecraft drove into Deerlake in Henry's Volvo on
April first. Henry had been invited to give his paper, "Window and Door
Imagery in *Madame Bovary*," at the University at Urbana-Champaign,
but Beth had prevailed upon him to come with her to Minnesota. "Just
this once," she said. For most of the trip Henry drove above the speed
limit and did not look at the passing scenery.

In Deerlake, Beth directed him past the gas company and the feed
mill, then across Main Street and the final two blocks to her mother's
house.

Above the slouched and faintly dirty snowbanks, the wide face of
her old house looked white and fresh. For a moment she thought the
house had been newly painted; then she decided it was just the cleaner
air, the brighter slant of smalltown light. The front sidewalk shone
gray and wet; it was the only bare concrete in the neighborhood.

"How does real estate move around here?" Henry asked.

"Move?" Beth said.

"Sell," Henry said, "sell."

"I . . . really have no idea," Beth said. She was looking through the
window into the living room. There were lights on. And blue striped
wallpaper. She didn't remember that wallpaper.

She walked onto the porch. The doorsill was sharp and square, a
new piece of varnished oak. The doorknob had changed from iron to
yellow brass. She tried her key. The tumblers turned. The door swung
open without squeaking. Inside music was playing. A radio. Some
country-western song.

She paused to knock on the door. "Hello?" she called. "Hello?"

The house smelled different. Gone were the brackish odors of old
carpet and furniture and stewed tomatoes. Now she smelled fresh
paint and lemon furniture wax and flowers. On the mantel was a white
vase with two red roses.

"Not bad," Henry said, steering her inside. "I'd buy this house."

Beth's heart began to thud. She followed the hallway toward the
yellow-lit kitchen and the music. She smelled fresh coffee. On the
table were two cups and saucers and, between them, a larger bouquet
of red roses with a note.

"Where's the bathroom?" Henry called.

"Upstairs," she murmured. She stared, then turned to speak to Henry but saw only his legs moving up the stairs, shortening as they climbed.

At the table she slowly reached down for the note. "Dearest Beth," the small handwriting began. She crumpled shut the note and caught her breath. There was noise behind her in the living room. Henry—she must quickly explain all this to Henry—so crazy, all of it, a big laugh for Henry, and of course she couldn't fault him for laughing because she was to blame really, completely to blame, she must take full responsibility for this terrible—Then the front doorknob turned and the door swung open. Sylvester Harjula, dressed in a blue cap, a brown jacket, a pink shirt, checkered pants, all clean and pressed, stepped inside.

They stared at each other. Sylvester removed his cap. He grinned and his face reddened in the same moment.

"Sylvester—" she began, and started toward him.

"Beth—" he said. "Oh Beth." He moved toward her and his arms came up.

At that instant, upstairs, the toilet flushed.

Sylvester froze. His arms dropped to his sides. Down the stairs came Henry's brown shoes, his argyle socks, his gray wool slacks, his black belt and small potbelly, his gray sweater, his shoulders, the salt-and-pepper tip of his beard, and finally his face. Henry stopped midway to stare.

"Henry . . . Sylvester . . . Henry . . . Sylvester," Beth said. The names went around in a circle and she did not know where, on which one, to stop.

Sylvester's jaw went slack.

"Sylvester," Beth said, "this is . . . my husband, Henry Ridgecraft."

It was late in the afternoon. Henry had made one joke about Sylvester and the roses, then went to the basement to examine the furnace. After that he went upstairs for his nap.

While Henry slept Beth sat alone in the kitchen. She made a cup of tea but drank little. She sat with her hands folded around the warmth of the cup, and watched birds come and go at the feeder.

Chickadees.

Little sparrows with red crests.

A fat blue jay that periodically chased all the small birds away.

Later she blinked as Henry stirred upstairs. The cup was cold in her hands; it was six o'clock. Soon Henry came downstairs whistling. "Hey, I'm starving," he called to Beth. "Let's go out for dinner, my treat."

He came into the kitchen with her coat. Beth stood up. She fitted her arms into the holes. Outside, they walked toward Main Street.

"Some little French place—or maybe Chinese—either will do," Henry said jovially, and put his arm around her shoulders.

It was heavy and she shrugged it off. "The Hub Cafe on Main Street is all that's open. It'll have to do," she said.

"Okay, okay," Henry said.

Late sunlight slanted low through the intersections and divided Main Street, already dusky in the shadow of the buildings, into a three-block lattice of blue and orange. A handful of cars, none together, sat here and there. The curved, cursive Kinder's sign hummed and clicked, then blinked on; one by one the letters flickered to pink. The final S buzzed, strained, but in the end could not muster itself to light.

Below the Kinder's sign, gleaming darkly, sat a long car with an orange For Sale sign taped to its rear window. Something about the car— the sweep of its fenders, the slope of the roof—did not release Beth's gaze. She squinted to see better. The black fins. The four doors.

"Hey, where you going?" Henry called.

Beth left Henry and crossed the street. A pickup with two teenagers passed. Its brake lights blinked on red as the teenagers swiveled their heads to stare at the Buick. Yes—the Buick LeSabre, their old LeSabre, the one her mother had bought, Beth realized. But it couldn't be. This LeSabre looked newer, shinier than their LeSabre had ever looked, even brand new. Slowly Beth walked closer. The Buick's paint gleamed deep obsidian black. In the curves of its chrome she saw Main Street both left and right, saw the asphalt below, saw the orange-and-purple sky above; saw her own face as if in a fun-house mirror, a wide face with round, open eyes, a face that for a moment she did not recognize. She looked behind her, but there was no one there. Only Henry across the street, and the pickup turning at the end of the block, coming back.

She turned back to the LeSabre and bent to look inside. The black seats, the dark carpet, the great jet plane dashboard with its round-eyed clock and the gleaming silver knobs—it was all exactly as she remembered. It was all the same except for, dangling from the radio dial, the Pine-Tree air freshener.

She suddenly looked up to Kinder's. In the frosted window, centered in the oval of frost-free glass, was Sylvester Harjula. He sat in profile. He did not see her because he stared straight ahead. His left hand, holding a cigarette, held up his chin. His brown eyes, unblinking, gazed far away. The only movement came from his cigarette, whose smoke curled upward white into the white frost.

"Hey, come on, I'm hungry," Henry called from across the street.

But Beth did not move. She stood in place and she stared at Sylvester Harjula. At the portrait of Sylvester Harjula. A living portrait but one already gone over into the future. As would she—she suddenly realized—if she moved from this spot. She who knew the answers to everything but had no knowledge—not one good clue—as to why or how or from where the questions ever came.

Behind Beth pickup doors slammed. Reflected in the Kinder's glass, two teenagers wearing letter jackets over sweatshirts, their gray hoods pointed up, walked quickly to the Buick. They bent to look inside.

"Man, it's cherry!" one said.

"Wonder what they want for it?" the second said.

"Plenty, I'll bet," the first said.

The closest one straightened and turned to Beth. In the shadow of his hood she could not see his face. "Hey lady," he said, "is this your car?"

Blaze of Glory

The young doctor scribbled the prescription; he had a beard and his pen scraped loudly in the small room where Dolores Johnson waited with her husband, Herb. Herb sat in his undershorts on the examining table. Clearly he could put his clothes back on now, Dolores observed; under the fluorescent light he looked white and sagging and chilly. Oddly she thought of "Caves of Mystery" (or was it "Mystery Caves") in South Dakota, a tourist attraction where she and Herb had stopped on their honeymoon more than forty years ago—the pale, humped, stalagmites in cold, harshly lit stone rooms. "Digoxin, Herb," the doctor said, ripping the prescription sheet from its pad and spinning on his chair toward Herb. "I see you've taken it before, right?"

Herb glanced at Dolores, then turned away to reach for his pants.

Dr. Field paused on his rolling chair. He wore blue jeans and tennis shoes, had a rumpled look straight out of those evening medical dramas on television. Herb's regular doctor had retired, and while Dolores tried hard to be charitable toward the young these days, she was fairly certain Dr. Field did not measure up. His gaze skipped from Herb to his chart. "How old are you again, Herb?"

"Seventy-one," Herb muttered, zipping, then reaching for his shirt.

"I presume you've had a good sex life?"

Herb paused with one arm in his shirt, one arm out. Dolores looked quickly away, toward the wall, to the bright red-and-yellow poster of the human heart—its valves and ventricles, its chambers and arteries; the artist had added little road signs such as "Free Direction" and "One Way" and "Detour—Under Repair."

"You could say that," Herb answered gruffly. Clothes rustled.

Dolores glanced back to find Herb angrily misbuttoning his shirt.

The doctor continued. "What I mean, Herb, is that the side effects— including impotency—are why some men don't like digoxin."

Herb refused to look at him as he fumbled with shirt buttons.

There was silence in the room. "Does that include you, Herb?" the doctor asked. He glanced at his wristwatch again. "Have you had problems getting an erection?"

Herb muttered something, jerked at his shirt, and began to redo the buttons.

The doctor turned to Dolores, who blushed scarlet and shook her head no. Herb looked up to glare at her this time.

"That tells me that you probably didn't complete the last prescription," the doctor said, "which is why you're having arrhythmias again, Herb."

Herb reached past the doctor for his socks and shoes.

The doctor drummed his fingers once. "Think of it this way, Herb," he said, standing, holding out the prescription, speaking in that overly familiar, first-name, too-loud manner which someone, somewhere was teaching young doctors nowadays. "You've got two choices: either your pecker or your ticker."

Dolores, holding the prescription (she had been the one to reach for it), stood in the hallway while Herb finished dressing. She was looking for the young doctor, intent on giving him a piece of her mind, but he was already in another examining room greeting someone loudly.

Dolores refocused herself, a skill that Herb did not have. "Are you all right in there?"

"I can still dress myself," Herb growled behind the door.

There was some rustling, the clink of a belt buckle. Then silence for a long time. She thought of the heart poster; she guessed he was looking at it. Then shoes clunked and then Herb opened the door. He was fully dressed now, in his red Pendleton wool shirt and his town pants, a leather belt tucking up his girth; there he was a man with pale blue eyes and a full head of platinum hair, someone she would still choose.

His eyes lightened briefly at her look, then lowered their gaze to her hands. To the prescription. He reached for it. "I've still got some pills left," he said with false brusqueness. "I'll get this refilled next week sometime."

"The doctor was right: you haven't been taking them."

Herb shrugged. For a long moment they held the little square of paper between them. In his blue pupils she saw a flicker, the tiniest gray shadow of fear. She let go.

And on Monday she let go of her job.

Gave notice.

Retired.

For twenty-seven years Dolores had been head clerk at the local electric co-op, but a recent *Reader's Digest* article titled "The Golden Age of Travel" and now a flare-up of Herb's arrhythmia convinced her it was time to go. "Retired" was a word she had always reserved for really old people—shuffleboard players, canasta types, corn-kernel bingo enthusiasts—yet Dolores herself, a straight, trim woman with lightly tinted brown hair was indisputably sixty-four, and Herb already seventy-one. As well, Herb had a brother in southern California, and Dolores a sister in Florida, both of whose children they had seen grow up only in Christmas snapshots. That plus the discounts for AARP members—as high as 20 percent—all were highlighted in the same article, which ended: "What are you waiting for?"

The days surrounding her departure from the office (she still couldn't call it "retirement") buzzed with energy. The reception, the stream of cards and letters, the solicitations to join Garden Club and Women Aglow (both of which she put off for now), the calls from her sister—it was almost too much. Even Herb seemed livelier, though he still muttered about the young doctor with the beard.

On the first Monday of her new life Dolores laid out the old Rand McNally on the kitchen table. It was important to be decisive. To make plans. She turned first to the United States map and slowly penciled a route toward California, then across to Texas. Herb said nothing.

As she worked Herb paced back and forth behind her, rattling the nutcracker and bowl, comparing window thermometer readings. Finally he said, testily, "Those maps are twenty years old. The roads have changed completely. You can't plan a trip with old maps."

Dolores got up and drove downtown. She brought home a bright, hefty twenty-dollar road atlas. Herb, as it turned out, was substantially correct about new roads, but his smugness served to soften his resolve on another, coincidental matter. "There's an ad in the paper," Dolores said, holding up a new *Herald*. "Clean used 18-foot Winnebago, one owner," she read.

A week later, thanks to Dolores's co-op profit-sharing check, the motor home was theirs. The Winnebago was part of an estate sale; the son and executor, a man balding already in his forties, came by with the keys. "At least my folks had one good trip," he said gravely. He held the keys out to Herb.

"Was there a spare set?" Herb asked.

The following four weeks Herb spent servicing, fine-tuning the motor home. Tires, battery, thermostat, brake lines—he left no mechanical part unworried. He insisted they sleep in it at least once before they left, which they did. The bedroom was cramped, with a low ceiling, but the mattress passable. "It feels like camping. Without the tent," Herb said. Luckily deer season came along and sent him to the woods, which allowed Dolores to finish packing the motor home.

Finally, on November 12, they left Lake Center at 6:45 in the morning with the temperature at 19 degrees and 11,041 miles on the odometer. Herb sat strapped in the rider's seat, exhausted from hunting, his cheeks windburned, his eyes open wide. He waved to Lake Center cars he recognized, which included nearly all of them; several drivers tooted their horns in a salute. "People honked their horns when the Titanic left Southampton, too," Herb joked.

"Yes dear," Dolores murmured; she concentrated on her driving.

They passed the lake itself, the community college, and, finally, the city limits sign. A thrill shivered through Dolores and she leaned forward in the seat. Ahead on the open road the day was November gray, and Herb drifted off to sleep almost immediately. Dolores examined everything that passed: a wooly cluster of damp and steaming cattle; a green checkerboard Christmas tree plantation; a single arched curl of snow that drooped from the power line; a gleaming crow along the shoulder picking at a dead deer. She drove, mile after mile, with a slowly increasing assurance, rising excitement, something akin to joy. At the Minnesota–South Dakota border the skies lightened and the sun suddenly blossomed in a brilliant, frosty corona. "Look!" she cried out to Herb, "look!"

Herb jerked awake and flung up an imaginary rifle. "Where?" he shouted.

After Herb was fully awake he began to worry about home. About the furnace. About the water pipes. About the bird feeder. He was certain the Bartlett boy would not put out thistle seed and suet; that all the birds that whistled and chirped in his yard would go across the street to Walter Anderson's feeder.

"They've been coming for years to our yard," Dolores said. "And Joey Bartlett is an A student."

"As don't mean what they used to," Herb said.

With Dolores driving they rolled on. Herb took a turn at the wheel that afternoon, but Dolores found it hard to relax; his driving had become less certain the last year, and today the motor home tended to ride the center line. What if? But she did not let herself think pessimistic thoughts. Rather, she consulted the map and calculated miles, hours, and driving time so that her shift would take them through Sioux Falls, South Dakota, the first major city on their route.

"Say," Herb said, swinging his gaze to a billboard. "Mystery Caverns. Didn't we visit those on our honeymoon?"

The billboard was faded but still stood straightly.

"Yes, we did," she said.

Herb squinted. "Closed for the winter," he read. Then he turned to look at her. "Too bad." She smiled, touched his arm.

Dolores kept the motor home rolling south and west. Herb was a retired highway engineer, and he provided state-by-state analyses of the road conditions: the seams in the asphalt, the pothole ratio per mile, the general layout of curves and overpasses. Dolores drove.

Through Nebraska, so large it ought to have been divided into two states, East Nebraska and West Nebraska.

Through Colorado and the bright, sharp eastern edge of the Rockies.

Through Utah, which had surprising natural beauty (Dolores had always thought it a desert state).

Through Nevada and its pale purple mineral hills, its bright casino oases.

Through frightening Donner Pass, and down into California.

They stayed a short week with Herb's brother in San Bernadino in an overly developed tract with identical ramblers and rock and cacti lawns. Barry was an aerospace engineer, or so they had been told via Muffy's Christmas letter every year. In truth Barry was swing-shift foreman at a tool-and-die plant that did occasional work for Boeing. This was let slip by Muffy, who talked incessantly, as if someone switched her on in the morning and left her on all day. That, plus their two Schnauzers which nipped at Herb's ankles whenever he passed, kept Herb and Dolores in their motor home for longer and longer periods each day. To Dolores, Barry and Herb appeared to be from two different families—two different countries, even. The brothers spent their afternoons playing gin rummy, slapping down their cards, venturing conversational gambits such as, "How you can stand those winters in Minnesota is beyond me."

"Me, I couldn't take not having a lawn. A real lawn, with grass."

A full week sooner than planned, Herb and Dolores were back on the road. "Well, that's over with," Herb said, even as they were waving good-bye to Barry and Muffy. Dolores felt her eyes well up, but refocused herself to find their way out the maze of cul-de-sacs and curving streets.

An hour later, heading east on Interstate 10 toward Palm Springs, they were as talkative as two escaped parakeets.

Only once did Herb look over his shoulder and mutter, "Aerospace engineer."

"Help me with the map, dear."

Heading to Arizona and beyond, they took secondary highways and stopped at every tourist trap. Dolores bought small turquoise jewelry items and salt and pepper shakers; Herb a silver belt buckle and an agate string tie. They turned in wherever they wished for an afternoon nap, and slept easily as 18-wheelers rumbled past. One day they covered only eighty-two miles. Often they did not know, even by midday, where they would park their RV that evening, where they would sleep that night. Arriving after dark on the outskirts of Las Cruces, New Mexico, and following notes taken from an uncertain AARP 800-operator, Dolores finally saw the sign for Fresh Aire RV Park. She checked her jottings; it was supposed to be Bel Aire or perhaps Mel's Aire, but Fresh Aire, set well off the highway and ringed by a hedge and tall wooden fence, looked quiet, orderly, and private. The man at the check-in booth, an older, very tanned fellow, was not wearing a shirt, which Dolores thought slightly odd, but then again this was not Minnesota. "You folks down here for some sunshine?" he said cheerfully.

"Yes, I guess we are," she said pleasantly. After getting a site map, she rolled the motor home inside the gate, found their spot, and parked.

In the morning Herb was first to awaken and crack the shade.

Dolores dozed.

"We're dead," Herb said.

"What's that?" she mumbled. There was a long silence, during which she probably fell back asleep.

"We crashed the motor home somewhere and we're dead."

Dolores sat up with a start; she peered out the window. A regular RV park, yes, with rows of campers and some nice trees and central commons area with showers and small grocery store, people here and there chatting and walking their dogs, nothing out of the ordinary. Except that the people were naked.

Naked.

Buck naked. Jay naked. AARP naked. A whole campground of white-haired naked people.

"I kept looking for wings," Herb would say later—but at the moment he and Dolores both shrank lower in the window.

"Welcome, neighbor!" a round-bellied man from next door called out to them.

Herb narrowed the shade. "Good morning," he croaked.

The man's wife appeared, a sturdy, very tanned woman wearing only reading glasses on a neck chain. Herb swallowed; his Adam's apple squeaked. "Heard you come in late," the woman said pleasantly, "coffee's on over here." With that the two of them began to set up folding chairs and a table no more than ten feet away. Their RV plates read Indiana.

"We might sleep a little longer," Dolores managed to say.

"Whenever you're ready," the woman added cheerfully, and settled into a sunny chair.

Herb and Dolores retreated to the center of the motor home. They stared at each other. "What are we going to do?" Dolores whispered.

Herb stroked his jaw. Looked out once again. They did nothing at all for several minutes. Every once in a while one of them would peek out the window again to make sure they weren't dreaming. Or dead.

It was Herb, finally, who took charge. He looked straight at Dolores. "Honey," he said, "I believe we're in Rome."

The first cup of coffee was a bit tricky, but the couple from Indiana, Ray and Arlene Davis, were the nicest, most normal folks one could hope to meet. The four of them sat in a half-circle of lawn chairs facing into the sunlight.

"Freshen that up for you?" Ray said to Herb, bringing around the thermos.

"Sure," Herb said; he sneaked a glance at Dolores.

"Just a splash," Dolores murmured, keeping her eyes on the cup as Ray stood before her and poured. She noticed that the Davises had draped bath towels over their lawn chairs before sitting down; she wished she had thought of that. After an hour, the plastic webbing of her own chair felt like a waffle iron across her bare butt, yet she decided against getting up and moving around. Shifting about she managed to sit there naked in the southern sunlight with complete strangers and talk about children and relatives and the open road and car accidents they had witnessed and interesting wildlife they had seen until Arlene began to lay out four paper plates for lunch.

"Let me help," Dolores said, hopping up. She had forgotten she was naked but the lawn chair had not: it stuck to her. It hung on her.

Herb laughed and kept laughing.

"Let me get that!" Ray Davis said gallantly, and hopped up to peel off the chair.

"Why thank you, Ray," Dolores said. She was certain she was blushing on unknown areas of her body, but she also threw an evil eye at Herb, whose smile faded.

"Now how can I help?" Dolores said, pressing quickly ahead, assisting Arlene with the picnic table, bringing pickles and fruit from their own refrigerator. In the fish-eye mirror of their Winnebago she caught sight of herself, a white, round woman with a red plaid butt. Well, red plaid her butt might be but round she was not. In fact she was in better trim than Arlene Davis or most any other woman she had seen so far at Fresh Aire—and she was certain that Herb and Ray Davis, too, were aware of that fact. She ignored the mirror and went right to the picnic table and stood there in full daylight and made egg salad sandwiches.

By midday both Herb and Dolores had loosened up enough to stroll, by themselves, into the commons area. Rubber thongs slapped on the shuffleboard court, and horseshoes clanged on steel posts. "I used to throw some good iron," Herb said, and made a ringer on his first toss. The matter of Herb's afternoon nap never came up; there was nude swimming in the little pool, nude cribbage in the shade, and nude potluck supper.

That evening, back at their little Winnebago, Herb opened the door. Heat washed over them.

"Whoa!" Herb said, leaning away from the blast. "We forgot to open the windows."

"But it's a dry heat," Dolores said dutifully.

They went inside nonetheless and sat down heavily and with simultaneous sighs. Herb mopped his forehead. Sweat trickled on both of them. They stared at each other. "Too hot for pajamas tonight," Herb said.

Dolores found two towels and they mopped themselves. Afterward they sat there in silence again. Dolores looked down at herself. "Odd," she said, glancing about the motor home. "All day, I've paraded around naked."

Herb watched her.

"But now that I'm here, inside, I feel like I ought to have clothes on."

Herb's eyes moved down over her body.

"Do you know what I mean?" she asked.

Herb swallowed. "Come over here."

She let her eyes move over his body. His shoulders carried pink epaulets of sunburn.

"Here," he said, pointing to their mattress.

She smiled.

"And don't be slow about it," he added, his voice suddenly throaty.

Dolores sat there a few seconds longer, living in, inhabiting the large, shimmering space of this moment.

Later Dolores worried that the motor home's clever little pullout bed would not hold up; that it was not designed for large-framed midwesterners; that the entire vehicle might turn over. She thought of a bumper sticker she had seen: "If this RV's rockin', don't bother knockin'." She held on and they did things that night that they had never done—things that were likely illegal in Minnesota—but she was not about to complain, not that whole long, hot southwestern night.

In the morning they slept very late. It was 11:30 before Dolores awoke. The window shades were gray, which meant an overcast day; a shiver of disappointment rippled through Dolores, that, or perhaps the chill of sunburn. She felt flushed and slightly achy, but got up, found warm clothes, and made coffee. She left the shades drawn as she fixed herself; made up her hair, her face. She wondered what the Davises did on a cool cloudy day; if they would seem like the same people.

Herb woke up at the gurgle of the percolator. He rolled over and let the shade rattle up. There was silence for a long awhile.

"What is it?" Dolores said, holding a hand mirror to her face. Behind her she saw him staring out their window. She turned, followed his gaze. The space where the Davises' RV had sat was empty. A blank empty space. All that remained was a smudged, dusty oil ring on a bed of crushed gravel.

They left Fresh Aire in the early afternoon. Both were silent. Herb went to sleep just after they entered the freeway. Dolores drove north to Albuquerque, then east again toward the Texas panhandle. A cold, east wind buffeted the Winnebago and she had to fight the wheel all the way. Tumbleweeds bounded and once a scrawny coyote darted right across in front of her; she did not brake. Later in the day, the wind swung round to the northwest, which allowed her to relax a bit. Herb stirred and put on some coffee. They slept that night behind a gas station called Cactus Pete's, in Tucumcari.

In the morning her hands were stiff and ached terribly, so Herb took the wheel. The freeway to Amarillo was straight and empty. "Why don't you go back and have a snooze?" Herb said.

"You're sure?" she asked. The bed was still warm and she fell asleep almost instantly.

Some time later she awoke to silence. They were parked. She imagined they were at a rest stop or a filling station, but a semi-trailer blasted past just outside the tin walls. She scrambled upright and went up front. Herb sat at the wheel, staring ahead. He was ashen and sweaty; his forehead glistened.

"What is it? Are you okay?"

He waved her off. "Not sure," he whispered. "I think maybe I have to lie down." She held her hand to his forehead: damp and clammy. She slid two fingers to his neck and felt his heartbeat; it surged and fell, surged and fell and surged like an engine racing.

"Here," she said, getting his pills, getting water.

He took them without complaint.

She helped him back to the bunk. "Just lie there," she said. "I'm going to drive on to . . ." She realized she did not know where they were.

"Amarillo" Herb said. "It's about thirty miles. I thought I could make it."

Dolores pushed the Winnebago to the limit, eighty miles an hour, and followed the blue, universal hospital signs to St. Anthony's. The emergency attendants were black men wearing white latex gloves and light blue jumpsuits and they knew what to do. Within a minute Herb was hooked up to oxygen and a monitor. It soon beeped fairly steadily; his sweatiness subsided.

Soon enough a doctor, a sturdy middle-aged black woman, came and listened to his heart with a stethoscope. She looked away, that faraway gaze that all doctors got when they listened, when they moved that cold steel button across the skin.

"Have you had any heart trouble before?" she asked at last, yanking the stethoscope from her ears. The doctor had a deep drawl.

"Yes he has," Dolores said. She gave a brief history of Herb's condition, his arrhythmia.

The doctor nodded once or twice. "Or maybe it's just too hot down here for a Minnesotan," she said, adjusting his blankets.

Herb managed a grin.

"I'm going to prescribe some pills to steady your heartbeat," she said, "and we're going to keep you overnight for observation. See how you're looking tomorrow, okay?"

Dolores slept that night on a cot in Herb's room. Twice she was awakened by a helicopter's *whop-whop-whop* low overhead as it settled onto the brightly lit roof of the hospital. In the morning Herb, pale but lively, ate a full breakfast, and soon the doctor came by on rounds; Herb liked her, and joked that she should consider coming up to Minnesota to practice there.

"Lord save me from snow and ice!" she said. After a lengthy listen to Herb's heart, she consulted with Dolores—and then Herb was free to go.

An attendant wheeled Herb out the door and made sure they were safely in the motor home, where Dolores took the driver's seat. Once they were buckled in, she turned to him.

"Florida is not all that far," Herb ventured. He was very pale.

"Next trip, I believe," Dolores said, and started the engine.

With Herb navigating, she drove the Winnebago out of Amarillo, then east on Interstate 40 to big I-35 north. There she balled the jack (as Herb would say) up through Wichita, Kansas City, and beyond, stopping only for gas, snacks, and the occasional catnap. Herb's color returned as the landscape paled. They saw snow in northern Kansas, a light skift on the fields that gradually deepened, whitened, as they reached Iowa's southern border; however, the roads remained clear, the sun shone, and the whiteness was reassuring. Herb's improved complexion was not an illusion, and, gradually, Dolores began to slow their pace a bit. They stopped a full hour for lunch. They even took a short detour to the Amana Colonies, where Herb's appetite reclaimed itself in a large plate of German sauerkraut and potatoes. But Dolores watched him closely, and kept her eye on the weather, the road conditions.

They arrived safely back in Lake Center, Minnesota, 5,893 miles behind them, on January third at 3:32 PM. The temperature on the bank clock read two below zero. There was more snow here, tall banks cut squarely by the plow, and their street looked narrower, their house so small under winter's heavy quilt. At the curb, she switched off the engine and let out a long breath.

"Well," Herb said, stepping down from the motor home, flexing his legs, "that's over with." It was supposed to be a joke.

Dolores stared at him. An enormous tiredness fell down her bones, a heavy curtain dropping, and she felt a burning in her eyes.

"You'd better check on the furnace and your bird feeder," she said. As the door closed behind him, she remained there, behind the wheel, fingers clenched on its big hoop.

For the next week Herb rested on the couch and took his pills at noon. Dolores laid them out alongside his plate, had a water glass ready. From the side of her vision she watched him, made sure he swallowed. Afterward Dolores kept up a cheerful chatter while Herb ate his lunch with his head down.

In the second week home Herb's pulse was just fine and he was back to form. "There are less birds every year," he said, coming from the feeder. Dolores suggested he clean up the garage after November's deer season; that he drive his deer hide downtown and exchange it for gloves—or donate it for Deer Habitat Improvement—one or the other. The hide had hung there, draped over a rafter, gray and stiff, day after day since early November. She also realized that they had this conversation about deer hides every January.

Upon his return, which seemed altogether too quick, Herb was indignant. "Two dollars!" he said, letting his coat drop in the hallway, "now for a pair of gloves they want the hide plus two dollars."

"But you got rid of the hide, yes?"

"No," Herb said. "I'm not about to give it away."

Dolores slapped her magazine rather sharply onto the coffee table. She went to the kitchen and began to wipe down the sink that was already shiny; she looked out the kitchen window to the white yard. To the motor home.

Herb stared out the back window to his bird feeder. "The purple finches should have been here by now. They probably aren't coming this year."

Dolores joined a club. Garden Club, she imagined, was about gardening, which she enjoyed. For her first visit she bought along a Canadian magazine that had a most interesting article about cold climate roses.

But the group of women gardeners, whose average age was at least eighty, was dressed in scarves and good sweaters and were intent on cookies—plate after plate of them—along with strong black coffee. Then came sing-along songs on the player piano, the ancient scrolls for which included Stephen Foster's "My Old Kentucky Home," with his lines about "darkies pining all day . . ." The women sang loudly and by heart; Dolores mouthed the chorus.

Finally came the centerpiece of this meeting: initiation of a new member. There was considerable disagreement about the process.

"Well I remember my initiation," one of the oldest members said.

"That was forty years ago."

"Thirty-five. I remember: Eisenhower was president. I still have that button somewhere, 'I Like Ike.'"

"I voted for Stephenson, myself."

Dolores glanced at the clock. Finally things proceeded. Giggling, giddy from black coffee and sugar, the white-haired ladies blindfolded Dolores for the first test, which consisted of reaching into a paper bag, removing a piece of fruit, and identifying it by shape alone.

Dolores purposely mistook a grapefruit for an orange, but honestly mistook an avocado for a large lemon. The game was actually more difficult than she imagined. When, groping, she removed a banana, all the old ladies laughed hysterically.

After the fruit test, which she "barely passed," her final task was to tell a secret.

"A secret?" Dolores said.

The ladies of the club nodded as one. Their eyes brightened.

"A secret." Dolores was buying time.

The ladies waited, smiling.

"An old secret or a new one?"

"Your choice."

Deciding with the bookkeeper's part of her mind that a new secret was less costly than an old one, Dolores grasped onto the first thing—

something away from Lake Center, it had to be, she decided on the fly—that came to mind. "On our trip, down in Arizona, near Las Cruces, late at night Herb and I pulled into this overnight RV campground."

"And?"

"Well, as it turns out—and we didn't know this—it was a nudist colony."

There was silence.

Emma opened her eyes fully. "So did you stay?"

"Oh dear, no," Dolores said, and faked a laugh.

"A nudist colony!" the women murmured. "What's the world coming to?"

On her way home (now a full-fledged member of the Garden Club), Dolores felt sad and false. The Pontiac was a nice car, but she longed for the motor home—for the big steering wheel in her hands; for the feel of her own little kitchen and living room tagging along no matter where she drove; for the curtained, cramped bedroom that held the day's heat—sunlight above, engine warmth below. For the sound, hour after hour, of the road unreeling behind.

She pulled into her own driveway. The motor home sat there, its windows frosted over, like a tin igloo. She remained in the Pontiac long minutes with the engine idling, staring. She looked down, to her hands on the wheel; finally she switched off the engine.

Inside the house, Herb was napping on the couch, on his back, his hands folded across his chest. From the light of the TV he looked blue. Quickly Dolores crossed the living room and changed channels. Herb snorted and woke up.

"How was your club?" he mumbled.

"Stupid," she said, turning away.

"That's good," he murmured, and let his eyes drift shut again.

In the kitchen she rattled her pan sharply as she began to peel potatoes, then rattled it again. She wanted to make noise. A lot of noise. She wanted to wake Herb up—wake up everybody and everything.

This house.

The Garden Club.

This whole damn town.

Potato peelings flew from her knife like mayflies hatching; they stuck to the sides of the sink, to her wrists, to the toaster. Wake them all up, shake their houses like an earthquake, a tornado, chase them outside—into the cold—naked!

"Ow!" She bit her lip and held her finger as blood oozed. She heard herself breathing—short shallows breaths—as she ran cold water on the little flap of skin. She had to sit down. Later, after drying the cut with a paper towel, she rummaged for a Band-Aid, then made herself sit down again. All the sweets and coffee—that's what made her so edgy. She forced herself to remain seated. To get a grip.

Herb continued to doze, once again on his back, once again snoring loudly. She sat there, watching him. When was, she wondered, the last time they had made love?

Of course she knew the answer: it was at Fresh Aire RV park in New Mexico.

Then came a darker thought.

Was that the last time? Was that part of their lives over?

She stared out the window. Herb sat up with a start.

"What is it?" Dolores said quickly.

"I must have been dreaming," Herb said. He stared at the blank TV, then at her.

"About what?" She went over and stood beside him.

"I don't know," Herb said. His voice sounded far away.

Later, during supper, he said suddenly, "I remember."

"Remember what?" Dolores said abstractedly. She was the silent one this evening.

"My dream."

She looked up at him.

"It was about finches. The feeder, the whole yard was purple with them."

Dolores began to weep.

A early-January thaw saved her. What little snow there was settled and hardened, making for good walking, which she did for at least an hour every day. More importantly, cars came and went easily on the lake that, from an earlier cold snap, still wore thirty inches of ice; and Herb decided to put out his spear house.

Dolores was most happy to help him load the little shack onto his trailer. She had long held the opinion that ice houses saved many a midwestern marriage: the husband was out of the house all day; when he came home he was sufficiently tired as to doze in his recliner through the evening (though Dolores had never understood how one could be exhausted from sitting and staring for six hours through a square, green hole in the ice); and the meals of fresh pike were always a treat (though more so in the earlier part of winter than later, when they became too much of a good thing).

Herb was reenergized. He got up early, ate a good breakfast, was off by nine o'clock. "Off to the office," he said every morning, holding up his battered box full of pike decoys as if it were a briefcase. He always chuckled at that joke.

She did not worry about him driving. On the lake there were no stoplights, no center lines.

When Herb came home with his first fish, a fine, shiny, seven-pound pike, Dolores made it a special occasion. She baked the fish whole, along with potatoes and carrots, and invited to dinner the Rybecks, a slightly younger couple who worked at the college; Herb brought out the trip slides of California, Arizona, New Mexico. Bill Rybeck drifted off during the second tray of photos; his wife, Helen, kept nudging him, though she, too, began to cant in her chair. Dolores realized that the Rybecks had worked eight hours that day; that they had to get up in the morning and do it again. That it was nearly midnight.

Later, in bed, Dolores snuggled against Herb. From the coffee, from the entertaining, she was not sleepy at all. Herb let his arm fall across her chest. After awhile, she put her hand over his, moved it to the fuller part of her breast.

"Well!" Herb said, feeling her nipple stiffen under his fingers.

She made a small humming sound.

They fooled around for a long time. An hour. More. With Herb, nothing happened; she was breathing hard with desire.

"Sonofabitch," he said, and sat up.

"It's okay," she said quickly. "We can just snuggle."

He swore again, flung his pillow across the room, and left to the living room couch where he slept that night.

After he had gone Dolores lay there huddled in the dark. She kept seeing the pillow, flying, like some heavy, white, wingless bird.

In the morning Herb was already gone to his fish house before Dolores awoke. She had heard him up and around, but thought it was a bathroom call. A bread sack and the luncheon meat pak and the mayo jar sat open on the counter; the empty coffee pot was still warm.

Mid-morning she thought of visiting him on the lake, but decided against it. Women did not do that. She had not been in his spear house since the first winter of their marriage. At dusk, 5:00 PM, he came home with another fish. "Here," he said, holding it out to her before she could speak.

"Well! Good luck or good aim?" she said brightly. She took the fish. It smelled and flopped once.

"Not as big as the last one," Herb said, stowing his gear.

"But still a keeper."

Herb nodded.

"Like you," she added, staring straight at him.

Herb looked at her, then lowered his gaze and took back the pike. "Hand me my knife," he said gruffly, "I'll take it in the garage and gut it."

That night Herb slept with her in the big bed, but there was no snuggling. He seemed to make it a point to drift off immediately. She lay a long time listening to his snoring. In the morning he was up before her, though she saw him off to his fish house.

"Do you have enough lunch? Enough coffee?"

"Yes."

"Your pills?" she said softly.

"Sure," he said, turning away.

After he was gone she noticed that the bottle of Lanoxin was still there. But some other things were missing.

A thick Christmas candle that had sat on the bookcase. One of her dining room chairs.

At suppertime Herb clumped onto the garage steps.

"Where is my good chair?" Dolores said first thing. "From the dining room?" She had practiced. She kept her voice even, nonaccusatory.

"The one in my fish house gives me backaches," Herb said.

"They're our good kitchen chairs."

"What are we saving them for?" he said sharply, matching her stare, her tone of voice. "Tell me that."

Dolores turned away.

And the next day, at noon, when she went to turn on the portable radio to catch the news, there was no radio.

She swore, words she had never used. Words she did not know she knew. Then she walked downtown and bought a radio, a small General

Electric nearly identical to the one missing from the kitchen counter. She put it in the same spot, behind the toaster and the coffee pot. That night, when Herb came home, she was friendly enough. Supper moved along. During it Dolores said, "Isn't there a high school hockey game tonight?"

"I don't think so," Herb said, his eyes flickering her way.

"Why don't I check the radio?" She rose and reached behind the toaster and turned the radio on high volume. She took some time, rolling the dial, the various stations blurting out parts of songs and commercials in ear-rending squawks. "I guess not," she said finally and turned off the radio. They finished supper in silence.

This went on.

The silence.

The things going missing from the house.

Smaller and smaller things: a towel, her eggbeater, some odds and ends of dishes, nail clippers. She stopped mentioning them, directly or on the sly; it always made for a long, tense evening. And every morning, Herb was up early and gone.

Dolores began to take longer walks. The light was better now, the end-of-January sun as bright as an egg yolk suspended in white vinegar, and she walked two hours every day. Her usual route was uptown. She did not stop at the cafés for coffee and gossip like other retirees, but went beyond, to the community college, where she stopped in the library and browsed for an hour. Afterward she had a hot chocolate at the student union, then headed back, this time a different, even longer route. She took the curving No. 29, or Lake Road.

Far out on the ice were little villages of ice houses clustered tightly above the sandbars. These were the walleye fishermen whose cars and snowmobiles migrated to the lake about the same time every day in the late afternoon. Walleyes were a schooling fish and their fishermen a sociable group. They drove a common, plowed road to the sandbar; they were not above painting their houses in bright stripes, adding small picture windows or planting cast-off Christmas trees by the door for an amusing, yard-like effect. Walleye fishermen did not mind daylight or loud radios or drop-in guests or close quarters as long as everyone was having some luck and no one was having too much of it.

The spear houses stood at least one hundred paces from each other—it was an understood distance—and closer to shore along the reedbeds. They stretched down the lake as regular and solitary as the footsteps of a passing wolf. As a class, spear houses were smaller, darker, more pointed—tall enough for a man to stand up in occasionally to stretch his legs. Owners of spear houses came and went on separate paths from the landing. Some arrived and departed at intermittent hours, guessing, playing the odds; others, like Herb, waited all day, every day, for a big northern pike to drift in from the weedbeds in search of perch and take a closer look at the bright wooden decoy fish hung in the hole.

Decoys were the only bright spots in spear house decor. Dolores had spent one interminable afternoon in Herb's spear house during the first winter of their marriage. Herb's decoys were variously red and white, yellow and white, silvery, green and yellow, all carved a hand's length long with a lead belly and shiny tin fins. She wondered if his decoys were still bright. Her memories of the spear house were mainly of darkness broken only by the luminescent ice and the green water, a hot dim space sealed against daylight even a ray of which could frighten off the pike. When a big fish was taken, it was spirited home in a gunny sack, or strapped on a sled and overlaid with gear lest someone see the catch and move right next door.

Today Dolores had her binoculars. She sighted them on Herb's house. A thin dark smudge wafted from the stovepipe. He had a portable kerosene heater; wood heat was too hot, too cold, too up-and-down, he had told her more than once. She kept her binoculars trained on the house for several minutes, until her eyes began to water and her lashes freeze inside the rubber cups. She believed that by concentrating her vision on his hut she could will Herb to get up, step outside, look around—at the sky, at the weather, at something. That he would emerge into daylight not knowing the sudden nature of his restlessness.

She wished, in passing fancy, that he had a telephone in his house; there were portable phones nowadays, the cellular kind, and she could call him. They could talk. They could say all the things that went unsaid in their living room during the evenings, in their bedroom at night. Maybe that's what they needed, a cell phone.

But Herb did not come out. Nothing, no one moved. On the flat, bright, curving lake the tiny houses were dark squares on irregular porcelain. Dolores secured her binoculars, wiped her watering eyes, and walked home.

That night she cried herself to sleep. Herb did not snore. She knew he was awake.

Mid-morning the next day (Herb had left at sunup), as Dolores made the bed and put away linen, she halted. From the closet there was a pillow missing. And the spare woolen blanket as well.

She went to the kitchen where she sat staring out the window at the bird feeder. She watched English sparrows and nuthatches and blue jays come and go. Then, abruptly, she rose and dressed for her walk. She chose only a light jacket and hat, and set out.

A half hour later she paused, puffing, on the road overlooking the lake. Their car, along with several others, sat at the landing. Herb was conservative that way (for which she was grateful); it had been unseasonably warm of late, and there was no reason to take chances driving on the ice.

Her eyes followed the narrow ice path that branched off to his house. Setting her jaw, Dolores walked down to the landing and set out upon the ice. As the shore receded behind, Dolores was surprised at the distance to his fish house. The great white space of the lake was tricky; perspective faded; it was difficult to see well. She kept her eyes downward, on the path, the frozen boot marks. Herb's boots.

Her own boots crunched one after the other. Slowly Herb's house grew until she could read his name on its side; see the dark flower of kerosene smoke on its roof; see the narrow, shiny door hinges and padlock clasp. Fifty paces away, the door swung open a crack.

Dolores held up a hand.

The door went shut.

Then, suddenly, it opened again, wider this time, and remained ajar. Herb's pale, squinting face leaned out.

"Hello!" she called and marched right up to his house.

His eyes widened. "Well!" he said, confused, blinking against the sunlight like a groundhog in March.

"May I come in?"

"Well, sure," he said. He stood up and something bumped and clattered. "Just let me make some room here." The door closed and she could hear him in there, for a full minute, rustling and shifting things.

"Ready," Herb said, swinging open the door full wide.

Dolores ducked her head and eased inside. Herb closed the door behind her. At first she could see only a green square, about a yard wide, framed in white. Slowly the frame deepened, paled, to smooth walls of ice enclosing open water; the water moved, almost imperceptibly, as if breathing. Down several feet on a plumb-straight line hung a battered red-and-white decoy.

They were silent.

Herb reached upward and cranked something. She squinted. Her eggbeater. Or what was left of it. One side, one beater had been removed, and the decoy line secured, in a complex knot, to the remaining beater; now as the line wound itself, the decoy below began, slowly, to move; to turn in a slow circle.

"Pretty slick, eh?" Herb said.

"I guess so!" Dolores said evenly, reminding herself that eggbeaters were not expensive.

They were silent as they watched the little fish follow itself, its phosphorescent image, in continuous, exact circle.

"How did you figure that out?" she inquired, squinting up at the eggbeater.

"In the fish house there's plenty of time to think."

She saw him glance her way, then look back down the hole.

At length she said, "Have you seen anything today?"

Herb shook his head sideways. "Slow," he said. "Very slow."

Dolores stared down the hole. The arm-deep sides of ice were buffed smooth by the far-off, slow breathing of the lake, the swell and sink of its water, and the translucent rectangle was shot full of tiny, trapped bubbles of air.

"So it's nice to have a visitor," Herb said.

Dolores looked to him, then back down the hole. "Are you sure?"

"Sure I'm sure," he said.

She smiled.

"Hungry?" he said.

"Maybe a little."

"It's never too soon for lunch in the fish house," he said.

And so they ate. Herb divided up his sandwich, shared his coffee; they passed a cup back and forth. As they dined, Dolores paused to hang up her coat, to look around the house. The missing pillow was secured at head level in the corner, the blanket folded neatly nearby.

"Sometimes I lean back and take a snooze," Herb said. The red Christmas candle, burned down halfway, sat anchored in the other corner. "It takes away the kerosene smell," Herb offered. By the stove was the small frying pan, along with a bottle of cooking oil and salt and pepper. "Sometimes I get tired of bologna sandwiches, so I jig up perch, clean them and fry them."

"I thought bologna was your favorite." She had been making him bologna sandwiches for hunting and fishing for forty years.

"Well, it's okay," he began

She laughed. She laughed for a long time.

"What's so funny?" he said.

"Nothing," she said.

They sat there several minutes watching bits of plankton drift through the water. A school of minnows angled past.

"Is it hot in here or is it me?" she said.

"My stove runs to the warm side. Plus it's a nice day outside."

Dolores took off her sweater.

"I might join you," Herb said. He took off his wool shirt, sat there in his white underwear top. He leaned down and made some adjustment to the stove, which only seemed to heighten the heat (she thought of their motor home after that day in New Mexico).

"You got a warm day plus two people in the house," Herb said, mopping his shining brow. "It makes a difference."

Dolores checked her watch.

"But there's plenty of room," Herb added quickly. "You don't have to go."

A yellow-and-green striped perch drifted through the hole.

"Not a good sign," Herb said. "If there was a big pike around, that perch wouldn't be here." He leaned back and relaxed. Shadows played under his chin and cheekbones.

She reached up and turned the eggbeater handle. The heat, gathered near the ceiling, made her squint and lower her face. Back in her chair she unbuttoned the top part of her blouse.

"It is hot," Herb said.

She fanned herself.

"That damn stove," Herb said. He fiddled with its thermostat again, then raised his arms and peeled off his underwear top. He leaned back over the hole to take in its chilled air. "I should go back to a wood burner."

Dolores mopped her brow. "Do you mind?" she said, unbuttoning her blouse all the way.

"Some days I'm down to only my undershorts," Herb said, chuckling.

Dolores shrugged out of her blouse. Sat there in only her bra. Herb looked at her. In the soft light of the water, the ice, they smiled shyly at one another. Herb's arms were still strong, his shoulders square. A bead of sweat ran down between Dolores's breasts.

"I don't know what to make of that damned stove," Herb said, looking down, fumbling with it again.

"The heat feels good, actually," Dolores said, fanning herself. "It's healthy to sweat once in a while. We should build ourselves a sauna someday."

Herb stared down the hole again and worked the decoy. "It wouldn't take that much," he said. "A sauna. It'd make a nice project."

"Once a week a good hot sauna," Dolores said.

"Like the Finns," Herb added.

"When it's twenty below outside we could throw off our clothes and bake like a couple of potatoes."

After a while Herb slowly looked up at her. "You don't look like a potato," he said. His gaze fell to her cleavage, her breasts.

She was silent a moment. "Neither do you."

He turned his gaze back to the water.

The stove continued to whisper its heat.

"Geez," Herb said, "I'm going to have to get out of these pants."

Dolores stood up at the same time. Leaning on each other, laughing, she, too, removed her slacks. The floor was cold so they kept their boots on.

"Now we're talking," Herb said.

And they did talk, at first haltingly, then with more ease, about things that had gone unsaid for too long.

Herb told of the quiet and the darkness of the fish house, how it allowed him to think about things; how his mind drifted to the past and their lives together; how sometimes it was so quiet that he could hear his own heart beat, and then he wondered, really, just how much time he had left in this world; that if life were a football game, he was probably in the two-minute warning.

Dolores told about feeling lost at home; of having nowhere to go, no office, real or otherwise. Her voice broke at the end.

Herb put his arm around her. She leaned into him for a long while. He was sweaty and slick, a clean, woody odor. They sat there staring down the hole—then looked at each other and suddenly they were kissing.

And more.

Herb pulled at her bra and Dolores took it off all the way. Herb pulled her closer; he nuzzled, kissed her chest. His underwear began to tent up.

"Holy cow!" he murmured, looking down at himself.

Breathing hard, Dolores tugged down his underwear bottoms. With her free arm she flung down the blanket but there was no room to lay down. And no time. They lurched to their feet and pulled each other tight and the little house began to creak and rock with sounds certain to scare away all fish within a city block.

At the end they both cried out—and, on four momentarily week knees, they sagged against the far wall of the little house.

Which tipped.

"My God!" Herb cried in alarm and joy—and they rode the house down together. Decoys clattered, fishing gear flew. The little kerosene stove tipped as well, along with its reservoir of fuel. Suddenly flames licked and crept just inches from bare skin.

"Fire! We gotta get out!" Herb shouted.

With a chair (her good one) he smashed away the thin plywood, broke open the side. Daylight burst upon them like an unending flash bulb, and seconds later they were standing on the ice naked but for their boots.

"Snow! Kick some snow on it!" Herb shouted.

The crusted snow refused to budge in any useful quantity, and huddling against each other, they were forced back from the heat.

"Your house, your decoys! Our clothes!" Dolores cried, as the fire grew.

Herb was silent. He put his arm around her and squinted at the blaze. "Let it go. I'll make new ones, we'll get new clothes. Are you all right?"

Dolores checked herself. But for a few scratches she was, and, surprisingly, she was hardly even chilly. Neither of them were. At first Dolores thought they might be in shock.

"Body heat," Herb said. He managed a shy grin, then looked toward the landing. "But we better make tracks before we do get cold."

So they headed quickly across the ice to the shore. The sun was shining.

Dolores kept looking to the road, to the landing. No activity, no cars arriving or leaving. So far, so good. Once or twice they looked behind at the narrow column of smoke, at their blaze of glory. The fish house was soon reduced to its bony framework and, even as they watched, caved inward in a shower of sparks and leveled itself with the ice.

"I needed a new fish house," Herb said. "I've been thinking of a better design."

"Hurry up, now," Dolores said, eyes on the landing again. "It would be just our luck—"

And, say no more, a pickup pulled down to the landing.

"Elmer Olson," Herb said.

"You go first," Dolores said, falling in behind Herb.

"He's eighty-four years old, got cataracts, and can't see worth a darn," Herb said.

"You better hope," Dolores said.

As they neared the shore, Elmer was on his way out to his own fish house, pulling a little black sled with lunch and spear on a path that took him a few paces parallel to Herb's and Dolores' trail.

As they drew even Herb held up his hand in greeting.

Elmer waved once and drew to a stop.

"For God's sakes keep walking," Dolores whispered, staying to the far side of Herb.

"Any luck today?" Elmer asked. He smiled across the few paces of ice—then suddenly squinted, blinked his rheumy eyes, and looked closer.

"Slow," Herb said. "Real slow."

Elmer's mouth drifted open.

"But then again it's been slow all winter," Herb added.

"Yes, yes it has been," Elmer murmured.

"Well, good luck to you," Herb said, moving on.

Elmer shook his head as if to clear it, mumbled something to himself, and continued onward to his house. Once Dolores glanced over her shoulder and saw the old man standing motionless on the ice as if thinking about something.

But by then they had gained the shore. Their car started as it ought, and, more than a little cold but huddling close together under the car's emergency woolen blanket that all true Minnesotans carried, Herb drove them fast away from the landing, toward home, hot chocolate, and a hot bath. Neither of them looked back.

Haircut

FOR TED AND JIM LAFRINIERE

Toby needs a summer haircut. Mom and Dad are busy—they're always very busy—so Harvey says, "I can take him."

Toby's mom, Marissa, glances quickly to Toby. He's a fair-haired, slender ten-year-old, all sharp elbows and knees, who takes after his mother; he's a tidy, stylish kid who likes things—especially his hair—"just right." At the moment Toby is madly thumbing a little "beeper game," as Harvey calls them (a term which always makes Toby laugh).

"Okay if Grandpa Harvey takes you, Toby?" his mother asks.

"Sure," Toby says, "as long as it's Kara and not that Sue Ellen."

"It's Kara," his mother confirms.

Toby nods. He's the kind of boy—like his parents—who is always doing several things at once. But he makes time for Harvey; he loves his grandpa. When Marissa, and Robert, Harvey's son, announced that Grandpa Harvey had sold the farm and was coming to live with them, Toby had clapped his hands, let out a whoop, and leapt into Harvey's arms. That was almost a year ago. For Harvey, living in town with his son's family has worked out all right. For the most part.

Robert and Marissa owned a large, ranch-style house in a nice neighborhood on the north side of Fargo; there was plenty of room (it seemed unlikely that Marissa and Robert would have more children—when would they have time?), and now that Grandma Helen was gone, it did not make sense—as Marissa put it—for Harvey to "rattle around in that drafty old farmhouse."

So Harvey had sold the farm in western Minnesota (Robert would never farm, that was certain), and moved the seventy miles to Fargo. And it was Toby, all the things he and the boy did together—snap-together villages, wood carving, homework (Toby was impatient with math), yard ball, plus working his giant collection of baseball cards—that kept Harvey occupied and kept his thoughts off his old life. Off Helen, though she had been ill for so many years that her passing was a blessing; off the wide space and horizon of his wheatfields; off his little orange Allis-Chalmers tractor, his coffee buddies at the Koffee Kup

Café on Main Street, his trusty Ford pickup. Some days, here in the city, his old life was like something he had watched on the History Channel.

"What time is Toby's appointment?" Robert asked, sweeping into the kitchen, tying his red necktie with a quick jerk, then reaching for the coffee pot. He was stocky, strong in the trunk like Harvey used to be, brown-haired, and, in expensive and polished brown oxfords, the same height as Marissa.

"Ten this morning. I've got a showing—it just came up—or else I'd take him," she said apologetically; in passing she straightened Robert's tie and gave him a quick peck on the cheek. Harvey looked away. Marissa was a beautiful woman—and the driving force, the accelerator pedal of the family; though she had changed Robert into a full-feathered city man, Harvey believed she was probably worth it. He, too, would have had little power against a woman like her. It was to Robert's credit that he held his own against Marissa in a tolerant, slightly amused, but steady kind of way. Their marriage seemed to work. It was their busy-ness, however—Robert, an attorney, was in several civic organizations, and Marissa, a realtor, was always on the go— that drove Harvey nuts. He got a headache just keeping track of them. They walked fast. Talked fast. Drove fast. How they did it, how they managed to live like that, was beyond him—but then again, most everybody rushed around nowadays.

"Where's he going?" Robert asked. Both husband and wife had to be involved in every detail of family life; nothing could be left to just one or the other.

"The Hair Affair at the mall, same as always," Marissa said as the two began their kitchen routine: bagels, coffee, wipe down the counters—no crumbs allowed on these counters.

"I'd take him but I'm headed the other way," Robert said with a frown. Husband and wife paused to glance at each other, then to Harvey. "Dad, you okay with going to the mall? I know it's not your favorite place."

"Sure," Harvey said. "I can get him there and back." He was a good driver; for Robert and Marissa, it was not about his driving, but about family routines. Heaven forbid there be any changes.

"The West entrance, Dad," Marissa said. "Near the blue flag in the parking lot?"

"Green flag," Toby said, watching TV and thumb-beeping.

"Sorry! Green flag," Marissa replied. "Toby knows the way. Listen to Toby."

"I always do," Harvey said. Toby smiled.

"And leave in plenty of time so you don't have to rush," Robert said.

"Take your cell phone along just in case," Marissa said to Toby.

"Yeah, yeah, yeah," Toby said. "We'll be fine."

Short minutes later, Robert and Marissa rushed off in different directions, and, in the big, immaculate living room with its white brick fireplace, it was just Harvey and Toby. "Want to play, Gramps?"

"No thanks. Hurts my thumbs. And anyway, I've got to study the maps so we don't get lost going to the mall."

Toby giggled and kept beeping. Yet, deep down, he was a serious boy, one who did not like loud noises or scary movies on television. Well before it was time for the two of them to leave for the mall he put away his toys without being asked, went to brush his teeth, then returned having changed into different warmup pants and a bright tee shirt that advertised some kind of tennis shoe. Toby checked his watch against the kitchen clock. "We should leave in about six minutes, Gramps."

In the car, Toby buckled his seat belt. Harvey was not a big fan of seat belts in general and the shoulder harness in particular, but he shrugged it on for the time being, or else Toby would nag him.

"Do you have money for my haircut?"

"Do I have money?" Harvey said. "Does your Gramps have money!"

Toby smiled. "Just making sure."

Harvey backed the Honda Accord, Marissa's old car that they had kept for Harvey's use, out of the tidy garage and onto the bright summer street. It was a fine June day. Though he always felt guilty driving the Honda (what if one of his old coffee pals from farm days just happened to be in Fargo and saw him driving a foreign make?), it was a good little car and he could see why people bought them over Fords and Chevrolets. "Well Sonny, we're off to the barbershop."

"Barbershop!" Toby laughed wildly, like it was the funniest thing in the world.

"What?"

"Barbershop! You said barbershop."

"Yes, what about it?"

"It's a hair salon, not a barbershop."

"Okay, okay, salon. Same difference: it's a place you go to get your ears lowered."

Toby giggled again. They rode along for a few blocks, past Oxbow Park, past tidy lawns and suburban-style houses. Behind them, to the east, lay the Red River, which separated Minnesota and North Dakota. Toby fell silent; his face turned thoughtful.

"Yes?" Harvey asked.

"Gramps, what's a barbershop?"

Harvey tapped the brakes, not hard but distinctly, then released the pedal and drove on, though slower. "What's a barbershop?" Harvey repeated.

"Yeah," Toby said, "I mean, what are they like?"

He turned to stare at his grandson. "You mean you've never been to a barbershop?"

Toby shrugged. "Mom always takes me with her to the salon at the mall. Dad gets his hair cut there, too."

Harvey concentrated on his driving. "I see." And he did, of course: there was city and country, there were salons and barbershops.

"I mean, how are barbershops different?" Toby persisted.

Harvey scratched his head. "For one thing, in a barbershop a man usually cuts your hair."

"A man?" Toby exclaimed. He had another major laughing fit; it was clearly the second-funniest thing he had heard his grandfather say that day.

Harvey turned again to look at the boy; the sunlight caught his blonde curls and glinted off his white, polished teeth. Harvey, driving south on Elm Street, approached Nineteenth Avenue, which would take them west to Highway 75, and around to the mall. At the last moment he did not turn.

"This is not the way to the mall," Toby said quickly.

"I know."

"Are we going a different way?"

"Sort of."

Toby frowned and fell silent.

"Actually, we're going to a barbershop," Harvey said in his most cheerful voice.

Toby glanced at his grandpa. His brow furrowed. "I'm not sure what mother would say."

"We could call her," Harvey said; it was a huge gamble—he held his breath.

Toby took out his little blue phone, then paused. He frowned. "She really doesn't like to be bothered during a showing. Unless it's an emergency."

"Is this an emergency?" Harvey asked.

"Not really, I guess," Toby murmured.

"Okay then," Harvey said, again in his cheerful voice, and turned the Honda left onto 75, which took them across the river and into Minnesota.

As he drove past the sewage lagoons and then into open farm country, Harvey entertained Toby with all the boy's favorite stories about growing up on the farm—the pony with a broken leg, the crabby cat in the hayloft, the time a crazy old moose wandered into the hay shed—but Toby was not easily distracted.

"We're heading back to your old farm," he said.

"Not the farm. Somebody else lives there now. We're heading to town to the barbershop," Harvey said.

"It's a long way," Toby said. He looked across the open fields.

"Fifty minutes or a bit more and we're there."

Toby glanced at his cell phone, then to his grandfather. "I'll miss Little League practice. My coach will be mad."

"We'll play yard ball all afternoon," Harvey answered. "I'll wear you out."

Toby fell silent and watched the highway. His gaze scanned the farms, the tiny towns and their rusted grain elevators, the highway behind them; he clutched his little beeper game but did not play it.

Harvey told him stories all the way and soon they arrived on the main street of town. Beyond, five miles north, was the homeplace, but that was for another occasion. When Harvey was more ready.

Louis and Tom Courbette's barbershop sat a half block off Main Street on Second Avenue, kitty-corner from the American Legion Hall, just up from the feed mill, next to a furniture store with "Everything-must-go" signs in the window; behind the barbershop were the weedy railroad tracks and the abandoned Burlington Northern Terminal. The faded, candy-striped barber pole was the brightest color on the block. Harvey parked the Honda well down the street. They got out, Toby slowly. Harvey came around and tousled his hair. "Here we are!"

Toby looked over his shoulder, then all around him. Approaching the shop, Harvey could see nothing much had changed. Behind tall window glass Louis and Tom, wearing dark-blue shirt smocks, stood, arms in motion, beside two barber chairs; two very old men sat in the chairs. Another man read a magazine as he waited.

"Looks full," Toby said.

"They move pretty quick here," Harvey replied. "Besides, it's summer. We've got all day."

Toby glanced at his cell phone, then slipped it into his pocket and trudged after Harvey. A tiny bell jingled on the door. Inside, country music played behind buzzing electric clippers and the *snick-snick-snick* of scissors. It smelled of cigarettes, aftershave, and the woody odor of hair that lay thick and horseshoed around the barber chairs.

"Hey, sailors," Louis Courbette called. He was a short, sturdy man in his sixties with a full dark crew cut and a bent, boxer's nose. He was active in the community and coached Golden Gloves boxers from the reservation. Louis looked again. "Harvey! I'll be damned."

Toby flinched.

"Morning, gents," Harvey said.

"Good to see you. Getting along all right in the big city?"

"So-so." Harvey kept his hand on Toby's bony shoulder and steered him toward the line of customer chairs. Louis kept his clippers moving around the old man's ears; his gaze fell to Toby.

"And who's your first mate?"

"My grandson, Toby." Harvey touched Toby's warm, small neck. "Son, say hello to Mr. Louis Courbette."

Toby managed a little smile.

Louis nodded and kept clipping. The old men under the chair-cloths looked sideways at Harvey by moving only their eyeballs; Harvey nodded to them, old men with hardly enough hair to bother.

"Find yourself a chair, Harvey, Toby," said the younger barber. Tom Courbette was the same general size as his father, though with a straight nose, smooth cheeks, and bit rounder in the face. He had been a three-sport athlete in high school. "Be just a few minutes." He gave Toby a brief smile before his eyes returned to the television.

"If Albert here had less hair I'd be done already," Louis said, winking at Toby. Albert, stiff-necked beneath the clippers, grinned over milky yellow dentures.

Harvey took a chair. Toby took the one beside his grandfather and closest to the door. A thin, younger Native American man gave them the faintest nod, then turned his eyes to the window, toward the street. The chairs had glassy-eyed cigarette burns on the varnished wood arms; beside them was a tall ashtray with a forest of butts stuck in white sand. A chipped cribbage board shaped like a walleyed pike, a well-thumbed pile of golfing and other sporting magazines on a three-legged table, some dog-eared *Playboy* magazines at the bottom of the pile. In the far corner a kerosene space heater left over from winter. Above, perched in the corner, a slightly purpled TV screen tuned to Country Cable and Tanya Tucker, whose mouth and blouse were both significantly open. Toby seized an *ESPN* magazine and ducked behind it.

"You okay?" Harvey murmured to him.

Toby, ever so slightly, nodded.

Harvey leaned back. It had been a year—right before Helen's funeral—since he had been to the barbershop. At floor level Albert's fine white clippings sprinkled the ring of darker hair—powdered sugar sifted onto chocolate. Above the heavy, filigreed iron footrest the barber chairs rose up curving, green-leathered and high-backed as fancy saddles. On the side of each chair dangled a leather strop; Tom's strop was several shades lighter and far less shiny than his father's. Behind the chairs the counter hung with squat, chrome clippers; on top, tall glass jars where combs and scissors stood in dusky alcohol solution. Near the till, catching window light, a jar of bright, translucent lollipops: orange, yellow, red, and green.

"So what's new over in Fargo?" Louis asked Harvey.

"Construction everywhere. Lot of young people. It's a college town now."

"Never used to be," Albert the old-timer mumbled. "Used to be just a railroad and cattle town. They went and ruined it."

"Over at the college, I hear they hand out rubbers," Tom Courbette said to Albert, with a wink toward the other men.

At the word "rubbers" the half-smile on Toby's face shrank to a frozen blankness. He raised his magazine an inch higher; his gaze flickered to the door, the street beyond.

The old-timer in the second barber's chair snorted, and nearly took a cut to his ear. "There's too much damned immortality among kids nowadays," he muttered.

"Immortality?" Tom Courbette laughed at the word choice. "Those young kids sure seem to think so," he said, his scissors never missing a *snick-snick-snick*.

"Well that, too. I remember feeling immortal when I was that young," Louis added, without missing a beat.

"And television. Take somebody like that Christina Aguilera," the old guy said, not listening. "Why she's no more than a damned cheap whore."

Toby's eyes widened.

"Now Emery," Louis Courbette said, "don't be getting your blood pressure up."

"Well he's right," Albert interjected, glaring straight ahead, "Like Madonna and those other girls, all they're selling is pussy—their own."

Toby tensed up like a runner at the blocks.

"Well, I don't know about that," Tom Courbette drawled. "But I do know that those girls aren't dumb. They've got way more brains and talent than I'll ever have." He slipped on the scalp massager, a buzzing, electric vibrator that strapped to the back of his hand, and gave Emery's skull a good working over. Harvey worried that the old man's dentures might pop out of his head. "There you go, Emery," Tom Courbette said, switching off the massager, sweeping off the chair-cloth. "Now take it easy on the those retired gals."

Emery, recovering his humor, smiled and began, very slowly, to thumb through an ancient wallet stuffed thick with greenbacks.

"Who's next?" Tom Courbette said.

Toby glanced to the Indian man with the long braid, who waited. His eyes were fixed on some unknown but interesting thing outside.

"Billy's just hangin' out," Tom Courbette explained. "He's a regular here."

Billy smiled. He had pure white teeth.

"So which one of you sailors is it going to be, then?" Tom Courbette waited beside his empty barber's chair.

Harvey looked at Toby. "Me. I guess," Harvey said.

He settled into the chair. Tom Courbette flipped out the chair-cloth and it swirled and settled over Harvey. He snapped the collar tightly around Harvey's neck.

"What do you need today?" Tom Courbette asked, glancing up at the TV.

"Just a trim."

Tom Courbette nodded, his eyes on the new Ford Taurus commercial. The electric shearers buzzed sharply in Harvey's ears. He flashed a smile at Toby, then closed his eyes. He kept them shut and listened to the country music.

"There you go," Louis Courbette said to Albert in the adjoining chair; Harvey opened his eyes to a fine snow of hair, a blue swirl of another chair-cloth, and then, beside him, an empty barber's chair. It was Toby's turn.

"Ready, son?" Louis said as he took Albert's money.

Toby swallowed.

Harvey nodded, ever so slightly, to his grandson.

Slowly Toby stood. Came forward. Climbed stiffly up into the chair.

"So how about those Twins?" Louis said as swept the blue sheet over Toby. "Who's gonna win twenty this season?"

"Brad Radke," Toby answered.

"No way," Louis said, beginning to comb out Toby's curls with short jabs of his stubby black comb. Toby's head jerked with each stroke. One of Louis's meaty hands was bigger, nearly, than Toby's face.

Louis reached for a scissors. "Radke pitches too much over the plate. Hitters just swing away on him." He began to cut great sheaves from Toby's head. (He did not ask Toby what kind of haircut he wanted.)

"So what do you like then, a lot of walks?" Tom Courbette threw back at his father. "At least Radke don't put runners on base."

"Nobody's ever on base with Radke," Louis said, "'cause they're doin' a home run trot around the bases."

Toby smiled just a bit.

"You play ball, son?" Louis asked, his eyes on the television.

Toby nodded quickly.

"Hold still," the barber said gruffly.

Toby froze.

"What position?"

"They make us rotate," Toby said cautiously, moving only his jaw this time. "Kind of every position."

Nothing was said for awhile. Billy, in the chair, turned to look out the window, but he was listening, Harvey knew.

"So which position do you like best?" Louis asked.

"Pitcher."

Louis nodded. "All the young boys want to pitch."

There was comfortable silence but for the TV, the scissors, the country music. Billy, the listener, said softly, "Louis used to be a catcher."

"In the old days," Tom Courbette added, with a sly glance at his father.

Louis shrugged. "It's true. In 1952 I played Double A ball in the Cincinnati Reds organization. The Tulsa Oilers, down in the Texas League."

Toby started to lift his face to look up at the barber, then caught himself in time. He looked into the mirror back toward Louis Courbette.

"The Reds gave me a good look," Louis said, keeping his scissors, his big hands moving. "But the Korean War was going then and I got drafted. When I came back, three years later, I'd missed my chance."

"He hit .288," Billy said to the window glass.

There was silence in the shop except for Reba McEntire and the electric clippers.

"Yes I did," Louis said.

Tom Courbette added. "My old man's even got his own baseball card. Not that it's in real high demand these days."

"That's pretty good—.288!" Toby said.

Louis paused and looked down at Toby. "Nowadays they'd pay me a million bucks a year to catch and hit .288, wouldn't they, pal?"

Toby nodded his head vigorously; Louis did not call him on it.

"But is he complainin'?" Tom Courbette said of his father, his eyes on the TV. "No-oooooo, I've never heard him complain." He turned and winked at Billy.

"And you never will," Louis said, bending to clip closely around Toby's right ear. "It was just a matter of timing. I did my duty. I served my country. I came back and I'd missed my shot. It didn't work out, and here I am."

By now Toby's yellow hair was mostly gone. He and Harvey got simultaneous, buzzing, scalp massages. "There you go, son," Louis said as he unfastened Toby's chair-cloth.

"That do it for you, too, Harvey?" Tom asked, spinning him around to face the mirror. Harvey stared. His entire skull, all its bumps and bones, stared back at him. Toby, with wide white sidewalls above prominent ears, looked like a kid escaped from 1950s, black-and-white-television days. He was staring at Louis Courbette's big battered hands.

"Sucker?" Louis Courbette said to Toby, as Harvey paid for the haircuts (twelve bucks total, fifteen with tip).

"Sure." Toby took an orange one.

"Gramps?" Louis asked.

"Why not," Harvey said.

Billy the watcher, smiled, then caught himself and looked away out the window.

Harvey and Toby soon found themselves outside on the sidewalk in the June sunlight. Toby had not yet thought too much about his hair—what there was left. By the Honda, he bent to the window glass; he squinted at his reflection, then leaned into the side mirror for a closer look. He tilted his face one way, then another.

Harvey held his breath.

"Wow," Toby said, turning back to his grandfather, "that's the best haircut I've ever had."

They were hardly buckled in the car when Toby's phone rang. After glancing at the tiny screen, he looked to Harvey. "It's Mother."

"Best answer it," Harvey said. He listened to Marissa's voice, tiny but increasingly faster and louder, and was glad he couldn't make out the words.

"Yes, mother. Yes, mother," Toby repeated. Afterward, he shut off his phone. He looked at Harvey.

Who kept driving.

"We're sort of in trouble," Toby said.

"I see," Harvey answered.

"When we missed our appointment at the salon, they called my mom's phone and she just now checked her messages. I told her where we were."

"In other words, we're 'busted.' As you would say."

"Yeah. Big time."

They were silent for awhile.

"Well then, I guess there's no hurry in getting back," Harvey said. Ahead was the Dairy Queen, and Harvey turned the Honda sharply into the lot. Toby smiled for real now; it was like something in his face and his eyes breaking open; some weight loosening, falling away.

The Dairy Queen had a new drive-through line, but he and Toby went inside and ordered at the counter. They sat in a booth and gurgled their straws and poked fun at the old-timers in the barbershop and did tricks with napkins—nearly all the napkins in the little table dispenser—until the manager came over. "Is there anything else I can get you?" he said, looming over their booth.

"Nope. All done, thanks," Harvey said. Back in the car they headed west to Fargo. Toby kept the window down to let the warm wind blow on his scalp. His little beeper game lay forgotten on the seat.

"When we get home I'm going online and find Mr. Courbette's baseball card," Toby called out. "Then do you think we could come back and get his autograph?"

"Maybe. After we're out of trouble," Harvey said.

Toby laughed like this was the funniest thing his grandfather had ever said, then returned to airplaning his skinny arm against the warm summer wind.

The Last Farmer

FOR JAY

It was the sheriff again, this time in person. Spencer was rolling in his John Deere when a black-and-white Chevy Blazer with a ski rack of lights crawled into his rear video monitor. Jakey—Sheriff Hanson now—easing up the section line road in Spencer's blind spot, making no sound, leaving no dust.

Sneaky. Typical Hanson maneuver. Spencer and Hanson had gone to high school together twenty-five years ago when there was no love lost (Hanson was a towel snapper, a hallway arm twister, a late hitter in football) and certainly none now. Here in "the Valley" of northwestern Minnesota, everything was about land.

Running his tractor by a GPS receiver, Spencer sat back to watch the Blazer's progress. The ungraveled line road was greasy and soft—the frost had gone out four days ago—and with any luck Hanson would slide into the judicial ditch and get stuck, in which case he could damn well call a tow truck from town. Kindly farmers on their tractors did not stop to pull vehicles from ditches; those days were gone.

The Blazer kept coming, slewing, but gradually drew even with Spencer's John Deere; then kept pace. Spencer did not slow until red lights flashed atop the Chevy. He swore without heat; taking his sweet time, he eased back on the RPMs, touched "neutral" on the finger pad, and let the thirty-six-foot seeder, like a sea anchor, drag the John Deere to a stop. He did not switch off the engine, nor was he getting down from the cab to walk the five hundred feet to the road, not in this cold, black gumbo.

"What, Jakey? Am I driving over the speed limit?" Spencer called over by cell phone.

"Very funny, Spence. Didn't think you saw me." Hanson held his mobile to his face but did not get out of his Blazer. "Big new tractor, tinted cab, cruise control, video screens. I figured maybe you were watching a movie in there."

"What's on your mind, Jakey? Spring has sprung. Fish to fry."

"The old Erickson house, that's what. You said last fall you were going to take care of it."

"True," Spencer said, glancing down the line road to the old farmstead—a few gray, empty buildings before a windbreak, the only bump on the horizon for a mile—then back to Hanson, "though I didn't say when."

"Don't be cute, Spencer. You might own all the farms around here now, but you're still responsible for the buildings."

Spence cracked his RPMs and sent Jakey a puff of black diesel smoke. "It's on my list, Jakey, not high, but on my list."

"Well move it up. Those empty old farm houses attract bad elements."

"Bad elements? You mean, like us back in high school, Jakey? Remember when we'd drive around looking for an old house or an empty barn to throw a kegger? Hey, remember that time when you fell—"

"Beer and a little weed is one thing," Hanson said. "We're talking meth, now, Spence. Meth heads are everywhere. They're like rats, always looking for a place to crawl into."

"Yeah, yeah," Spencer said.

"Not kidding, Spence. An abandoned house like Iver's is a public health hazard—which makes you liable. You don't want some meth head to fall down Iver's stairs, break his neck, and sue the shit out of you. Then he'd own all your land and you'd have to get a job like the rest of us."

Spence glanced at his watch. "I'll try to take care of it this summer."

"See that you do, Spency."

"Over and out, Jakey-boy." Spencer clacked shut his cell phone, slipped it into his shirt pocket. After a quick glance at his dashboard LCDs to make sure he was still autotracking, he brought up the RPMs to 1800; in a flower of dark smoke the John Deere leaned into its seeder and headed downfield. Once rolling, Spencer poured a cup of lukewarm coffee, then swiveled his seat to watch Hanson, who, sure enough, drove into the Erickson place, which is what it would always be called even though Spencer had owned it for years.

In the bare, empty yard Hanson got out. Stretched. Walked slowly to the narrow, steep-roofed farmhouse. Tapped on the boarded, first-floor windows with the butt of his long flashlight (what was it with cops and those long-barreled flashlights?). Mounted the concrete steps, inspected the front door. "It's open," Spence said to no one.

Hanson disappeared into the house. Stayed inside for a long time. Spencer thought of calling Jakey on his cell and asking if he was spanking the old monkey in there, but didn't. Hanson was high school, always would be. Back then, Spencer was a scrawny, 145-pound, second-string running back with a rust-bucket Ford truck and only one clear thought in his head: to get the hell out of Dodge the day after high school graduation. Which he did. However, after a couple of wild years out west, plus fitful starts at college, Spencer came back into town on the Greyhound, and walked the final five miles home. There was something about that walk—the close-up look at the ditches, the fields, the horizon of spring wheat—that spun his brain with possibilities.

"I figured I'd see you again," his father had said, and got Spencer started farming by renting him a line of older, smaller equipment and forty acres (with his father there was no free lunch). Spencer, on his own, gradually worked out a deal with Iver Erickson, a cranky old bachelor, to farm his place on shares: the first year forty acres, then eighty, then, eventually, the whole quarter.

Twenty years and two divorces later, Spence now owned Iver's place and several more farms. Iver had stiffed his relatives, giving them each $500 but the bulk of his estate ($400,000 in savings) went to the U.S. government to help pay down the national debt. A patriot and then some. Spence owned his family's farm plus six more sections (including one that used to belong to the Hanson family), which made his operation one of the biggest in the Valley. He didn't hang out with anyone from high school days; they brought him down, made him indecisive, threw him off his game.

At field's end, Spence overrode the autotracking GPS system, which was "hands-free steering" up to a point—he still had to make the turns—then settled back in his seat as the tractor locked onto its new, parallel coordinates. By the time he passed the Erickson place again, the Blazer was gone.

At 2:00 PM he met a co-op fuel truck in Iver's yard and took on a tank of diesel. The driver was one of the Larson boys, Gary, the term "boy" being relative in farm country; Gary's father, Henry, was at least eighty, and showed no signs of slowing down or stepping aside, and Gary, wearing his usual mirrored sunglasses, was already in his early fifties.

"That new 9520T working out for you?" Gary asked as he dragged the hose up the bright green ladder-steps to the fuel port.

"So far so good," Spencer said cheerfully from ground level.

Fuel stiffened the hose; the meter on the truck spun like a runaway slot machine. Larson adjusted his sunglasses and leaned back on the little platform like he owned the tractor. "They say rubber tracks are harder to turn than with regular tires."

"No difference, really," Spencer said and stepped away. He tried to limit his time around diesel fumes and losers. He walked over by Iver's granary where he leaned a palm against the weathered boards (long hours in the John Deere's cab gave him sea legs) and took a good long piss. His urine was darker than he liked. Too much coffee. Afterward, he opened the granary door and poked his head inside. From a leak in the roof, the granary smelled like a fraternity house, like beer soaked into the wooden floor. Bins, built around a scoop shovel, one of which still hung on the wall, rose up straight and square with yellowed, twelve-inch, white pine boards; mice, however, had chewed through the corners of the bins, rounded out knotholes in the floorboards, gnawed crazy spirals in the scoop shovel's smooth handle—they loved the salt in men's hands—and from their work left a layer of black, thistle-seed droppings on the floor. High up in the granary's peak a fist-sized barn owl swiveled his head to stare down at Spencer. "Hey mister," he murmured; the little owl did not blink. Spencer withdrew.

Back at his tractor, the fuel port gurgled louder as the truck's meter slowed: the dial stopped at 255 gallons.

"Ouch," Spencer said.

Larson capped off the port, climbed down, racked up his hose, then produced a battered metal clipboard plus a pocket-sized calculator.

"Just let me sign, I don't want to know the damage," Spencer said. It was an offering, a conversational gift to Larson, who continued to write up the ticket in silence.

"Looks like 710 bucks today," he said, handing over the clipboard and pen.

Spencer scrawled his name. "Easy come, easy go."

"I wouldn't know," Larson replied. He tore off the receipt for Spencer.

Spencer paused. "How's your Dad these days?"

Larson shrugged. "Same-o. Still farming."

"Amazing. That guy's going to live to be a hundred."

Larson stared at Spencer long moments, then got in his truck, started the engine and backed out of the driveway.

***

The day was lightening, and Spencer took a brisk walk about the yard to stretch his legs. His daughter, Sara, who was twenty-six and lived out East, warned him about blood clots; about drinking enough water—about staying hydrated so he didn't get kidney stones. Warned him when she called, that was, which was not often.

For Sara's sake he briskly walked the two-acre square. He had not gotten it mowed last summer, and the dead grass, long and tangled, thickened at the edge of Iver's windbreak, which stood at perfect right angles to the farmyard: three tall rows of poplars on the outside; two rows of box elders closer in; a row of weeping willows; two rows of lilacs; and, finally, a bushy, prickly wall of caragana. Every tree and shrub was planted offset to the previous row in order to form the densest possible wall against the northwest wind. The poplars were fifty feet tall; at least half had died and fallen (the earth here was too rich and dense for some types of trees), and chilly Canadian air flowed through the gaps and bare branches.

Along the edge of the windbreak, overgrown by brush and bull thistles, were remnants of Iver's machinery. A rusty, orange Case tractor with engine and seat missing—a rattling, muffler-less tractor Spencer had driven many an hour when, as a boy, he worked for Iver. A dump rake with its iron seat also gone. A harrow with sharp, rusty tines (once Spencer had turned the Case too sharply and the harrow rode onto the rear tire and almost onto him, but he had braked in time, and never told Iver). Piles of scrap iron. Mounds of broken concrete blocks. Iver's crazy self-propelled mower made from scratch in his shop: four Model T rubber wheels attached to a welded-pipe carriage, a Wisconsin engine (frozen up, or it would be gone by now), a seven-foot sickle scavenged from an old hay mower, an iron steering wheel that pulled cables on pulleys. Spencer remembered Iver puttering around his yard on the contraption, laying down perfect swaths of hay that he later gathered with the dump rake and fed to his cows. With Iver, nothing was wasted.

Spencer kicked a tire on the old mower. Cracked, brittle rubber fell away from the rusty rim, which was missing its hubcap. He pushed aside weeds with his boot and looked closer; Spencer was sure those hubcaps—heavy, antique aluminum disks—were there last fall, but everything nowadays was collectible.

He walked alongside the broken-backed barn, its red-painted sides faded to blushed smoke, and stepped through the gaping front doors. Pigeons rattled upward—he flinched—through a bright raw star of daylight in the roof. Below, the same light fell dimly on concrete gutters filled with rotted straw, and skeletal stanchions made from ¾-inch water pipe (no town-bought stanchions for Iver), their drinking cups drooping slack-jawed and rusty. He had milked Iver's cows for a couple of weeks one summer when Iver got pneumonia; the cows did not like him and the feeling was mutual.

There used to be a pile of planks in the corner and a thick haymow rope overhead. Maybe if he closed the barn door people wouldn't feel free to scavenge. He leaned into the wide panel of boards that made up the big door, its rollers squeaking sharply along the metal track, and would have latched the thing but its iron hook and clasp were gone.

The exterior of the house showed no additional theft or vandalism; the front door still worked. Inside the dim kitchen he wrinkled his nose at dankness and, faintly, the oily-wool smell of old man. Wallboards around the kitchen were kicked in. People still believed Iver had hidden money in the house, but Spencer knew better. Iver was a scrooge but not a fool: it was banks, not walls or mattresses, that paid interest on savings and certificates of deposit.

In the living room by the old green couch was a fresh scatter of Bud Light cans. He went upstairs, careful on the narrow risers. The handrail was glass smooth from fifty years of use; on the wall where the stairs turned hung the dark, caked, constellation print of Iver's left hand. Not the cleanest guy in the world.

The upstairs bedroom was close with the smell of beer and damp cotton. A stained, exploding mattress lay askew on a rusty coil spring. One sock-foot of black nylon peeked out from underneath the bed; Spencer fished it out with his boot, a torn pair of panty hose, slightly stained and ripped off in a hurry. He remembered that desperate feeling of driving around with a girl, looking for someplace to be alone in a small town where everybody, including the motel owner, knew him and his parents. He straightened, careful not to bump his head on the steeply pitched ceiling. Evidence of screwing, yes, but drug use, no. He kicked at a pile of trash, stooped to pick up a rusty harmonica. Iver played harmonica? He tapped dust from its little square holes, a C harmonica, then went to the west-facing, narrow window and yanked up the sash; he lay the harmonica on the sill, then drew the window down on top. A crack of fresh air, not so large as to let the pigeons in, would do this room good. He kicked once more through the trash, took a last look around. The only thing he had saved from Iver's house were his farm logbooks, a stack of brown, narrow accounting journals into which Iver had logged every dollar of expenses and income since 1939. Neither Iver's family nor thieves had wanted them and it seemed a shame to let the mice get them, so Spencer had taken them home. In general, he was superstitious about keeping a dead man's things, but the logs were fun to look through on occasion—along about 1975 Spencer's own name showed up in the books—plus they were a good record of prices not to say one man's life. In June of 1947, Iver had stopped smoking; near Christmas he paid fourteen dollars for a radio.

On his way out of the house, Spencer peeked down the basement stairs, which were rotted off where they hung in two feet of black, fetid water. He covered his nose and got the hell out of there, back to daylight and fresh air. Iver had never married. Spencer's mother said more than once, "I don't want you kids in his house—ever!" They obeyed, and Spencer was not sentimental about Iver, who, to be honest, was a smelly old goat; however a house was a house, even this one.

Spencer was glad to climb back into the comfortable, new-smelling cockpit of his John Deere. He fired the engine and cranked up the stereo. A little Springsteen—"Divorce Music," he called The Boss's songs—but at least Spencer didn't have to worry about that anymore.

At 3:00 AM he finished Iver's quarter, then headed home. Spencer's parents had retired to Fargo, his two brothers and two sisters lived out of state, and Spencer lived with his daughter's cat in the homeplace where he'd grown up. In the mercury-vapor yard lamp, his metal grain bins lined the driveway in an ascending row of size and brightness. Beginning, nearest the house, with a squat, gray, 1,000-bushel Butler cylinder (the first departure, in the 1940s, from wooden granaries like Iver's), continuing through the 10,000-bushel size of the 1980s; his recently added 25,000-bushel bin dwarfed them all. Billy Craddock's pickup was parked by the Quonset machine shed. Spence was dragging, but he walked across the chilly yard and stepped inside the hangar-sized building. Billy, a high school kid and wizard with a welder, put in hours for Spence whenever he could; centered on the wide concrete floor, his blue jeans and boots poked out from underneath the field cultivator, his welding rod splashing a fountain of sparks. Spencer averted his eyes though not quickly enough.

"Billy, dude, everything goin'?" Spence asked when the sparks died.

"Under control, Spence," Billy said, voice muffled. He sat up and tipped up his hood partway. Molten suns floated inside Spencer's eyeballs; he couldn't really see Billy at all.

"What's your schedule this week? I need to dig that west eighty."

"Not good," Billy said. "I can give you twenty hours maybe."

"Beggars can't be choosers. Plus I was thinking. You know the old Erickson yard?"

Billy nodded.

"I got to do something with those buildings. Maybe get the house fixed up and rent it out, or sell it to some young married couple. You know anybody?"

Billy sat up straighter and laughed for real this time, his teeth white and wet beneath the lip of his mask. "One problem Spence—there aren't any young married couples. No young people period. I mean, hey, your own daughter—she's gone and she ain't coming back here."

Spencer shrugged. "That's because the only guys left are redneck welders driving beater pickups."

Billy chuckled and shrugged down his mask.

Spence tapped Billy's boot with his own. "There should be a couple of cold ones in the office fridge."

"No thanks, got my Dew," Billy replied.

"Kids nowadays," Spence said, turning to the door. "Jesus."

Billy's laugh was muffled as the welder hummed louder. Sparks sizzled.

In the house, which was pretty well empty after his brothers and sisters had divided up the stuff—Spence had a kitchen table, two chairs, a couch, a television, and a bed upstairs—he took out a Schwan's roast beef dinner and nuked it in the microwave. Fred, Sara's old cat, whined at the door. Spencer let him in. He was orange and white, half wild, a great mouser, and not hungry tonight. He let Spencer pet him briefly, then headed upstairs, *bump, bump, bump.* Spencer showered, came back to eat his crinkled aluminum plate of roast beef, then headed to bed himself. He was a dead man; never made it out of his bathrobe.

Much later he thought he felt Fred rustling around on the bed in the dark, then smelled old people.

"Hey, baby," he mumbled, "aren't you working tonight?"

"Yeah, but I'm on break and was horny."

It was Sandy, his sort-of girlfriend. She was head night nurse at the local rest home, and since their schedules never matched, it was catch-as-catch-can. She was also married.

"You must have been dreaming about somebody special," she murmured, her hand inside his robe.

"You, honey," Spence said.

"Yeah, right," she said. In one of those sweet moves that only women can do—crossing her elbows and lifting her arms—she shrugged off her smock. Twenty minutes later Sandy was gone and Spence spent; he fell back asleep immediately, and then his alarm rang. 5:00 AM. Time to roll.

Three weeks later, planting his last forty acres of soybeans, Spencer believed that the far windbreak was not a windbreak but a gray line of welding that held earth to sky, and if that weld broke there would be hell to pay: the field would come unstuck from the horizon, tilt backward, and Spence and his new tractor would slide off the edge of the earth. Good-bye cruel world, Spence thought—when his phone rang. Area code 617.

"Hey, honey!" he said immediately. He tried not to sound eager.

"Hi Daddy."

"Where are you, baby?" He powered down, killed the engine.

"Boston. Like usual."

"Are you all right?"

"Sure. No trouble. Just thought I'd see if you were done planting."

Spence swung open his cab door and climbed down. "You still got good radar, honey," he said, dropping to the earth, grabbing the rail to steady himself. "I'm on my last few rounds."

He could feel her smile, though she didn't laugh. She was not the laughing type; there had been too much trouble, too much pain in the divorce, all of which was Spencer's fault. "You coming home?"

Sara was silent. Spencer winced. It just slipped out.

"Where's home, Daddy?"

"I know, I know, honey. I mean home as a figure of speech. Are you coming back? For a visit? That's what I meant."

"Not sure," she said. "I have business this summer in Minneapolis. Maybe we could meet there for dinner."

"Tell me when, I'll drive down," Spencer said. "Right now, I'd get in my truck. You know I would, honey." His voice broke.

"Oh Daddy, it's all right. I know how you get in spring and fall."

Spencer honked his nose.

"How much sleep have you been getting?" she asked.

"Four or five hours."

"Be honest."

"Three. Maybe."

Sara clucked her tongue. "Well, when planting's done I want you to get rested up, all right?"

"I promise, honey, I will." Spencer could not stop weeping; this was a disaster.

"I'll call you about Minneapolis, all right? It'll probably be July. Maybe August."

"I'd love that," Spencer said. "You know I would."

"Okay, Daddy. Sleep, rest, all right?"

"I love you, honey," Spencer said.

There was silence. "Bye, Daddy."

Spencer stumbled back up into his tractor. In the cab he had himself a good long cry—he was in way worse shape than he realized—then finished the field and went home to bed.

It took him two weeks to recover from planting. Long binges of sleep. Days of naps, of a groggy, nobody-home, wading-through-slurry kind of feeling. He could barely muster himself to call the Schwan's man, who came and went while Spence dozed on the couch. He found an invoice on the kitchen table and a handwritten note. "I couldn't wake you, so took a guess."

Spencer looked in the freezer compartment. Chock-full of entrées, mainly roast beef, but a couple of chicken potpies that looked decent.

"Lucky I don't lock the house," Spencer said to Fred.

Like there's anything to steal, said Fred's blank-eyed stare.

"True," Spencer allowed, and headed back to the couch. He dreamed he was drowning in a bin of flax seed, which was finer and more slippery than quicksand—flax seed was every farmer's nightmare—and awoke to find Fred sleeping heavy on his chest, his fluffy tail twitching in Spencer's face.

By June first the scales sloughed off his eyes, the shutters lifted from his brain; the sky inside his head lightened by degrees, and the backaches from too much couch time receded. His energy returned. There were fish to fry.

Small ones, at least, to start. He called the bulldozer guy to knock down the buildings on two farms he owned west of town. It would be enough to keep Jakey off his back.

"No problemo," the young Cat-skinner said over the phone. "You want them piled to burn or you want me to bury it?"

"Bury it," Spence said. "Otherwise, Hanson will nag me about a burning permit."

"He would do that," the Cat-skinner said. "Windbreaks too?"

Spencer paused. The trees on both farms were craggly and crappy, well past their prime. Like Iver's place, lots of dead trees. "Okay."

"And as long as I'm rolling, do you want me to do the old Erickson place too?"

Spencer was silent.

"I mention it because Hanson said he was after you about it."

"He did, did he?"

The Cat-skinner paused. "I mean, it's no big deal . . ."

"No rush on the Erickson place," Spencer said. "Maybe later this summer."

"Sure," the man said quickly. "I'll do the other yards first. When I get done you'll be able to farm right over them. Like they were never there."

As the spraying season approached, Spencer stayed inside the house. Took care of paperwork. Made phone calls. He contracted out all his herbicide applications, pre- and post-emerge, because he couldn't own a sprayer or a crop duster for what it cost to hire it out but also because the chemicals made him sick. Made his face puffy, his eyes baggy. Not sick sick. Not something he could name—no rashes or dizziness or vomiting—but when everybody was spraying he just didn't feel good. Even inside the house, with the windows closed and the air conditioner running, he got thick-brained, stiff, groggy. This year he had vowed to get ahead of the curve—not feel shitty for three weeks—and when Jeff Broker and his spray rig rolled up the long driveway Spencer met him in his pickup, suitcase packed.

The spray rig with its tall, skinny tires and folded, fifty-foot boom wings and pull-behind chemical tank looked like a giant praying mantis on life support; at night, far out on the fields with running lights on, rigs like his were downright scary.

"All set?" He spoke with Broker by cell phone.

"All good," Broker replied. "Got your new satellite maps down-loaded and I'm ready to roll." He was fiddling with his laptop even as he held the cell to his ear.

"Okay, I'm outta here for a few days," Spencer said.

"What, you don't like how I smell?" Broker grinned behind sun-glasses and his narrow, tinted-glass cockpit.

"Nothing personal," Spencer said. "And hey, feed my cat if he looks hungry, will you? House is open."

Broker gave a thumbs-up, and Spencer headed to the highway.

At the blacktop, he paused. Winnipeg and the Fort Garry Hotel were an hour and a half to the north. Winnipeg had good restaurants where he could get borscht and pasties, and Canadian girls were pretty, but there was the border, which always made him nervous, plus all that flat prairie land—the north end of the Valley—in between. He turned south, toward the lake and pine country of Bemidji, which was about the same distance away.

On the way through town, he swiveled his head to stare. He could swear it was smaller these days. A car dealership now had only a bare, cracked, asphalt parking lot. A downtown restaurant's windows were papered over. On the south edge of town, the old grain elevator, tall, square, rusty, galvanized tin—the kind that photographers loved—had been torn down and bulldozed into a pile. Dump trucks were hauling it away even as he passed. He knew the old elevator was a dead duck. All the small-town grain elevators under 100,000 bushel were doomed be-cause ADM was building a "super-regional" grain storage center near Argyle, one with a circle of railroad tracks big enough to hold a double-unit train, 220 carloads, of wheat. Knocking down this old ele-vator felt a little like shooting the last buffalo.

He turned up Springsteen and rolled southeast, passing gradually over the Agassiz Ridge, the slight rise (most drivers never noticed it) that ran north and south, the old oxcart trail of last century's settlers and voyageurs heading to Canada. On the back, east side of the ridge was the transitional zone where long-ago glaciers had left fields full of boulders—some as large as his truck—that cattle farmers had pushed into piles like Stonehenge. Black Angus grazed around the big rocks. No crop farming here. In the Valley a mile or two made all the differ-ence, and the smartest farmers on the ridge had switched from cattle to large gravel pit operations where trucks rumbled night and day.

In another half hour he passed sloughs and potholes as he entered lake and pine country. He took back roads through Gully and Gonvick, stopping for a burger at a café where the girl was plump, young, and friendly but barely able to look away from *Days of Our Lives* on the television over the bar.

In Bemidji he checked in at an AmericInn and fell asleep in his clothes. Much later—almost 11:00 PM—he roused himself and went out to find food. He drove around to find the bar that had the most cars, in this case Dewey's, a log-sided steak house at the edge of town. Inside it was loud—very loud—and crowded; he was lucky to find a stool at the bar, where he ordered a burger basket and a Labatt's. Everybody here seemed to know each other. He watched the people as they laughed and talked and bought drinks and danced. The jukebox was impossibly loud and the laughing voices of a table of women pricked like fish hooks inside his ear drums (too many years around high-RPM equipment). He discreetly made a couple of napkin spitballs to buffer the noise, which made the bar *Cheers* on mute. One of the women at the table caught his eye and smiled briefly; he nodded, and eventually she came over, unsteady on her feet (no wedding ring), but the music was too loud for good conversation, and, in bad timing, his food arrived; when Spencer turned back to the woman, she was moving down the bar.

Spencer stayed in Bemidji for four days, sleeping a lot, once walking over to the college to look at the coeds. He followed a girl in shorts and a tank top into the campus bookstore, where he pretended to read while he watched her return some books. When she left, he couldn't very well follow her, so he lingered with his book, *The World is Flat* by Thomas Friedman. Back home he read the *New York Times* online, and kept up on world events—particularly as they affected wheat prices—but he hadn't read a real book in years. This one felt heavy in his hands, its sentences too long; he wondered if his brain was beyond the point of reading a full book again.

The following day he hired a local guide to take him walleye fishing on Lake Bemidji, but the lake was plate-flat and waveless. "We need that walleye chop," the guide kept saying, and Spencer ended up with a bad headache from the sun's glare on the water.

At the local Perkins the next morning, his waitress with smoker's teeth brought him coffee with two creams. "The number five?" she asked. After breakfast, Spencer checked out of his hotel.

He had hardly started toward home when his cell phone rang. "Hey Spencer, it's me."

"So I see, Jakey."

"Where are you?"

"I could be anywhere."

"You're not home; I was just there."

"Everything all right?"

"Sure. Just checking on the Erickson place. Which, now, I hear, is haunted."

"English, Jakey."

"I heard some kids talking. They went out there to drink beer, I guess, but kept hearing noises, voices, something. They got all freaked out."

"That's a good thing, right? If they think the place is haunted, they'll leave it alone."

"Kids maybe, yeah, they're afraid of ghosts. The meth heads are the ghosts, Spencer. They ain't afraid of anything, which is why that house has to go."

"Okay, okay, Jakey. Here's my plan. I think I have some leftover ammonium nitrate. I thought I'd haul a couple of barrels of it over there, soak it with diesel fuel, and blow Iver's house to Kingdom Come. What do you think?"

There was silence. Then Hanson said, "You blow up anything with ammonium nitrate you're in deep do-do."

"With who?"

"With me. With Homeland Security. With everybody in law enforcement. There was a little thing that happened down in Oklahoma City, if you recall."

"Geez, Jakey, when did you get so serious? Can't a guy have any fun anymore?"

"You got ammonium nitrate, you call it in and get rid of it. People want to steal that shit—then who knows what they'll use it for."

"You worry way too much, Jakey."

"Not kidding, Spence. I can get a warrant."

Spencer scuffed his phone across the seat, then held it at arm's length. "You're breaking . . . Jakey. I'll . . . touch." Then signed off.

He drove on in much better spirits.

On his way back into town, he slowed at the city limits, which felt closer in than when he had left. The old elevator was completely gone. Like it was never there. On the north side of town, wheat and soybean fields rolled up closer than he remembered. And what happened to the old drive-in theater and the bowling alley? The fairgrounds was gone, too—all that in four days. But he was looking through his rearview mirror and his sunglasses, which he peeled off; however, the brilliant June sunlight, made hazy by the humid breath of miles of wheat and soybean fields, made it difficult to see well, or even very far.

He turned his truck west, toward Iver's place. On the line road, skinny, fresh car tracks wove ahead of him; the road was dry now except for a few black puddles, and the car tracks turned into Iver's driveway. No vehicle to be seen. Probably Jakey come and gone on Homeland Security detail. Jakey or scavengers.

He parked and got out. Stretched his legs after the drive from Bemidji. He took a leak and was about to leave when he heard music. A swell of breeze and a weak ghostly chord of music—in C—came from the upstairs window. He laughed and walked toward the house—and into the path of a skinny, pale woman coming from the other side. She was carrying a small camp stove. Behind her two rail-thin guys were unloading stuff, including a propane cylinder, from a battered station wagon parked inside the barn.

The woman called out to the men—who straightened. They all froze.

"Who are you?" the woman said. She had very bad teeth.

"I'm . . . a farmer," Spencer said.

Nobody moved. The woman glanced backward, then again to Spencer. She grinned with her lips but not her eyes. "So, you want to party with us?"

"I don't think so," Spencer said.

"Come on baby, you look like you could use some fun." She let her bony hand slip to her shirt buttons. Teased one open.

"Listen. I own this place and you shouldn't be here," Spencer said. He swallowed. "I'm gonna walk back to my truck and drive away, and you better do that, too. Like right now." He didn't wait for an answer; he moved with even steps back to his truck, ready to bolt if he heard anything—a clank of metal—behind him, but there was nothing. Purposefully not looking back, he turned his truck around and drove, slowly, back down the line road.

In his rearview mirror he soon saw the station wagon throwing dust behind him, then turn south on the blacktop and disappear. He let out a breath.

Arriving at his own driveway, he paused, by habit, to check the mail. A few bills, including one from the Cat-skinner, plus an invoice from

Broker for spraying. Nothing serious. In the house, there was no Fred to be seen; he was probably out mousing. While a chicken potpie hummed in the microwave, he toyed with his cell phone—"who you gonna call"—then he punched up the bulldozer man.

"Turns out I could be there later this afternoon," the man said.

The days were long now, and the lowboy and Caterpillar rumbled up in tawny, humid light at 8:30 PM. Spencer was waiting in his truck, windows up, air conditioning on. The least he could do was be there. Watch.

He got out and stood near as the man tipped down the ramps and loosened the required come-alongs and chains. "As if they'd keep this baby on the trailer," the guy said, his head ducked low as he worked. The fellow was young and quick on his feet; he hopped upward into the cab, closed the door on his own air conditioning. As the Cat's engine surged and its tracks clanked down the steel ramps, Spencer returned to his truck. Inside the cab he tuned in to public radio, which he didn't often listen to. Tonight was chamber music by Dvořák, a Czech composer who had once come to Iowa and composed there, the announcer said; he listened and watched the Caterpillar dig a long trench about twenty feet wide and six feet deep. No gravel, no sand to be seen, only glistening black dirt, rolling up blacker than crows' wings. After Dvořák came Copeland, a long piece by the American, during which the trench was completed. At sundown, the Caterpillar turned toward the buildings. Spencer cranked up the music; he preferred not to hear the crunching sounds. The Caterpillar pushed Iver's house forward as if it were weightless—tipped it into the trench in an explosion of dust and broken boards—then drove over it and back several times. Afterward he turned to the granary; then the barn and sheds; then the old machinery; and lastly, the windbreak. Samuel Barber now, Adagio for Strings, as the dead trees tumbled soundlessly into the hole—it was like he was watching a movie—and by 11:00 PM, with headlights below and starlight above, the Caterpillar lurched back onto its lowboy. Its engine died.

In the gathering blue darkness Spence walked back to the rig. The air smelled strongly—a yeasty rankness—of fresh dirt and wet tree bark, and the night air swelled in freely from the now unbroken field.

In the darkness, Spencer wrote the man a check. "Buy you a beer in town?"

The man shrugged. "Gotta be honest, I can't do that anymore. Plus it's late, and the wife . . . you know."

"Sure," Spencer said. "No problem."

After the rig rumbled away, he took a last look around. He could farm over this—it was remarkable how small a rise was left in the blackened yard (people not from here would never notice it). No more worrying about hooking his cultivator or his seeder on a tree, no more scavengers, no more meth heads. It really was simpler this way.

Hungry, he turned his truck toward town to see if anything was open; if anyone was around. He stayed with the symphonic music—it seemed right tonight—but must have gotten lost in it. Or made a wrong turn somewhere. For the more he drove, the fewer lights he saw on the land. He kept driving far beyond the time when he should have reached town, driving until he understood that there no longer was a town. It was all gone. As far as the eye could see, there was no one home.

Sweet Land was designed and set in type by Mike Hanson and Will Powers at the Minnesota Historical Society Press. The type is Legacy Serif, designed by Ron Arnholm. Printed by Thomson-Shore, Inc., Dexter, Michigan.